The Mural

Lauryn A. Brooks

Be Proud. Stay You. Publishing

For information contact :
laurynabrooks@gmail.com

Cover design by Lauryn A. Brooks
Formatting by Derek Murphy
ISBN: 978-1-7363648-1-9 (paperback)
ISBN: 978-1-7363648-0-2 (Ebook)

This novel is dedicated to the ones who believe in me and my dreams, the pioneers for my beloved and resilient queer community, and to my inner child, who never thought these dreams of mine could come true.

One

I CAN'T BELIEVE THIS. I mean, don't get me wrong, it's not like I have to stay. I could very well just leave, head to my classes without any regard for... whoever I'm supposed to be showing around today, but I'm worried about how bailing on them would look. Not that the new student seems to care about first impressions, anyway, considering they're now ten minutes late.

As I sit in the front lobby, my knee impatiently bouncing away, I check my watch. Okay, I would give them five more minutes, and then after that, they're on their own.

Then they'll be lost on their first day, thanks to you.

Well, I have classes too!

Yeah, but we both know you won't get in trouble for missing them.

Who's "we"? We're the same person. And besides, just because the faculty favored me didn't mean I was okay with abusing the privilege. Also, I want to go to my classes to claim my seat.

I check the time again. The starting bell had rung thirteen minutes ago, *meaning* the new kid is now thirteen minutes late. I continue tapping my foot.

After I tuck a strand of hair behind my ear and exhale irritably, I send a quick text to Gwen, my best friend, for her to save me a seat next to her in English class. The counselor at the front desk clears her throat, suggesting I put my phone away.

The bell rings one last time, signaling the start of classes.

I stand to leave. Maybe the new kid isn't coming today. Maybe they aren't coming at all. At this point, I didn't care. I have a class to get to.

That's when they, or should I say *she*, barrels through the front doors loud and not-so proud. She's tall, possibly between five-foot six and five-foot seven, and her slim build reminds me of a runner. She wears her summer tan well, and she has this kind of natural beauty about her, and this crazy vibe I can't seem to ignore...

Get it together, Peyton.

"Hi, uh..." she mumbles to the lady at the front desk.

"I'm looking for Peyton Kelly. He's supposed to be showing me around."

I roll my eyes. Well, she certainly won't find any male bits around my part of town.

"Yeah, that's me," I introduce myself sharply. "Peyton Kelly."

Hazel eyes pull their attention away from the front desk and land on me. Her eyes widen, probably out of embarrassment from realizing Peyton Kelly is in fact a girl, but who knows? Her cheeks turn red.

"Shit, I'm sorry," she apologizes as she runs one hand nervously through her dark-brown hair. "I didn't know..."

"It's fine," I reply.

She stands still for a minute, looking at me almost dumbfounded, until she realizes my purpose in being here. That's when she fishes for her schedule in her black backpack.

"I'm Jamie Kendall," she finally introduces.

As she struggles to find what she's looking for, I find my anger over the whole late situation subsiding. There's something about her that's intriguing, to say the least, but I couldn't put my finger on it. But judging by her outfit that consisted of tight, black skinny jeans, a pair of Converse shoes, and a white t-shirt with the word GIRLS on it, I immediately pin her as a city girl. They were few and far between here at Branton High because, well, we're a small town located in north-central Georgia. I silently wonder how she's ended up here.

She finally finds her schedule, which is now a little crumpled, but still intact. She hands it to me.

"Great," I say while turning on my heels. "Let's go."

She falls into step next to me, which would've been more difficult had she been shorter, but the extra inches give her an advantage. I had always been told for a girl not over five-three, I sure was fast.

It came in handy for soccer season.

"This is the English hall," I start. "Your class is in this room."

She takes note but doesn't seem all that interested in the tour. If anything, she seems more interested in me. I can't help but feel the nerves bubble in my stomach.

"The school isn't as big as it seems on the outside," she assesses. "My old school was huge."

"Where are you from?"

"Chicago."

I hadn't expected that, but I knew she surely wasn't from around here.

"You're pretty far away from home," I say.

"Yeah, well..." She sighs, expressing obvious disappointment. "Trust me. It's not by choice."

I continue to show her around school, realizing halfway through her schedule that we have the same elective in the same hour block. Fourth hour art.

"Well, we have art together," I tell her. "So, you'll see a friendly face in there."

"Oh, we're friends now?" she teases. "Or is that just the

4

famous southern hospitality they talk about?"

I'm besides myself at the flirtatious look Jamie's giving me. Instead of saying anything I just laugh and show her the room our art class would meet during the year. After, I lead her to the middle of the school grounds.

"And this is the quad," I finish.

The "quad" consists of four massive oak trees that were planted when the school was built many years ago. You can follow the cement walkways to the different trees that, during lunch, became the meeting grounds for different groups of students, like jocks, preps, band kids and so forth.

"Lemme guess," Jamie observes. "It matters what tree you hang out at?"

I purse my lips at her quick observation. It was true. Whoever designed it hadn't considered how high schoolers would treat it, or maybe they had, who knows.

"Yeah." I point. "That's the prep tree, that's the freak tree, the band tree and the tree we used to call no-mans-land."

"What is it called now?" Jamie wonders.

"Uhm, it's called the pride tree," I say through a chuckle. "Believe it or not."

"What's so bad about that?" Jamie asks seriously.

"N-Nothing," I stutter.

I secretly hope I haven't offended her, but she looks at me with a playful expression instead that makes my heart flutter. I try not to let her see.

She smirks. "What tree do you think I'll end up at?"

I know exactly where she'll end up, because if I were being honest, her flirting with me made it pretty obvious. It would be weird if she didn't end up at the tree where most of the LGBT crowd congregated at this school.

"You know what, don't answer that," she interrupts my thoughts. "I'm afraid you'll say the freak tree and I'm still not sure how I feel about everyone calling it the "freak" tree. Like, what makes the kids that hang out there so freaky?"

I laugh it off, but I'm really just relieved she didn't make me answer her question.

"Nothing," I answer. "They're not freaks. Well, some of them do hiss at you if you get too close, but most of them are regular people just trying not to get involved with the social hierarchy of high school."

Jamie lifts a brow.

"And I don't blame them," I finish.

She gazes out at the quad while I watch the sunlight dance in her irises, bringing out magnificent hues. Then I notice the small nose ring that wraps around her left nostril. I find it hot, but know she'll have a hard time getting away with wearing it during school.

"Well, if I do end up at the freak tree..." Her eyes meet mine again. "I won't hiss at you."

I just keep deflecting her flirting with laughter, but I'm losing my composure. I've never been so blatantly flirted with by such an attractive person before, much less a *girl.* The shock of the situation results in me bailing on the invitation to flirt back and stepping away from her.

"L-Let's find your locker," I stutter.

I quickly start back to the main campus and attempt to stay ahead of Jamie so she can't see the red on my cheeks. I know what I'm feeling. I've felt it many times before. The emotions multiply rapidly until I feel the fire all over inside.

As my heart pounds in my chest, I decide that Jamie Kendall has been sent here to demolish the illusion that senior year would be easy sailing.

And maybe I kind of like that.

Two

SO, I'M PRETTY SURE I'M GAY. No. I'm *definitely* gay. Peyton Kelly likes girls because she is gay. I've thought it a million times.

Most times were when I was trying to convince myself that I wasn't. That it was a phase, or something that all girls probably experienced at least once in their life. Other times, when I was finally coming to terms with what a lesbian was, and I realized the truth.

But I've never said it aloud, and I wasn't planning on starting now.

Of course, there are other LGBTQ+ people here at Branton High. The fear of being the only one wasn't what was preventing me from coming out. No. But *one* of the reasons is because the group was small, and everyone knew everyone's business, and all the drama went to the head of the group.

Jacqueline Ross.

There are many reasons I haven't come out yet, not even to my best friend, but the main reason was because of Jacki.

See, Jacki Ross is your typical pretentious, high school mean girl, and I appreciate and cherish my status here at Branton High too much to jeopardize it. And *maybe* I am a fraud for encouraging people to be themselves while I actively refuse to do the same, but there were ways for the truth to leak through the cracks, and Jacki was the last person I wanted to know I was a lesbian.

Now, Jacki and I go *way* back. We grew up here in Branton, Georgia, went to the same schools, were on the same sports teams, and ended up in the same clubs. She's in every yearbook that I own. That's how far back we go.

Her feud with me started sometime between middle and high school, but I have no factual idea why she doesn't like me. Maybe it's because I'd beaten her out for class president ever since we were freshmen. Or maybe her competitiveness started earlier on, like when I made the all-star soccer team when we were twelve and she didn't. Or when I beat her at our sixth-grade spelling bee. It didn't seem like a reason to *hate* me, but it's all I could think of.

Moral of the story: Jacki can absolutely *not* know that I am gay because she would certainly use it against me, and

I couldn't have that.

"Have you met the new girl?" Gwen asks, which pulls me out of my thoughts.

"Uh, yeah, vaguely," I reply, trying a little too hard to seem uninterested. "I gave her a tour this morning."

"She's pretty out there." She laughs. "And by out there, I mean, she's clearly gay and doesn't care who knows."

Oh, trust me, I think to myself. *I noticed.*

"She's in Bio with me, but Jacki couldn't stop talking about her in theater class."

I'm not surprised by this. Gossip about the new kid always happens, and since Jamie is clearly gay and from Chicago, she's all everyone would talk about, at least for the next week.

Plus, Jamie *is* really cute.

"So, I'll see you after fourth?" Gwen wonders. "We can leave for lunch. I'm sure Darian and Gibbs wouldn't mind."

"Sure," I agree.

Gwen leaves my side and I scan the area for Jamie. I know she has this class with me, and the starting bell is about to ring. This girl sure likes to be late, huh?

I walk into the familiar classroom I've come to every single year since I started high school. It's a personal safe haven because art is something not many people know I enjoy, so it allows me to be able to shut off for at least an hour of my day.

Then the late bell rings and I roll my eyes. Jamie is late. Again.

The teacher begins taking attendance as I get comfortable in a chair. My eyes glance at the door occasionally, anticipating the arrival of a cute brunette with pretty, hazel eyes.

"Peyton?" Mr. Zephyr calls. "Fourth year in a row?"

"Of course, Mr. Z," I answer.

He just gives me a quick smile before continuing.

"Jamie Kendall?"

No answer.

"No Jamie today?"

I sigh. "She's here..."

"I'm here!" Jamie calls as she barges through the half-open door. "I'm here. I'm sorry. I got turned around and..." Her voice trails off from exhaustion. I find it adorable that she ran here.

"I'm here," she finishes.

"First days are tough, kid," Mr. Z says. "Have a seat anywhere you'd like."

The class itself is small. There are maybe ten of us altogether, but there are plenty of seats in the spacious room. I usually sit by myself and away from everyone because it helps me relax.

But Jamie chooses the seat right next to me.

"Hey," she greets. "Do you mind if I...?"

"N-No, go ahead," I stammer.

Jesus, get it together.

She sits and I get a whiff of her perfume. It's strong, but not too strong. I recognize the scent of lavender.

11

"Were you gonna cover for me?" she asks with a teasing smile.

I blush. "Yeah, I was."

"Thanks." She leans back in her chair. "This school is more confusing than I thought."

I smile to myself and determine that if she had paid more attention to the tour this morning rather than to me, she might've remembered her route. Although, I can't say I'm disappointed over it.

Mr. Z finishes with attendance and begins handing out flyers that include a list of supplies we would need. I accept mine even though I've practically memorized it from being in his class over the last three years.

As I place my list in a folder that's returned inside my bag, Jamie struggles to shove her list between two notebooks, crinkling the sides. When she's done, she leans back and looks at me.

"I meant to say this earlier but, I wouldn't have pinned you as an art geek," she says.

Having her attention makes me feel like I'm on a stage.

"I can say the same about you," I reply.

My answer unintentionally ends the conversation.

She scans the class. "Do we do anything or...?"

I shrug. "Not usually. He gives us a few days to get our supplies and stuff."

"Sweet."

The conversation dies again. I can't blame her for ending it. I'm not being particularly talkative. It's just weird, and she's cute, and usually I'm more confident and outgoing.

"S-So, why Branton?" I ask.

She pulls her eyes away from her phone. "My mom's job laid her off and she decided to move back to her hometown."

"Your mom is from here?"

"Apparently." Jamie laughs. "I can't picture my mom growing up in a town like this."

"Don't write it off just yet," I suggest.

She tilts her head. "I've been here since the beginning of July. What the hell do you do for fun around here?"

"Lots of things." I defend. "Parties, pool days, go to the lake, fishing, hunting..."

"You've lost me."

"We find ways to entertain ourselves." I laugh. "Besides, Atlanna isn't too far."

"Nice accent," she teases.

"What do you mean?"

"The way you say Atlanta," Jamie informs. "It's cute."

I'm caught off guard by her comment and my face heats up. While I fumble a response, she just gives me a smile before returning to the lengthy paragraph she's typing. I assume it's probably her friends back home checking in on her first day.

I retrieve my notebook and begin doodling, all while picturing Jamie in my head. I can't deny that I might be *slightly* infatuated with her. I mean, she's a cute girl from a big city that's far away from this small town. She's considered a rarity around here.

The bell rings after about thirty minutes of me doodling, and when I pull back, I realize the figure resembles the girl I had been daydreaming about. I quickly close the notebook, so she doesn't see.

"So, I think the only place you haven't showed me is the cafeteria," Jamie says as she walks next to me.

"Right, well, it's just across the quad," I answer.

We walk together in silence, but the feeling of underlying tension surrounds us. And only for a moment does her hand graze mine, which sends electric currents throughout my body. I refuse to look up at her because I'm afraid she'll be able to see the red on my cheeks. It happens a few more times before we finally make it to our destination.

"This is the cafeteria..."

"Chicago!" I hear a familiar voice yell. I immediately recognize it as my friend Darian.

Both Jamie and I look up to see Gwen, Gibbs, and, of course, Darian walking in our direction.

My three closest friends couldn't be more opposite. We have Darian Martin, the six-foot, bulked-up jock with a killer smile and warm, brown skin. I notice from afar that he's gotten stronger from summer football conditioning.

Then there's Gwen Richardson, your typical blond, captain of the cheer squad that stands at about my height and wears different color nails every week. People used to think we were sisters when we became best friends sophomore year.

And Hunter Gibson, AKA Gibbs, who stands just a bit taller than Darian – who also plays football. He's a brick wall compared to Darian, with shaggy brown hair that sticks out from under his backwards baseball cap.

Jamie tells my friends hello as I wait for Darian to explain his sudden outburst. He must've seen the confusion on my face.

"Chicago sits next to me in English class." He drapes a muscular arm over Jamie's slim shoulders. "She's the coolest lesbian at this school and she just got here."

I feel my face redden.

"Uh, Jamie, this is Gwen," I introduce.

They exchange smiles.

"And this is Hunter, but we call him Gibbs."

Gibbs shoves his hands into his pockets. "Maybe we can be each other's wingmen."

Jamie laughs. "Maybe so."

Darian slaps Gibbs' chest. "He needs all the help that he can get."

Jamie seems to mesh well with my friends, and I'm not sure how I feel about it. Being around her brings out emotions I've been able to hide so well, and it scares me.

"Do you have a fifth hour?" Darian asks Jamie.

"Nope."

"Perfect, 'cause we're leaving for lunch if you wanna come?" he offers. "It'll be a lot better than the food they serve here. I promise."

All my friends verbally agree that she's welcome to tag along except for me, but no one really notices with all the excitement. Jamie inevitably agrees to join us.

We pile into my car, filling it to max capacity.

"Where are we going?" I ask.

Everyone shouts different places, and as they hash it out, my eyes find Jamie in my rearview mirror. She sits in the back, between Gibbs and Darian, but doesn't seem to mind as she throws me a smile. I tear my gaze away as I back out of my parking space.

As much as I like Jamie, I hadn't expected her. She's like a sudden downpour on a beautiful summer day. It's threatening, but deep down, I love the rain. I can see the clouds in the distance, the wind's invisible force shaking the trees while lightning and thunder crack.

And this storm has the potential to dismantle *everything.*

Three

IT'S TRADITION TO THROW A PARTY at Gibbs' family's lakehouse on the first weekend of the school year. This tradition had been established sophomore year by Darian and Gibbs, and inevitably, Gwen and I became accomplices, sucked in by association.

Gibbs' family's lake house is a hidden gem for us. His parents aren't your typical hard handed, by-the-bible kind of Baptists, if they even *consider* themselves Baptists at all. They're hard workers that trust their children to make the right decisions, and with trust came the responsibility of hosting safe parties.

We're allowed to gather there and drink if everyone who did stayed the night. On top of that, Gibbs is, surprisingly, the second most responsible of our friend group.

We all consider the lake house a small miracle, really.

I walk side by side with Gwen into school, wondering what this year's bash would hold. Last year was the first time I had gotten really drunk, courtesy of Darian pressuring me to do a keg stand, and ended up puking behind a tree. I made sure no one saw.

"What are you wearing tonight?" Gwen asks as she hugs her calculus book to her chest. "I was thinking either some black shorts with a tank or that burgundy dress..."

My mind is somewhere else as I spot Jamie getting off a bus. She was attempting to untangle her earbuds, and then trips after stepping on an untied shoelace. She looks up in frustration, then kneels to tie it.

She's cute when she's annoyed...

"Hello? Peyton?" Gwen snaps her fingers. "What the hell are you staring at?"

I shake my head. "N-Nothing I uh, I think you should wear the shorts and tank."

She contemplates my suggestion for a minute.

"I think I'm gonna wear the dress," she counters.

I narrow my eyes and give her a nervous look. "Are you sure that's a good idea?"

"Why?"

"Because the last time you wore a dress to a party, you flashed everyone when you fell off the back of the couch," I remind her.

"Now *that* was a sight," Darian's deep voice bellows as he swings both of his arms around our shoulders. "I vote for the dress."

"Get away you *creep*," Gwen teases as she shoves Darian.

I just smirk to myself.

"Yo, Gibbs!" Darian calls out to our friend in the quad.

I look back to search for Jamie but can't find her. I wonder if she's heard of the party tonight, and whether it was my place to invite her. It *is* my job to be inclusive, and inviting the new girl would be a good political move... but how would I feel having her there?

That's when I crash into a body, and by the smell of coconut lotion and cinnamon gum, I already know who it is.

"Jesus Peyton, could you watch where you're going?" Jacki hisses.

"It was an accident," Gwen defends. "Chill out, Jacki."

Narrow brown eyes watch me as a manicured hand flicks a strand of tight, bouncy curls behind an exposed, light brown shoulder. Jacki radiates, but not in good taste. Her aura is something of angst and anger mixed together, which makes me stand on my toes. If it weren't for her crappy attitude and conniving ways, I would consider her one of the prettiest girls at this school. Maybe being raised by an extremely strict, overly critical, single mom did that to you.

"I'm chill." Jacki holds her hands up in a fake defense.

"Guess I'll see you girls tonight?"

"Of course," is all I say. I never personally invite Jacki to the lake house parties because of her weird, unexplainable beef with me, but I'm used to her bad attitude, and fighting fire with fire isn't a good look for me.

Then Jacki's brown eyes light up. "Jamie!"

The name makes my heart stutter, but hearing it come out of Jacki's mouth ruins it. It had taken Jacki exactly four days to sink her claws into Jamie. I can't help but roll my eyes at the thought and walk away, but not before Jamie and I lock eyes for a split second. I quickly pull away when I feel my face heat up.

"I kinda feel bad for Jamie," Gwen reveals. "Jacki isn't gonna let her out of her sight."

"She'll probably turn into one of Jacki's little minions," I state bitterly.

"I don't know..." Gwen shrugs. "Jamie seems different. Y'know? Down to earth."

I know, I think. *She seems so at ease with who she is...* I envy it.

● ● ●

Jamie beats me to art every day since the first day of school. Since I'm coming from the upstairs physics department, and she's already downstairs in calculus, she has the upper hand.

And yes, I know her schedule. Sue me.

So, by Friday, I had already begun to fall into the routine of expecting to see her in the seat next to mine. I even pace a little faster down the hall, hoping to beat my previous arrival time Thursday.

I walk in and spot her. She's pulling her long, dark hair back into a high ponytail to keep it out of her way, which exposes her delicate facial features. I find a part of me wanting to run my hands through it, imagining how silky and soft it probably is...

"Peyton?" Mr. Z asks, snapping me out of my daydream. "Are you waiting for inspiration or are you having a heat stroke?"

I just laugh in embarrassment, then find my seat.

Jamie gives me an understanding smile. "I wouldn't blame you if you *were* having a heat stroke. It's really hot in here."

I nod. "Yeah. The art department doesn't get much funding."

"Not even for proper A/C?"

I sigh. "No. It's really unfair."

"Well, you're like the boss, right? Doesn't the senior class president have some political leverage?" Jamie asks.

"Trust me," I start. "I've tried for years to get the art department some support, but the athletic department has priority considering they bring the school money."

"Politics," Jamie scoffs. "It's all bullshit."

I bite my lip at the curse word and find it mildly attractive. Hell, I find a lot of what Jamie does attractive. Who am I kidding?

We fall silent again and I grow frustrated. I can't figure

out why I lose my words around Jamie, because I'm always so good at making conversation with other people. I do it all the time. And then there's Jamie, who probably has a wonderful story to tell, and I find it impossible to form a coherent thought!

Eventually, I no longer feel so bad for the silence because both of us become engrossed in our daily task. Our assignment today is to draw the object in the middle of the room, which is, cliché enough, a fruit bowl.

After about thirty minutes, I lean back and glance over, seeing Jamie's sketch. It's great. Like, *really* great. Nearly realistic, if not for the fact that it was just black and white on her paper. I find myself impressed.

She glances at me.

"Hey, no peeking!" she teases while covering her sketchbook.

I smile. "You're really good."

She nods over to my own book. "You're not so bad yourself."

I blush in response, and then the bell rings for dismissal. I sigh and silently wish that my other classes passed as fast as art did.

I pack my bag and stand, but before I can leave, Mr. Z stops me.

"Peyton, can you hang out for a bit?" he asks.

Jamie looks back at me before disappearing out the door. I find myself disappointed that I can't walk with her out of class.

"What's up?" I ask Mr. Z.

"Okay, before I even tell you, I need you to know that I'm not trying to overwhelm you, or pressure you into anything," he starts rambling. "I know you're probably the busiest student at Branton, and you have a hard time saying no..."

"Mr. Z," I interrupt his ramble. "It's fine. What is it?"

He smiles, and there's this tangible excitement in his light eyes. He walks over to his desk in the back of the room and picks up a flyer and hands it to me.

"There's a competition," he reveals. "Between our school district's art departments."

I study the colorful flyer as he speaks.

"A mural competition. Whichever student wins will get twenty-*thousand* dollars for their school's art department. There's criteria, of course, but I really think you're our best bet," he finishes.

A mural competition.

Criteria: Must be at least twelve-by-twelve feet, incorporate symbolism, and finished by the end of the school year. Number of persons allowed to participate for one mural is no more than two. Winners will be determined based on how well they meet the criteria and how creative the mural is.

"Let me sleep on it?" I ask with a smile.

Mr. Z reciprocates with a grin and nods. "Sure thing, Peyton."

I hold on to the flyer and bolt out the door. This sounds

big, and important, and *time consuming*. But it also sounds like a lot of fun.

I search for Jamie when I make it out of the classroom, but unfortunately, she isn't there waiting. Instead of dwelling on the disappointment, I make my way to the cafeteria, knowing that it's taco day, and Darian and Gibbs love taco day.

I find my three friends sitting already, and watch Jamie take her place at the table. For some reason, seeing Jamie so comfortable with my friends makes me nervous. It makes me nervous because it's different when it's just us two, without the presence of an audience.

"Well, look who decided to show!" Darian calls.

Gwen moves over. "We grabbed you some food."

I sit next to Gwen and across from Jamie.

"Thanks," I say.

My knee touches another under the table and I look up to see who it is. Jamie also looks up and allows her smile to grow just a bit wider. I find my stomach full of butterflies as she presses the rest of her leg against mine in response.

"So, tonight..." Gwen voices. "It seems like the entire senior class plans on coming."

"Nice," Darian boasts.

"Thank God the folks are out of town." Gibbs shoves half a taco into his mouth. "What time are y'all comin' over?"

"I was thinking ten," I include, watching Jamie's reaction. She seems confused.

"Chicago, you comin'?" Darian wonders.

"I have no idea what you guys are talking about," Jamie reveals.

Darian then looks at me. "Peyton you didn't tell her?"

Everyone's attention is now on me, and suddenly I'm hot with embarrassment. Crap. Crap, crap, *crap*. Why hadn't I invited her? She's going to think I don't want her there.

But do you really want her there?

Yes, of course! Right?

"I-I'm sorry," I stammer. "It totally slipped my mind."

I can tell Jamie isn't buying it, but she looks more hurt than offended. I want to believe it's because I hadn't personally invited her, and she instead had to hear about it secondhand. I feel the weight of her leg move away from mine under the table and suddenly I'm cold.

"It's whatever." She shrugs. "I won't have a ride there anyway."

"Really?" Gibbs asks.

"I don't have a car and my mom's also gonna be out of town until tomorrow," Jamie explains.

"Where do you live?"

Jamie mumbles something that I don't catch because I'm too hung up on my embarrassment for not inviting her. That's when Gwen kicks my foot under the table. I snap out of my daze.

"Peyton?" I hear. "Can you pick Jamie up before you come over? You live the closest to her."

I look at Darian and then Jamie, seeing an expression on her face I didn't like.

"Yeah, definitely, I can do that," I agree.

Jamie seems unimpressed with the fact that I agreed, but relieved at the same time. I wonder what she's thinking. Does she think I feel obligated to bring her since I forgot to invite her? Does she think I don't want her there?

"I'll uh, text you my address." She pulls out her phone and hands it to me. "You can just put in your number."

I type it in silence while desperately wanting to escape this situation. I'm a total mess around this girl and other people are surely starting to notice. When I receive her address, I force myself to look at her.

"I'll pick you up around nine-thirty," I claim.

"Sounds good." Jamie nods, and then takes a deep breath. "I uh, forgot... I have to check in with the counselor." She stands. "I'll see you guys tonight."

"Later."

I watch in silence as she leaves, aware that she, in fact, does *not* have to check in with the counselor because the counselor doesn't come in on Fridays. I wonder why she felt the need to leave but assume it's because I had messed up and made her uncomfortable.

"Tonight is gonna be awesome," Gibbs says.

"Agreed."

My silence probably worries my friends, but I can't find the will to be excited. Instead, all I feel is nervous. Like my stomach is currently caving in on itself.

Jamie is infiltrating my life without any idea how much it's breaking me down. My defenses are crumbling, my mask is cracking, and the closer she gets, the more she would unintentionally reveal.

Four

I'VE BEEN SITTING IN JAMIE'S DRIVEWAY for almost five minutes now. My heart pounds and my thumb hovers over the "send" button on my phone. If I had known my friends would volunteer me to pick her up, I would've skipped out on taco day.

Before I can hit "send", Jamie walks outside. She's dressed in a white t-shirt with the sleeves rolled, accentuating her delicate shoulders. She's paired the shirt with blue skinny jeans and white Converse high-tops. I think the outfit makes her look so...

"Hey," she greets half-heartedly as she joins me in the car.

"H-Hey... I uh, just got here..." I lie, showing her the

unsent text message.

"Yeah." She nods. "I saw you from upstairs."

I put my car in reverse and back out of her driveway, knowing the drive to the lake house will be longer coming from Jamie's house.

We sit in silence for a moment. I figure it's because of what happened at lunch earlier today when my friends called me out for not personally inviting her. The embarrassment still makes my cheeks burn.

"So, what did Mr. Z keep you after class for?"

I sigh in relief, grateful Jamie's broken the awkward silence.

"There's this competition going on between the art departments of our school district," I inform her. "A mural competition. He asked if I would do it."

"What's the reward?"

"Twenty-thousand dollars."

"Damn," Jamie says. "That could definitely fix the A/C problem."

I smile at her humor.

"Are you gonna do it?" she wonders.

I shrug. "I don't know, I mean, I want to..."

"But?"

"But... I don't know if I'll have time."

"Peyton," Jamie starts. My heart flutters at the sound of her saying my name. "You *have* to do it."

I glance at her. "Yeah? Why?"

"Because... Mr. Z thought of you for a reason. Out of

all his students, you were the one that came to mind. Plus, this could benefit so many kids after you graduate..." Jamie tries to contain her excitement. "It's an opportunity to leave a legacy."

"I guess..."

"Well, do you have to do it alone?"

"What?"

"Does it have to be just one student to work on the mural or can you have a helper?"

"Two students max can work on it," I reveal. "But, like I said, I'm not sure if I even want to, much less involve someone else."

Jamie leans back into the passenger seat.

"I have a month to decide," I finish. "The competition doesn't start 'til the middle of September."

The car falls silent again, but now I can feel the negative tension that had previously surrounded us begin to fade away. It's replaced with a kind of tension I'm becoming more familiar with. A pull that makes me a bit uncomfortable but... *excited.*

Then a song that's blue-toothed to my phone comes through my car speakers, the volume is too low for my liking. I reach to turn it up.

"I love this song," Jamie says while also reaching for the dial.

Our fingers touch and a jolt of electricity and warmth touches every cell in my body in a split second. I pull away like she's fire.

"Sorry," she apologizes.

I try to play it cool. "I-I love this band."

"Yeah? Have you seen them live?"

"I haven't. Have you?"

Jamie lights up. "Yes. Like, five times. They're from Chicago so they play there often."

"Lucky."

The conversation falls again, forcing us to sit in silence. Jamie shifts in her seat and I drum my fingers against the steering wheel with angst. I can feel something bubbling but I'm unsure what it is.

"Don't take this the wrong way but..." Jamie pauses. "Did you not want to invite me tonight?"

I feel my words leave me. I figured she felt that way, but I hadn't expected her to be so direct about it. I frantically search for an explanation.

"I get it if not," Jamie continues. "I kind of just barged into your friend group, and you really don't know me..."

"It's not that," I interrupt.

I glance over and see a look on her face that makes me regret ever making her feel left out. It has to be hard, coming all the way from Chicago and leaving everyone she knows. My insecurities shouldn't have the power to isolate her.

Only for a moment do I want to tell her the truth, but of course, I chicken out.

"I've just been overwhelmed," I lie again. "And mentioning the party really did just slip my mind."

My response seems to soothe her, but I know she's smarter than that. She's reading me, and I'm convinced she knows that isn't the whole story. But instead of pestering, Jamie allows the conversation to end.

I pull down the familiar dark, gravel road and slowly crawl to the lake house that sits at the end. I know every curve like the back of my hand despite the darkness that surrounds the beams of light from my car. I've been here *many* times, so I'm used to it, but Jamie's eyes are wide with caution.

"Are you sure we're not about to end up in a murder movie?" she nervously asks.

I laugh. "*No.*"

Finally, we park under a large white oak tree and I exit my vehicle. Jamie follows me in close pursuit. I feel her ease up when she spots my friends through the windows. When we walk through the doors, they give her a warm welcome.

"Chicago! You made it!" Darian shouts and hugs us both to his sides.

I escape his grasp and walk over to Gwen, who's already drinking some concoction from her plastic cup.

"Hey," she greets. "Want a drink?"

I nod eagerly even though it's a bit early, but my stress levels are high.

"Yes, please. Whatever you're drinking."

"Brave soul."

Gwen pours me a cup and hands it over, all while I watch Jamie converse with Darian and Gibbs from afar.

I didn't know what tonight would bring. All I knew was that I would most likely be drunk by the end of it.

● ● ●

As I rest against the handrail of the staircase, I attempt to focus on the story Gwen is telling. I've heard it already, which might be why I'm uninterested. Or maybe I can't focus because I can see Jacki and Jamie sitting together on the couch having a grand time.

I realize the drunker I get, the more courage I find to just head over there and tell Jacki to piss off. I know it's dangerous, so I choose to keep my distance instead. Except I can't manage to stop looking for Jamie in the crowd.

I stand straight and head down the stairs, making my way to the kitchen. My cup is empty, and I can't stand the sight of Jacki's hand gliding over Jamie's thigh anymore. I need another drink.

As I shove my way through the crowded lake house, I realize there's *a lot* of people here. Even people I don't recognize. The walls rattle with bass from the music. I pass a beer pong table and watch the guy shoot and miss, the ball bouncing right in front of my face.

Eventually, I make it to the kitchen and open the fridge to retrieve the mix Gwen had made before the party. The stuff is good, but it's also *really* strong.

"Woah there, Peyton," Darian warns. "That's like what,

your fifth?"

I roll my eyes. "I'm fine."

"You're a lightweight."

"And?"

Darian's expression lets me know that he's onto me, and that he's worried. Can he tell I'm not having a good time? Can he tell it's because of Jamie?

"Have you seen Chicago?"

I take a large sip. "Yeah, she's being felt up by Jacki on the couch."

The animosity burns my tongue and I know I'm giving myself away. Good thing Darian is also drunk, or he most likely would've noticed my jealousy.

"And I'm *missing* it?" he jokes.

I just scoff and walk away.

I push my way through the kitchen crowd and head back to the living room while the picture of Jacki's hand on Jamie's thigh burns my brain.

Why do I care, anyway? I'm just infatuated with the new girl. And *so what* if she's gay! Eventually, the things I feel will wear off, and I'll be left feeling embarrassed for obsessing over these stupid thoughts.

Then, as I round the corner I clumsily bump into a familiar figure. It's, of course, Jamie.

"Hey," she says. "I feel like I haven't seen you all night."

My heart pounds. All my previous thoughts are immediately thrown out the window. I realize I'm not as nervous as I usually am around her, which I find dangerous.

My nerves are my only defense against her. They protect me from saying too much. They make me *think*. But now they're gone, along with my inhibitions.

"Y-Yeah," I stutter. "Well, I'm just making rounds."

"Jacki's trying to convince me to join in on her game of truth or dare." She nervously glances over her shoulder. "I'm kinda scared."

"You should be."

Worry and confusion cross her features.

"Sorry." I shake my head. "Jacki's just... a lot."

"I'm noticing..."

I lean against the wall for support due to the alcohol's side effects or... Jamie's. I'm not sure yet.

"Are you at least having fun?" I wonder.

Her glossy hazel eyes find mine. I can tell she's also a little buzzed. She shrugs.

"I'd be having more fun if I were hanging with..."

"Jamie!" Jacki shouts, interrupting our conversation. "I thought you wanted to play?"

Jamie gives me a desperate look and silently begs me to join her or get her out of this situation. I'm not sure what to do.

"Oh, hey Peyton." Jacki taps a nail against her plastic cup. "You wanna play too?"

"Truth or dare?" I confirm. "You do this *every* time we throw a party."

"Because it's a crowd pleaser."

More like a Jacki pleaser, I think.

Jacki's free hand grabs Jamie's. "C'mon, we're starting as soon as I find one more victim."

"O-Only if Peyton agrees to play, too," Jamie claims.

Jacki doesn't seem thrilled. No one says anything for a second as Jamie begs me with her eyes. I'm terrified. Jacki's version of Truth or Dare is relentless, and it always attracts a crowd. There's no telling what could happen.

"Please," Jamie pleads.

Jacki smirks. "Yeah. Come and play, Peyton."

It could be my low inhibitions, or Jamie's pitiful expression, or the desire to shove Jacki's smugness back in her face, but I follow them to the living room.

"I got two newbies to play!"

The circle cheers in excitement. I feel ready to puke.

I sit across from Jamie, who sits next to Jacki. Gibbs has also decided to play, while Gwen and Darian observe from the outside, looking surprised that I've decided to join the game.

The rules are... *somewhat* simple, but there are also twists. The oldest in the circle always kicks off the game. Of course, it was usually Jacki because her birthday falls in November. She then chooses a candidate and, of course, asks "truth or dare?" There are seven of us altogether. Never more, never less. For every two truths, you must do a dare. Also, if you chose "truth," only to be caught lying, the punishment is to do a dare instead. If you bail on a dare, you're eliminated.

Now, any smart, *sober* person would refuse to play

altogether if they wanted to avoid social embarrassment, but with low inhibitions, people tend to feel invincible. The game can get funny, or serious, or even vindictive.

I'm aware of this. Yet, everything between Jacki and me seems to be a competition, so I *have* to one-up her.

"Okay everyone," Jacki announces. "To begin, we need to figure out who the oldest of the group is."

Everyone blurts their birthdays. The only people whose birthdays are in November are Jacki, and surprisingly, Jamie. Jacki's birthday is November thirtieth. Jamie's is November twenty-second.

"I guess the new girl will start us off," Jacki says, sounding slightly displeased.

Jamie isn't sure who to pick on, but I find her eyes switching between me and Gibbs. Jacki places her hand on Jamie's thigh. I feel my blood start to boil.

"If you have trouble choosing..." Jacki places a bottle in the center of the circle. "Just spin."

Jamie eyes the bottle and shrugs before looking straight at me. My heart pounds in my head.

"Peyton: truth or dare?" she asks.

My hands shake in my lap, but I try to hide them.

"Truth."

God, please don't ask me something embarrassing...

"What is your worst habit?" she questions.

I sigh in relief. Is she going easy on me?

"I bite my nails." I flash my hands to the group. "Sometimes, to literal stubs."

A few people murmur "*ew.*"

"Peyton, it's your turn," Jacki directs.

I look at Gibbs. He gives me a drunken smile.

"Gibbs: truth or dare?"

"Y'know I gotta pick dare, Peyt."

I smile. "Run around and scream that you farted."

The group giggles in response.

Gibbs rolls his eyes. "That's *easy.*"

He proceeds to get up and run throughout the lake house for thirty seconds, screaming, "I JUST FARTED." Once he's done, he sits back down with a huge smile.

"Jacki," Gibbs says. "Truth or dare?"

"Truth."

"Who do you think is the hottest teacher at our school?"

Jacki just laughs along with a few other people, and then thinks about her answer for a second. My eyes find Jamie's, which are already looking at me. She gives me a nervous smile before returning her attention back to Jacki.

"Probably Miss Burke," Jacki answers.

Miss Burke *is* hot. If you're into the whole older woman thing, I guess.

Then Jacki looks at me, and for some reason I know it won't matter if I choose truth or dare, because both will be equally difficult. The challenging look in her eyes makes me want to show her up.

"Peyton," she addresses. "Truth or dare?"

I refuse to break eye contact.

"Dare."

Even though I'm drunk, I know a power move when I see one. Jacki is always trying to show me up. She hadn't expected me to choose dare and the shock on her face satisfies me.

"Down the rest of your drink."

I look down into my nearly full cup I had fixed only minutes ago. There's no way I'm backing out this early in the game, but I'm already drunk. I'll be in dangerous territory if I do this.

My eyes find Jamie before I lift the plastic cup to my lips. Then, I watch Jacki's smug grin grow as I begin to down the concoction without any hesitation.

Darian and Gwen, who are sitting behind Jacki, watch me with worried but impressed expressions. They seem convinced they'll most likely be taking care of me later.

As the last sip of my drink slides into my mouth, I take a deep breath and swallow, successfully completing my dare. Everyone in the room is impressed.

"Damn," someone mumbles.

I wipe my mouth and take my turn with pride, picking on the others who haven't had a turn yet. Everyone seems to be having a good time, and after about ten minutes, the alcohol is setting in. People are becoming brave and taking chances. It makes the game exciting.

But it also makes it risky.

A few rounds later, it's now Jamie's turn again as she sips on her own drink while attempting to choose her next victim. I have a feeling it'll be me again. This time, I have no choice but to pick a dare because I had done two truths in a row.

"Peyton." Jamie smirks behind her cup. "I don't even have to ask, do I?"

I feel my cheeks heat up.

"No." I sigh. "Dare."

The room is warped in my periphery. The alcohol from my previous dare has now set in, so I try my best to focus on Jamie. She has this look on her face... Is it smug? Is it flirty? I can't tell, and I want to find it annoying, but only find it annoyingly attractive.

"You have to make out with the person on your right," she states. "Or the person on your left."

My heart somersaults in my chest at "make out." Then I realize to my right is Courtney Wilcox, an attractive cheerleader who I wouldn't mind making out with in my dreams. On my left is Micha... something. He must be a junior because I can't place him. Or maybe it's the alcohol again.

If I base the decision on attractiveness, Courtney wins by a landslide. *But* my decision is more personal. Is Jamie testing me? Is she trying to get me to reveal the fact that I'm gay? The thought makes my palms sweat.

"You have to kiss for *at least* ten seconds."

Everyone in the circle seems eager for my decision. Mumbles of excitement float around the room. My heart feels as if it's about to beat right out of my chest. I can pick

Courtney. She'll understand. But she's wasted... and will people suspect something? Will there be a rumor come Monday morning? Can I afford to do this?

"Are you refusing...?" Jacki presses. "Because if you are..."

I anxiously turn to Micha and grab the back of his head, probably a little too rough, and mash our lips together. He seems shocked, but apparently intends to enjoy it.

Those ten seconds couldn't have passed fast enough.

"Time."

I pull away and look at Jamie. She seems disappointed and refuses to look at me.

"Damn," Jacki jokes. "Peyton, that kiss was a little aggressive, huh?"

I feel a flame of anger ignite in my stomach.

"Jacki." It's my turn anyway. "Truth or dare?"

Intense brown eyes stare me down.

"Dare."

"Make out with your hand."

Jacki lights up at the words "make out", then scoffs at the rest of the dare. She rolls her eyes and momentarily refuses.

"Seriously?"

"Do it or you're eliminated," I state.

"I know the rules, Peyton," Jacki mocks. "I made them."

The room grows quiet as she narrows her eyes at me and shakes her head. The last thing she wants to do is forfeit, especially when the game was her idea in the first place. Without any more hesitation, she presses her hand to her mouth and proceeds to tongue it awkwardly. I can hardly stand the sight.

When she's done, she glares at me.

"Peyton: truth or dare?" she asks sharply.

"Truth," I say without hesitation.

"Is it true you're still a virgin?"

The question elicits mumbles and snickers from the group, but I try not to let it get to me. I clench my jaw.

"Yes."

I refuse to look around because I can already feel Jamie's wide eyes on me. The last thing I want is to see the look on her face.

"Jacki: truth or dare?"

At this point, the game is solely between us and everyone is drunk on the drama.

"Truth."

"Who was your first kiss?"

I watch the stern look on her face falter as she remains quiet. Jacki wants to say something, but instead, holds back. Weird.

"Are you refusing to answer?" I press.

"Yes," she says through clenched teeth.

"Then finish your drink."

She does without hesitation as I wonder why she's refused to reveal who her first kiss was. It seems like a simple question to answer.

"Peyton."

"Truth."

If I weren't so drunk, the negative tension in this room would surely kill me, but I'm too focused on winning. Jacki has embarrassed countless people during her games of Truth or Dare. I just felt it was time to give her a dose of her own medicine.

"Do you pee in the shower?" Jacki asks me.

"Who doesn't pee in the shower?" I feel the tension thicken. "Truth or dare?"

"Dare."

"Lick the floor."

The growing crowd murmurs with disgust.

Jacki refuses to back down and quickly leans over and runs her tongue over the wood flooring.

"Peyton."

"I know. Dare."

"Post on every social media platform saying, 'I'm a raging homosexual'."

She laughs at the dare, but I feel hot under the gaze of my peers. Time seems to stop for me, and I wonder if anyone notices. People around me laugh and I suddenly begin to panic under the spotlight.

"Why the fuck would I do that?" I spit.

The response exits my mouth before I can stop it, and I know what this means. I stand as Jacki laughs in victory. My stomach churns as the room spins. Suddenly, I feel sick.

I stumble up the staircase and try not to let myself puke before I make it to a toilet. The embarrassment of forfeit burns my skin as I slam the bathroom door and lock it behind me. My reflection meets me at the sink as I try to compose myself. Deep breaths help my churning stomach because all I can think about is people making fun of me for opting out of a seemingly stupid dare.

Then there's knocking on the door.

"Peyton? Hey, c'mon, let me in..."

I can't tell who the voice belongs to because of the muffled music, but I hope it isn't Jamie. I feel too embarrassed to face her right now.

"Peyton," the voice demands. "Open the door."

I reach and unlock it, only to reveal Gwen on the other side. I sigh in relief.

"Are you okay?" she asks. "That was intense."

"Y-Yeah," I stutter. "I think all the alcohol just hit me at once."

"Do you need to puke?"

"I thought I needed to," I admit. "But I'm okay now."

The answer seems to settle her worry, but I know she's curious as to what the hell just happened between Jacki and me. I feel the need to explain my reaction.

"Gwen I..." My words stop. Do I really want to tell her the truth? While I'm wasted?

She turns around. "What?"

My body goes numb with fear. What if I tell her, and she thinks differently of me? What if it freaks her out? We've slept in the same bed and we share secrets like sisters. Of course, I feel no sexual attraction for her whatsoever... but what if she didn't believe me? What if she pushes me away and convinces herself I had only gotten close to her because I liked her?

"Nothing..." I internally scold myself. "I'm just... really drunk."

"Then let's get you some water," she suggests.

I follow behind her in silence and realize that if I can't even find the courage to tell my best friend the truth, how could I ever tell anyone else?

● ● ●

The next morning, I wake in a bed that isn't mine. This isn't shocking. Usually, when we had big parties like this, I crashed in a guest bedroom with Gwen. Except this morning is different.

This isn't the bedroom we usually sleep in. The sheets are different and there's this chair in the corner of the room that I've never seen before. I spot my jeans on the floor, but nothing else.

Then, someone stirs next to me.

I peer over my shoulder. The sunlight peeks out from behind the curtains and makes my eyes ache, but not before I notice a blanket of silky brown hair. My breath catches in my throat.

It's definitely a girl. There's no doubt about that. But it *certainly* isn't Gwen, unless there had been another game of Truth or Dare and she had been challenged to dye her blond hair brown. Part of me hopes that's exactly what had happened after I blacked out last night.

The figure fights waking up. She groans and rolls over to face me. And when she does, I nearly jump out of my skin.

It's Jamie.

Shit.

How the hell had I ended up in the same bed as her? I couldn't remember anything after Truth or Dare. I couldn't even remember talking to her after that! What the hell happened? And had we somehow...?

I move to leave. I need to get out of this bed. Maybe, if I go downstairs, I can get away with claiming I had passed out on the couch, or in the hammock they had out in the back yard. Either way, I couldn't let anyone know I had spent the night in the same bed as Jamie. Not after the whole Truth or Dare fiasco.

My jeans are half-way on when a floor panel creaks, and Jamie is awake.

"Peyton...?" she says groggily while rubbing her eyes. "Are you..."

Her sentence trails off as her eyes take me in. I stand there like a deer caught in headlights and feel exposed. Vulnerable. And just a *little* turned on.

"Sorry," I apologize. "I just... I wasn't..."

Her confused expression only makes her look hotter. The way her bed head clings to her face paired with that sleepy look in her eyes...

"I have no idea how I ended up in this bed," I confess.

"I think you thought I was Gwen?" Jamie says as she sits up. "You stumbled in and fell onto the bed but kept tossing and turning because you couldn't get comfortable."

I notice my jeans are still half-way up my legs and decide to finish putting them on.

"Did I take off my jeans? Or...?"

"I did."

My face must've screamed a million words.

"You asked me to. You couldn't get them off and..." Jamie rubs the bridge of her nose. "That's all it was. I promise. You passed out right after."

I believe her. As much as Jamie could get cocky, especially when drunk, I didn't believe she had taken advantage of me. Besides, I still have most of my clothes on, and so did she. There's no sign anything had happened between us.

Yet, I still feel compelled to cover my tracks.

"Please don't tell anyone," I say.

"Tell anyone what?"

"That I... That *we*..."

Our gazes meet, and I immediately know I have nothing to worry about. Jamie isn't the one to do something like that, but my assumption clearly hurts her feelings. Suddenly, I'm nauseated again, and not from my raging hangover.

"That we slept in the same bed," she finalizes. "Got it."

I quickly button my jeans and nod in agreement, trying to mask the guilt I feel for hurting her.

"Thanks," I answer. "I'm leaving in a few. I can drop you off back at home if you want?"

Sad eyes force themselves to look at me, but only for a second.

"Alright."

Then I bolt out the door before anyone else decides to wake up.

Five

AFTER THE BACK-TO-SCHOOL PARTY, things between Jamie and me aren't the same. There's a distance, or disconnect, which shouldn't bother me as much as it is.

I know it's because of the incident the morning after the party. I know *exactly* what it is but can't seem to find the courage to address it and apologize. Now, weeks have passed, and she rarely hangs out with me and my friends, refuses to sit next to me in art class, and to top it all off, she's been hanging out with Jacki way more than usual.

Deep down it kills me but, in the end, I know it's my own fault.

Maybe I am a coward. Maybe, I really am terrified of how people will look at me if I tell them the truth. That

Peyton Kelly is, in fact, a lesbian, and has been since she could first remember.

Maybe, I had successfully convinced myself that it's because I had too much at stake to ruin my reputation when really, it's because I'm petrified of change.

And I had hurt someone because of it.

As I walk into school, the early September morning consists of humidity, fog, and gloom since the sun has barely risen. I had arrived a few minutes early to meet with the speech and debate teacher. I let myself into the hall and enter the classroom, greeting Miss Burke with a smile.

"Peyton," she greets "Good morning."

"Morning," I reply, involuntarily remembering the embarrassing game of Truth or Dare because of Jacki's lustful remark about Miss Burke.

"Listen, I'm glad you stopped by, because I want to talk to you about something." Miss Burke leans on her desk. "This year's team..."

"Is gonna be great. I know." I slip my annual registration form onto her desk. "I've already started preparing my first speech..."

"Peyton," she interrupts. "Have a seat."

I sit cautiously when I realize she and I aren't on the same page. Am I in trouble?

"I just want to start off by saying you've been an absolute treasure to the speech team," she compliments. "I remember how fierce of a competitor you were when you were just a freshman..."

For some reason, this feels like a breakup. What the hell is she getting at?

"But our freshmen this year are *so* promising, and there's one student who I'll have to say no to if I let you participate this year."

At first, her words don't register.

"Wait, what?" I ask.

She repeats herself. Confusion and anger boil in my stomach while white noise fills my head. But I won't lash out. That would look bad.

"You've done phenomenally, and if you decide to do speech in college, I have no doubt in my mind that you'll excel," Miss Burke finishes. "I just think your speech potential has surpassed high school level, and these freshmen need coaching."

A sacrifice. That's what she's asking me for. Three years of busting my ass on this team, taking them to regionals and *winning*... and this is what I get? Nothing but a "thank you" and a bitter send-off!?

I stand abruptly.

"N-No problem," I stutter as the betrayal pierces my heart. "Good luck this year, Miss Burke."

I catch a glimpse of her guilty expression but storm out before it can make me any angrier. Speech had been one of my favorite pastimes! And it looks amazing on résumés! I feel cheated.

As I storm through the hall all I can see is red. I hadn't expected to run into someone, especially since it's still early. And I surely hadn't expected it to be Jamie, of all people.

Our bodies collide. The book she's carrying falls to the floor with a thud. I fumble clumsily into her and feel her soft hands grip on my shoulders. Everything inside of me freezes.

"Shit, s-sorry..." I stammer, attempting to hide the embarrassment on my face.

"It's fine," she answers. Within that moment she realizes she's still holding me. Her hands release me quickly. "Are you okay?"

"Yeah," I lie. "Yeah, I'm fine."

"Are you sure? Because *most* people look up when they're walking."

I roll my eyes. As much as I appreciate the interaction with Jamie after weeks of being starved, my morning is ruined from Miss Burke. The anger is slowly subsiding, but she's honestly the last person I want to see me like this.

"What are you doing here so early, anyway?" I ask.

Her cheeks turn pink. "I uh... I missed the bus. So, my mom dropped me off on her way to work."

There seems to be a lingering tension, as if both of us have something to say to the other but are too afraid to do so. I know what I *want* to say and can't help but wonder if there's something on the tip of Jamie's tongue.

"Darian keeps asking me why you don't hang with us for lunch anymore," I blurt. "And Gibbs still needs a ton of girl advice."

Her stone demeanor softens at the comment about our friends, but not much. Her walls are still sky high around me. I don't blame her. She doesn't bother addressing my comments, probably because we both know exactly why she isn't coming around. She just forces a half smile, indicating that we are, in fact, on the same page.

"Jamie, I..."

"I'm gonna head to the library," she interrupts my apology. "I have some things I need to print before class."

I swallow my sentence and give her a stiff nod. She brushes past me without another word, leaving me to soak in shame and the early morning fog. I must've really hurt her, but why do *I* feel like the one who got the short end of the stick? Everything inside of me aches simply because Jamie is icing me out.

Suddenly, I fear the damage between us is now beyond repair.

● ● ●

The day passes slowly, and my classes seem to drag on for hours. Everything is monotonous. The teachers, the subjects, my friends... I find myself eager to make it to fourth period just so I can distract myself with art.

By art block I find myself crawling to class and no longer expect to see Jamie sitting in the seat next to mine. Every day since the party, I had walked into class with a small sliver of hope that she would change her mind. But, as expected, she'd be across the room, sitting alone. When I walk into the classroom, today is no different.

I try to ignore the burning in my chest as I make my way to my seat. I should just apologize. Apologize for assuming she would lie and tell people we slept together, and apologize for icing her out around my friends, apologize for acting like something I'm *not*...

Ok, no, the last one still scares the hell out of me.

Class begins and Mr. Z starts his lecture with some art history while I sneak glances at Jamie and try not to get caught doodling in my notebook. We're slowly making the transition from sketching to painting, and I'm way too excited about it.

Which reminds me...

Today is the cut-off date to enter the mural competition.

I hadn't given it much thought because I didn't think I would have time to do it, which had been true up until Miss Burke kicked me off the speech team. Now, my schedule had opened significantly, but do I really want to do this?

The conversation Jamie and I had the night of Gibbs' party resurfaces. Jamie had nearly convinced me to enter right then and there...

The ringing of the bell pulls me out of my thoughts. I shut my notebook and shove it into my backpack. My eyes watch Jamie leave without looking back. She always makes it a point to beat me out of the door.

I stand and make my way to Mr. Z's desk and hope that

when I mention the mural competition, my brain will finally decide if doing this is a good idea.

"Peyton," he greets me "You were quiet today. Is everything alright?"

I just nod. "Yeah, I just... I was thinking about the competition."

He raises a brow. "You know the entry deadline is today..."

He still seems so hopeful. Why is everyone so sure that I will do great? Don't get me wrong, I consider myself an exceptional artist, but murals are different. They're big, and make statements, and are sometimes even a bit controversial. Could I *really* pull this off?

"Do you have a back-up?" I ask.

"A what?"

"A back-up. A second choice."

He shakes his head. "No."

Great. So, if I say no, that means Branton High is automatically out of the running and has absolutely no chance at winning the prize money. Why hadn't he asked someone else? Does he believe in his decision *that* much?

"Peyton," Mr. Z starts. "You're a magnificent artist. Do you know that?"

There are only a handful of people who know my love for art. My parents, my sister Alyssa, Gwen, and Mr. Z, and out of those five people, Mr. Z is the only one who ever compliments me in ways that resonate. He critiques me, he educates me, and never embarrasses me if I make a mistake.

Instead, he teaches me to be a better artist. I look to him as a mentor instead of a teacher.

So, when he compliments me, it's always more than that. It's affirmation. It's confidence. It's a push whenever I really needed it.

"I don't know the first thing about creating a mural," I confess.

"Then we'll work on that," he promises. "But your mind works in ways most others don't. That's talent. And I really think you won't walk away empty handed."

He's right. I can do this because I'm not alone. If I need help, I can always come to him. Besides, it's not like he wouldn't be overseeing the progress.

"Okay." I agree. "I'll do it."

"You will?"

I just nod nervously.

He smiles. "You can start as soon as possible, but I would brainstorm for a few weeks. Come up with a brilliant idea. Draw it out. Color it in. *Really* put some thought into it. And then, when you're confident, start painting."

I sigh heavily, aware this is going to be a challenge on all fronts.

"I believe in you, Peyton," Mr. Z says.

I smile hard and attempt to contain my excitement and fear. Nervous isn't a strong enough term to describe how I feel right now, but I settle for it anyway.

"Thanks," I say. "I'll see you tomorrow."

Then I turn to leave.

So, I'm doing this. For real. Mr. Z will let whoever is overseeing the competition's candidates know Branton High now has a champion. I feel adrenaline burn through my veins at the thought. What if I *do* win?

I'm no longer in a crappy mood from this morning and decide to find my friends. If they aren't hanging out at the prep tree, then they're most likely inside the cafeteria. My hands push the doors open with excitement.

But when I spot Jamie laughing with Darian and Gibbs at a nearby table, a part of me tells my legs to stop. They look like they're having a good time. Even Gwen. I know my friends like Jamie. That's a given. And she's been avoiding them for my sake. Or for hers. I'm not sure.

If I join them, I'll just ruin it. Negative tension will surround the table, and everyone will notice. Then, once Jamie's had enough of it, she'll leave. In hindsight, me joining them is a bad idea.

So, instead, I turn right back around and head for the parking lot.

Six

FOR ME, RUNNING IS THERAPEUTIC. Now, don't get me wrong. It hurts like a bitch in the beginning, but if you can manage to get past the pain, everything after feels like autopilot. It's soothing, and my mind is free of any thought or worry in the world, even if it is only for a small amount of time.

"So..." Gwen pants. "Have you gotten any ideas?"

We're in sync, left and right steps together as we make our way around the track. Conditioning for soccer doesn't start until late October, but for Gwen this is prime time because of football season, and she hates running alone.

"Not one," I confess. "I'm overthinking it."

In exactly two weeks since accepting the challenge of

the mural, I haven't produced a single idea that's inspired me. Hell, the only thing I can seem to think about is homecoming, and the dance, and the pep rally tomorrow that I still have to paint posters for...

"Well, what's something you wanna say?" Gwen interrupts.

I shake my head and try to focus on my breathing. What the hell *do* I want to say?

"I don't know..." I wipe my forehead. "Something like... be true to who you are..."

We finally reach the end of the mile and stop to catch our breath. I place my hands on my head and inhale. The Georgia heat strangles my exhausted lungs.

"Okay..." Gwen doesn't sound impressed. "Those are just words... but you have to *show* it. Y'know?"

"Yeah."

We begin walking back to the locker room, but not before a figure in the stadium catches my eye. It's Jamie, in short running shorts and a muscle shirt jogging up and down the steps. The muscles in her legs protrude with each step and her biceps glisten...

"Is that Jamie?" Gwen asks, pulling me out of my trance.

"Looks like it."

"You missed lunch today," she starts. "But Gibbs and Darian invited her to ride with us to homecoming."

My heart threatens to burst from my chest. *Why* would Darian and Gibbs do that? We always went as a foursome, including whoever we decided to bring as dates! But now they had invited Jamie and thrown off the balance, and I wasn't sure how to feel about it.

"Great," I say. "That's great."

"Darian asked me to be his date."

I almost don't catch Gwen's comment because I'm stealing last minute glances at Jamie and wondering what I'm going to do about the dance this Saturday. It takes a minute for her comment to really register.

I look at her. "Wait, as in like a *date* date?"

She just nods, as if she's nervous for my reaction.

"It's about time he's made a move," is all I say.

"What?" Gwen laughs in confusion. "About *time*?"

"Darian has liked you for a while now," I confess. "Everyone knows it. He's just finally getting over his pride and doing something about it."

"But he made it seem like it wasn't a big deal..."

"Well, he's lying." I give her a smile. "He's definitely freaking out inside."

Gwen just blushes as we make it to the locker room.

As we change, I wonder if Jamie has been asked to the dance by anyone, and, if so, by whom? I want to be excited she was coming with us, but all I can think about is the underlying negative tension. All because yours truly had royally screwed up and hasn't found the courage to apologize.

But Jamie actively avoiding me didn't make it any easier.

We change in no time and begin making our way to the parking lot to leave. My mind is racing with thoughts about all I have to get done in the next few days. Then I realize I've forgotten my water bottle at the stadium.

"Crap," I express. "I forgot my water bottle."

"Okay." Gwen throws her bag into the backseat of her car. "I'll see you tomorrow?"

"Yeah, see you tomorrow."

Then I jog back to the track.

It remains where I had left it. I sigh in relief as I pick it up and take a sip.

"GSU?" I hear behind me.

I turn to see Jamie also drinking from her own bottle as loose strands of dark hair cling to her neck and face.

"Georgia State," I reply. "Over in Atlanna. My older sister goes there."

Jamie seems intrigued by the mentioning of my older sibling. She wipes her forehead with the back of her arm and moves under the shade of a nearby tree. Her hazel eyes glow when she no longer has to squint from the sun's glare.

"Did Gwen force you to run with her or do you enjoy self-torture?"

I can't help but release a small smile at her playfulness because it's something I miss. We haven't talked like this in weeks.

"I'm actually the motivator," I confess. "She hates running."

"You run track, or...?"

"Soccer." I watch her slim eyebrow raise. "I'm just getting a jump on conditioning season."

She smirks. "Always the overachiever."

There's a lull in the conversation. I want to say so many things to her but I'm not sure where exactly to start. I could apologize, or I could ask her if she has a date to homecoming yet. But that seems inappropriate considering past events...

"So, Gwen told me you're joining us before the dance Saturday."

She looks up from the ground. "Yeah. Darian and Gibbs kinda put me on the spot...." She pauses. "Is that okay or...?"

Cautious. She's still cautious and it's killing me inside. Why had I let her believe her presence made me uncomfortable, rather than the truth?

"It's fine," I reassure her. "The more the merrier."

"Yeah well, I'll probably be the only one without a date, so..."

Jamie doesn't have a date. *I* don't have a date. I'm not sure why my heartbeat speeds up at the information, because I know I won't make a move. I know we won't go together. But if Jamie doesn't have a date, then I won't go out of my way to find one either.

"Dates kinda hold you back," I lie, as if I hadn't been planning to find one before this conversation. "It's more fun with friends."

She smiles but doesn't say anything. Suddenly, I feel the need to apologize for what I had said to her the morning after the party.

"So..."

Then her phone rings in her hand and cuts me off. She glances down and types a quick response.

"And my ride's here," she says. "What were you gonna say?"

I shake my head as the apology falls from the tip of my tongue. "Nothing. I'll see you tomorrow."

She gives me a look of uncertainty but refuses to press me before walking away. I watch her disappear from the stadium as I try and deal with my rollercoaster of emotions.

We seem to be on decent terms again, and both of us are currently without dates for the dance. It has the potential to be a fun night together, and maybe I can finally apologize for assuming she would tell the entire school we had slept together at Gibbs' party.

After weeks of being uncertain if Jamie and I would ever be okay, things were starting to look up, and maybe, I could get things right on the second try.

● ● ●

Friday approaches quickly and I find running on three hours of sleep easier said than done. As senior class president, it's my responsibility to make sure all events run smoothly, from setting up for the homecoming dance to making sure the pep rally was a hit. Which it *was*, of course, thanks to yours truly. I have no time to even *think* about sleep until after the football game tonight, which is a huge deal considering it's against our rivals.

"*Are you on your way?*" Gwen asks.

"Yes, I'm pulling up now," I answer while pressing my phone to my ear with my shoulder.

"*Are your parents coming?*"

"Yes." I close my car door. "They're just waiting on Alyssa. As usual."

"*Ugh. I love when your sister is in town.*"

"Of course, you do."

Gwen and I continue the exchange for a little while longer before I hang up and hurry to the field. People are flowing in and the atmosphere feels electric. Everyone is excited for the game, but all I find myself doing is searching for Jamie in the crowd.

I occupy myself with helping the concession stand and then meet with some of the yearbook crew before the game starts. It isn't until I'm making my way to the student section that I run into Jamie.

"Peyton, hey," she greets.

"Hey." My heart flutters. "I didn't know you'd be here."

She looks over her shoulder. "Yeah, I didn't think I would be either but... here I am."

I smile. "Not a football fan?"

She just shrugs.

Even though we're speaking again, I still sense underlying tension. As if she doesn't want to give me the wrong impression. I find it annoying.

"Peyton!" I hear behind me. I immediately recognize the voice but refuse to turn around. "*Peyton!*"

I continue to ignore the voice and hope she'll just find me later when I'm *not* talking to Jamie.

"PEYTOR TOT!"

I cringe at the nickname. The look on Jamie's face makes me blush. *Why* would she say that aloud here? Of all places?!

Jamie looks past me. "Is that...?"

"Peyt, what the hell?" Alyssa asks behind me. "Are you really ignoring me?"

I turn around. "Alyssa, why on *earth* would I do that?"

"Because that's what you do."

I roll my eyes at my older sister before I pull her in for a hug. I hadn't seen her in a few weeks since she had moved back to Atlanta for college and I had missed her.

"So, you *do* miss me!" Alyssa exclaims.

"Of course I do, you loser." The hug ends. "Where's mom and dad?"

"Talking with Gwen's parents." Alyssa silently glares behind me and at Jamie.

"Hi...?" Jamie says nervously.

"This is Jamie," I introduce. "Jamie, this is my older sister, Alyssa."

They exchange quiet "hellos" as I stand and watch from the outside. My sister studies Jamie in a way that makes me feel embarrassed.

"Chicago, huh?" Alyssa says as she points to the flag on Jamie's beanie.

"Yeah," Jamie brags. "I grew up there."

After that, Alyssa has this look of approval stamped on her face, as if Jamie *not* being from Branton, Georgia was a trait worth having. I swear, my sister is so *weird* sometimes.

"So, I'm hanging with you guys tonight," Alyssa informs. "Are we goin' to the student section or what?"

And with that, she brushes past us and heads up to the stadium. Jamie looks at me with a humorous expression.

"Peytor tot, huh?" she teases.

"Don't," I warn as my face heats up. "Only she is allowed to call me that."

Jamie smirks. "Yes ma'am."

Even though my three best friends can't join me in the stands on homecoming night, I find joy in my newfound company. Without Jamie and Alyssa, I would feel alone, despite knowing every single senior in my class. I guess there's a difference between being popular and being genuinely liked.

After a minute of getting comfortable in the stands, we have kickoff. The game is on. I watch as Darian throws pass after pass and Gibbs blocks and pummels through the opposing team. Gwen instructs her girls throughout the entirety of it, cheering on the boys and hyping up the crowd in the process. The score stays neck and neck most of the game, and after half-time, things get even more intense.

One of our receivers runs the ball in for a touchdown

and the crowd cheers.

"Yes!" I shout while clapping in excitement.

"You're really into this game," Jamie says.

I look at her. "Of course I am."

"She *has* to be," Alyssa teases. "It's her job."

"I *like* football, Alyssa."

"Meh," my sister replies.

I roll my eyes. "Why'd you come to the game if you don't like football?"

Alyssa wiggles her eyebrows. "Because hot boys in tight pants, duh?"

I don't react, but apparently Jamie finds the need to make a sound of disapproval. This catches my sister's attention. I hold my breath with anticipation.

"What, you don't like that?" Alyssa asks Jamie.

"I prefer watching the cheerleaders," Jamie responds. "If you know what I mean?"

"Oh." My sister smiles. "So, you're gay."

My heart clenches in my chest at her brash comment. I cringe internally and hope she hasn't offended Jamie.

"Peyton, you've never had a gay friend before!"

"Alyssa, be quiet."

And just when I didn't think she could get any worse...

"What's it like?" My sister locks eyes with Jamie and ignores me all together. "Y'know, sleeping with girls? I mean, I've made out with my friends 'cause you know, alcohol, but..."

I can't help but look at Jamie. I'm too appalled to tell

my sister to shut the hell up, but too intrigued *not* to listen to Jamie's answer. God, why is this *happening?*

"Uh, well I've only slept with one girl..."

I sigh in relief, either from Jamie's confession or the fact that she hadn't told my sister to fuck off.

"Well?" my sister presses.

"Alyssa..." I warn.

"She was older than me, and more experienced so..." Jamie pauses. "It was actually pretty great."

Pretty *great?* Jamie's been with someone experienced that had exceeded her expectations. The information makes my body grow hot with envy. I'm convinced it's noticeable. Jamie is out and she's happy. She's comfortable with herself.

And then there's me. A hopeful but spineless girl who's nowhere near the caliber of Jamie Kendall.

The cheering of the crowd pulls me out of my trance, but my mind is no longer at the game. There are only a few minutes left, and it feels like it'll last an eternity. Then, to make things worse, Jacki and her squad move to the bleachers right in front of us. I roll my eyes.

I'm torn. I should just let go of the idea that Jamie and I have a chance, because I'm *not* out. Jamie wouldn't be willing to sacrifice her freedom to hide again! It's selfish of me to even consider asking that of her...

"Jamie!"

I snap out of it to see Jacki and Jamie exchange smiles, which makes everything I'm feeling right now even worse.

I just swallow my pain.

"Are you okay?" my sister asks. "You got really quiet."

"Yeah, I'm fine," I lie. "Just into the game."

There isn't a lot of time left on the clock and we are losing. Thankfully, we have the ball, and we just need a touchdown on this final drive. Everything is on the line. That's right. Focus, Peyton. This is what you're here to do. Enjoy the game. Not worry about Jacki, or Jamie, or your sister bringing up Jamie's sex life...

The ball is snapped. Darian steps back and looks around for a target. My heart pounds. The crowd goes silent. Even Jamie tenses up next to me.

Then the ball is in the air. I hold my breath.

It spirals over the players and far down the field. I feel my hand gripping something soft and realize it's Jamie's hand. She doesn't react, which encourages me to stay in that position.

The ball lands in the hands of one of our players and the crowd goes nuts. He dodges and jumps around opposing colors. My heart is in my throat. Then, he dives, and we score.

We won!

Everyone goes insane. The screams coming from the bleachers are deafening. Yet, all I can think about is the way my hand seems to fit into Jamie's. It's soft, and it feels... *right*. Like they're matching puzzle pieces.

Her hazel eyes find mine in the moment of chaos, but she doesn't say anything. I don't either, mostly because I'm too afraid to ruin it.

"Woah," Alyssa says.

I release Jamie's hand instantly.

I turn to see what she's talking about, but notice Jacki standing right in front of us, looking at Jamie with huge and hopeful eyes. Then I read the sign her friend is holding next to her.

It reads: *"Jamie, I know it's not a Cubs game, but will you go to hoco with me?"*

I can't stand to watch the rest, so I leave Jamie's side and head to the exit with Alyssa.

Seven

I FEEL SICK TO MY STOMACH. I know I shouldn't care that Jamie is going to the dance with Jacki or that Jacki had somehow managed to infiltrate the night Jamie and I were supposed to enjoy together. I shouldn't care.

But I do.

I pull up to Gibbs' lake house and try not to let it get to me. After all, this is my last homecoming. I had worked hard to make sure everyone has a great time, including myself. I will *not* let Jacki ruin that.

I tug down the sun visor and check my makeup. Alyssa helped me, which I was grateful for because I'm not a makeup guru like most of the girls I go to school with. I'm a minimalist whenever it comes to my appearance. After studying my reflection, I take a deep breath and exit the safety of my car.

Everyone is here. Gwen and Darian's vehicles sit next to Gibbs', and then there's Jacki's. I feel my body burn with annoyance.

I walk in and immediately find my friends in the kitchen, including Jacki. My eyes find Jamie's, and I want so badly to be annoyed with her for allowing Jacki to enter the equation, but God she just looks *so good.*

Those hazel eyes are rimmed with long, mascaraed lashes and just the right amount of smokey eyeshadow. Her dark hair falls in perfect loose curls over her slim shoulders. She's chosen to wear a navy suit that hugs every inch of her perfectly. I'm surprised at how well she pulls off the gender-bending look.

"*Damn* Peyton," Darian sings.

"Yeah, damn Peyt," Gwen agrees.

Darian leans to the side in exaggeration. "You servin' looks, ma."

I roll my eyes and blush at the realization that while I was checking out Jamie, everyone else was admiring me. Everything would be perfect if Jacki weren't hanging all over Jamie and looking at me like that. God, why is she here killing my vibe?

"Gibbs, is Courtney coming?" Gwen wonders.

"Nah." He takes a big sip from his whiskey glass. "She thinks going to homecoming together will make too big of a statement."

We all just look at him unsurely.

"Which I agree with, by the way," he finishes.

Everyone just looks around at each other, aware that Courtney and Gibbs have been fooling around for a while now, but adamantly refuse to make it official. Apparently, neither of them want a relationship.

I feel like they were both full of it.

Gibbs slides me his glass. "You have some catching up to do."

Honestly, I need a drink. I pick up the glass and throw back the rest. It burns the hell out of my throat and makes me cringe, but I hide it well. Even Jacki's unyielding expression shows she's impressed.

"We should go," I advise. "We're already late."

The group looks around at each other, probably noticing the tension from my mood, but follow along anyway. Gwen drives Darian's car since the boys have been drinking, and we make it to the venue in no time. I had worked my ass off this morning getting everything ready, so I pray homecoming turns out great. I need it to.

When we enter, the bass from the music rattles the walls. We're late, which means we've arrived in style now that everyone is here and already on the dance floor. Part of me feels relieved, but there's another part that hangs on to the idea that Jamie and I would've enjoyed this together had Jacki not wedged herself between us.

Then, before I can escape into the crowd, a strong grasp pulls me back. I turn to see Gibbs flashing a leather flask.

"Here," he offers.

I'm inclined to accept, but shrug it off. "I'm good."

He tilts his head. "Just a little. It'll help."

"Help what?" I ask.

But he doesn't say anything else. I try to read the look on his face in hopes that it'll give away what he's referring to, but nothing. I take a swig and then watch him shove it back into his pocket.

I part from my friends and obsess over the whole Gibbs situation. What had he meant by "it'll help"? Could he know...?

I shake away the nerves and end up socializing with a few of my peers from student council, all while stealing glances over their shoulders to watch Jamie. She seems like she's having an okay time. I wouldn't say a *great* time, because I believe no one can have a great time with Jacki clinging to their side.

Then I watch Jamie finally wander off and her eyes find me in the crowd. She makes her way over, which causes my heart to somersault.

She makes it to my side. "Hey, can we talk?"

"About?"

She hesitates. I can tell something is on the tip of her tongue, but the pause becomes too long. It's long enough for Gwen to find us and barge into on our short conversation.

"What the *hell* are you two doing off of the dance

floor?" she fumes. "It's senior homecoming!"

Then she proceeds to pull us into the massive crowd of dancing teenagers.

I'm only slightly buzzed from the liquor earlier tonight, but Gwen is right, and her mood grows contagious. I feel my body moving to the music and I catch Jamie watching. The nerves and adrenaline from her attention are enough to encourage me to continue.

Eventually, Darian distracts Gwen and gives me a chance to restart our interrupted conversation.

"What did you wanna say earlier?" I ask Jamie.

Her moves grow nervous, but she tries her best to loosen up.

"I uh, I just wanted to apologize," she admits. "For saying yes to Jacki."

My heart stops. "What..."

"I just know you two don't necessarily like each other, so I shouldn't have said yes and brought her along," she finishes.

I quickly swallow my confusion.

"She just put me on the spot, and I didn't want to say no to her in front of all those people..."

I feel the dullness surrounding my heart warm up at the confession. Jamie had only said yes to Jacki because she didn't want to say no and embarrass her. Now she feels bad because she thinks she has possibly ruined homecoming for me. She cares about how I feel, and *apologized*, even after I had been a bitch after the back-to-school party.

God, why does she have to be so perfect?

"Jamie, I'm sorry too..."

That's when the song ends, and we're interrupted. Again. The DJ turns up the mic for an announcement, and our attention is pulled to the stage.

"Hope everyone is having a good time, but we all know what time it is," the junior class president says, eliciting cheers from the crowd. "It's time for the homecoming king and queen to finally be crowned!"

Everyone goes nuts, but I personally hate this part. We do anonymous voting, and whoever wins is always a massive surprise. I personally hate surprises. I mean, most people do, right?

"Can I have the following guys join me onstage, please?" he asks. "Darian Martin, Hunter Gibson, and David Lowell."

Two of my best friends are welcomed onstage with huge smiles on their faces.

"And the following ladies..." He reads the card. "Courtney Wilcox, Jaqueline Ross, and... Peyton Kelly!"

I'm stunned. It doesn't register that I've been called up. That's until Jamie pushes me to the stage.

"Peyton, that's you!"

I snap out of my dazed state and make it to the stage. My friends cheer loudly as we join the guys. I can't help but think that, out of everyone I could be up against, it has to be Jacki?

Suddenly, I want to beat her.

"For the duke and duchess..." he continues. "David and Courtney!"

The crowd cheers, but I know this is going to be rough. Especially if Jacki loses to me. It's just another thing that she'll hate me for. Plus, I have a feeling she's starting to catch on to how much her relationship with Jamie bothers me.

Everything always feels like a competition with Jacki, but when it comes to Jamie's attention... well, that's a competition I care about winning.

"And now, for our king and queen..."

The crowd goes silent. So silent, I'm afraid they can hear my heartbeat through the microphone. I'm not sure if I care about being homecoming queen or not, because all I can really focus on is Jamie, who is staring up at me. She gives me a reassuring smile.

"Darian Martin and Peyton Kelly!"

My heart squeezes but I refuse to look at Jacki. I can feel the anger radiating from where she stands. She's fuming, and doesn't even wait for her plastic, and exceptionally smaller, crown before storming off the stage.

Darian and I are congratulated and shuffled offstage and back into the crowd. I search for Jamie, but instead, find her and Jacki talking. I stop and figure it's best not to interrupt.

Then Jacki glares at me, while Jamie remains oblivious to my stare, grabs my friend and pulls her in for a kiss. My stomach churns at the sight, but I know what Jacki's telling me.

I may have won the crown, and class president, and soccer captain... and virtually everything else.

But I didn't have Jamie.

Eight

AS I STARE UP AT THE BRICK WALL that's supposed to be my canvas for the mural competition, I can't help but feel slightly intimidated. Of course, the wall is bigger than my required size, so I had taped off twelve-by-twelve feet for the project. The next step is to clean and prime the wall before doing anything else.

"So, you're finally starting?"

I jump at the voice behind me. Jamie stands there holding the art hall pass in her right hand. Did she leave class to come and find me?

"Just prepping," I inform. "I still have to clean and prime the wall."

Jamie steps closer. "They picked a good spot."

She's right. The wall Mr. Z picked out is perfect. It sits in a closed corridor, but the cool thing about it is that the ceiling has skylights. There are also glass double-doors that lead outside. When it's a beautiful day, the sunshine reflects throughout the hall and makes the space wonderful.

It'll only look better once there's a nice mural painted.

"Is Mr. Z excusing you from class to work on the mural?" Jamie wonders.

"Yeah." I start scrubbing the wall. "I've taken his class for three years, so the administration doesn't have a problem with it."

As much as I love having Jamie's attention, homecoming is still severely burned into my brain. I've noticed she and Jacki are growing closer, and it was probably only a matter of time before they got together. I didn't want to be anywhere near Jamie when that happened, especially after the look Jacki had given me the night of homecoming.

It was like she was trying to tell me something, or threaten me, and it had terrified me.

"You and Jacki..." Jamie starts. My blood runs cold. "Is there a reason you two hate each other?"

Hate. It's such a strong word. Before Jamie showed up, I never would've described my feelings toward Jacki as "hate." Now, after coming to terms with how Jamie makes me feel, and how Jacki seems to be flaunting her in front of me every chance she gets ... hate now seems to suffice.

But I have to be the good guy.

"I don't hate Jacki," I lie. "And I don't really know why she has such an issue with me."

"Well, she says you do."

I stop scrubbing and turn around. "I do, what, exactly?"

"She says you do know why she has an issue with you."

I feel myself becoming defensive. My arms cross upon my chest as I allow my weight to rest on my left leg.

"Is that all she told you?" I press.

I can tell I'm intimidating Jamie by the worry in her hazel eyes. Is she scared of me? Or is she scared of getting on my bad side, afraid that I'll ice her out again? I try to calm myself down.

"Y-Yeah," she stutters. "Jacki's very secretive."

Yeah, well, so am I, I think.

I take a deep breath and turn back around. My scrubbing intensifies as I picture Jacki brainwashing Jamie about me during their time together.

"Yeah," I agree. "She's also manipulative."

Jamie remains silent after that. I don't bother turning around and hope she's left to go back to class. I don't want her to see how angry I am. I hate that I'm showing my jealousy. It's probably super obvious. After a few minutes of silence, Jamie eventually breaks it.

"You say you don't hate Jacki, but every time she's brought up, or comes around, I can tell you don't necessarily like her, either."

God, why is she pressing me so hard about this? Does she like Jacki that much? That thought alone infuriates me.

"Why does it matter?" I find myself asking. It's the only thing my brain can think up as a response.

Jamie looks stunned when I abruptly face her again. I wait for an answer, but her words seem to fail her. Or she's scared of telling me the truth.

"Why do you care if I like her or not?" I repeat.

How had we gotten here? I feel as if we're standing on the edge of a cliff, and I don't like it, but I feel like she's trying to make me admit something that I'm not ready to. I feel threatened. And when I feel threatened, I get defensive.

"Because I feel like I have to pick a side."

"*I* make you feel like that?"

She sighs. "No, I just..."

"So, *Jacki* makes you feel like that."

"Peyton." Jamie says. "I'm just saying, there's a lot of tension and I don't get it."

"And *I'm* saying... I don't ever talk about Jacki to you behind her back," I inform. "It's obvious who's wrong in this situation, isn't it?"

I turn back around for the final time. It's probably best that we end this conversation here, because if we continue, I will surely give away how much I truly do hate Jacki. Especially after learning that she talks about me to Jamie. She's probably trying to convince her that *I'm* the manipulative one.

What a *bitch*!

"Peyt..."

I feel her hand gently fall onto my shoulder, but I'm too

worked up. My body instinctively pulls away.

"You should probably head back," I coldly advise. "Mr. Z is nice, but he doesn't like people ditching his class."

There's a small moment of hesitation and silence. Then I hear footsteps disappear behind me, meaning Jamie's taken my advice. The weight squeezing my lungs releases as I take a deep breath. What the hell just happened?

And why do I feel as if things between Jamie and me have turned sour again?

● ● ●

Organ music echoes through the church and reflects off the tall brick walls, giving me the sense of fire and brimstone days. It's not that I didn't *like* church, but, well... no. I don't like it. Who am I kidding?

Being raised in a Catholic family, within a predominantly Baptist and Protestant community, it's hard to skip out on Sunday mass. It's like the hardcore Catholics have something to prove. Sometimes, I can lie and say I have an extracurricular commitment to get out of it, but today is not one of those days.

Alyssa, who has come home to visit this weekend, sits on my right while my parents sit on my left. We're about halfway through, but I can't stop myself from continuously checking the time.

"It'll pass faster if you stop checking your watch,"

Alyssa says.

"I can't help it," I answer.

"Be quiet you two," my mother orders.

I roll my eyes. It's not that I'm not religious, I just don't believe in the institutional aspect of the church. Plus, it's hard not to notice the persecution of anyone who identifies as LGBTQ+ openly, especially when it's outwardly condemned without shame.

Eventually mass ends and we exit the church. The morning weather is miraculously nice and cool now that October is well underway, but I don't expect it to last long. Georgia is hot most of the year.

I head for the car, but instead, my mom expresses that she wants to talk to the priest.

"Hold on, Peyt," my dad says.

I groan as I lean against a brick pillar.

"You're in a mood today," Alyssa observes.

"No, I'm not."

"You're *totally* in a moody mood."

I know she's right, but I don't want to talk about it. Ever since the talk with Jamie at the beginning of the week, I haven't felt like myself. There's this constant worry of what Jacki is telling her, and then there's the tension I've created by refusing to admit that I hate Jacki because she has something with Jamie I desperately want.

I'm just too cowardly to do anything about it.

When my mother *finally* finishes talking, we head for the car. It isn't until we're all settled in that Ms. Stanley, the owner of *Stanley's Sno-Cones*, walks by holding hands with her spouse, who is also a woman. I've always secretly admired how brave they both are for still showing up to church regardless of the stares and whispers.

"Now, I'm not sayin' homosexuality is bad..." my mom starts.

Here we go, I think to myself.

"But at church? When there are children around?"

"Mom..." Alyssa groans.

"I'm just sayin', it's not somethin' I would want my young to see!" she defends her ignorant comment.

I remain silent, because I feel like if I chime in, it'll only make things worse for my situation. Of course, that doesn't stop Alyssa.

"Why?" my sister fumes. "Why is love something you wouldn't want your children to see?"

"Children copy," my mom claims. "And I just don't think young, susceptible eyes should have to see that. It's confusing."

"You sound *really* homophobic."

"I'm not homophobic."

I just stare out the window while my sister argues with my mom. Cars and trees pass but I've zoned out. I feel myself going numb. Then my eyes meet my dad's in the rearview mirror, and I pull them away quickly. I don't want him to see how badly this conversation is hurting me.

I don't want anyone to see how much I'm hurting, no matter the cost.

Nine

RIGHT. LEFT. BREATHE. RIGHT. LEFT. Exhale. Even though soccer conditioning doesn't start for another week and a half, there's too much on my mind for me not to run today. I had even managed to convince Gwen to tag along, which she isn't happy about, but she joins me anyway.

Lately, there's been this relentless ache in my chest, and it hurts to breathe. I know what's causing it, but I refuse to admit the truth to myself. I refuse to admit that, maybe, if I just *told* someone, it would at least take some weight from my chest.

I glance over to my best friend. I can tell Gwen. She should be the first person to know. If I come out to anyone else, and it somehow got back to her, it would hurt her a lot. But how on earth do you even *start* that kind of conversation?

"How're you and Darian?" I pant in between steps.

She just sighs. "Could be better."

"Why?"

"He's just... a guy. I mean... I know we're best friends... but..." She exhales heavily. "He gets so *awkward* sometimes."

I can't help but laugh to myself.

"Give him time," I tell her. "To adjust."

We round the block of our high school and return to the student parking lot and head for the locker room. Unfortunately, I hadn't been able to sort through anything in my head, but at least the run had distracted me for a short while.

We walk toward the locker room, but not before someone sprinting around the track catches my eye. It's Jamie, of course, kicking up dirt as she makes her way around the track.

"Damn," Gwen says. "She's fast."

I watch her tall legs propel her thin body forward. Muscles protrude, her skin glistens, and her hair swings from side to side. She looks magnificent. I wonder why she hasn't tried out for track, or any other sport, for that matter.

Then she meets her goal. She slowly brings herself down as she jogs around the rest of the track. The look on her face says she's satisfied, but there's something else there. Something... *sad.*

In my trance, I hadn't realized Gwen had started for the locker room. I quickly catch up with her.

"You didn't wanna say hey?" I wonder.

Gwen shrugs. "I just..."

She stops. I'm confused as to why she's suddenly gotten weird. My skin turns cold. Could she possibly suspect that I...?

"Just... what?" I press while I begin to change clothes.

"I'd rather change before she comes in here."

I feel my heart stop. Did Gwen really say that? The look on her face alters.

"God, that sounds so bad," she confesses.

"Uh, *yeah*. It does."

"It's not that I don't like Jamie." She quickly slips on sweatpants. "It's just... I know she's gay and we get pretty naked..."

I'm appalled that my best friend is saying this. If this is how she really feels, I can only imagine how she'll react if I ever told her the truth! I've seen her naked *plenty* of times, for Christ's sake! And I had never once thought anything of it.

But as much as it infuriates me, I keep my mouth shut.

"I don't think of it that way, I guess."

That's when Jamie herself walks through the locker room door, gulping from her water bottle. When she's done, she gives us a quick smile and a wave before heading for her own bag. Gwen is done changing and is searching for her car keys. I find myself wanting to hang back.

"Are you comin'?" Gwen asks me.

"I'll see you tomorrow," I say. "I've gotta talk to Jamie about our art project."

Jamie overhears the lie, but Gwen doesn't suspect anything. She shrugs, hugs me goodbye and leaves the locker room. The pain in my heart grows. I know Gwen is a good person, and she isn't homophobic, right? She's so accepting of everyone! Yet, I can't seem to wrap my head around what she had just said to me.

"Art project, huh?" Jamie jokes. "Guess I missed that announcement."

I face her. All she has on is a sports bra and the spandex that had been under her running shorts. Heat runs through my body at the sight. If my mind weren't such a mess from Gwen, it would surely be from the sight of Jamie. It takes me a second to realize I need to respond to her.

"Uh, y-yeah I just..." God, *why* am I such a mess? "I needed a moment away from her."

Jamie looks at me with a concerned expression. "Are you okay?"

"Yeah," I lie.

She isn't buying it but refuses to press me. Her phone vibrates in her bag, and when she checks it, the look on her face lets me know it's bad news.

"Great," she mumbles.

"What?"

"My mom can't pick me up right now."

"She's your ride?" I ask.

"Yeah." Jamie rubs her forehead. "You think a forty-five-minute walk is too much?"

"I can bring you home."

The words leave my mouth before I can think about them. I blame it on the fact that Jamie still hasn't put a shirt on. I force my eyes to stay above her neck.

"Are you sure?"

She's hesitant. I can't blame her. Ever since the conversation about Jacki, there's this obvious negative tension between us. Of course, Jamie constantly hanging out with Jacki doesn't help the situation either, because it gets to me, and hiding it is more difficult than ever.

"Sure." I grab my gym bag. "It's on my way home, anyway."

She realizes this is her chance at a free ride and quickly gathers her things. I start for the exit to the locker room and attempt to hide my nerves. Being alone with Jamie always has a way of making me feel things I'm not used to feeling.

But despite the fact, I still *really* like it.

We climb into my car and I pull onto the road. We sit in uncomfortable silence until Jamie decides to break it.

"So, why'd you lie to Gwen?"

I should've known better than to bring Jamie into this. I should've just said something else, but no, I'm a moron. How am I going to explain this and not upset her? Would she think of Gwen differently like I did?

I drum my fingers on the steering wheel. "She uh... she

just said something that I didn't expect her to."

I make the mistake of glancing over at Jamie. Those curious eyes are locked on me. They're all but glowing from the sun's reflection on my dashboard. Thin strands of hair frame her face, making her natural beauty more prominent. My heart thuds against my chest at the sight.

"Like what...?" she asks.

I hesitate to answer.

"I mean, you don't *have* to tell me. I can just tell you're really upset about it."

"Have you ever had a straight best friend?" I blurt. "That knew you were gay?"

It's scary how easy it was to say that aloud to Jamie, but there's no taking it back. I pray she doesn't read into it too much.

"My best friend back home is *very* straight," she informs.

"Did she get... *weird* when you came out to her?"

Oh my *God*, Peyton, what are you *doing*?!

Jamie sighs. "A little. We had to talk about a lot. I mean, we shared just about everything."

"Like...?"

"Like, I had to tell her I was not at all attracted to her. Physically or emotionally. That I literally looked at her like a sister," Jamie explains. "I don't know why, but a lot of straight girls have this delusion that gay girls want any girl that crosses their path, and it's just absolutely not true."

I want to explicitly agree but feel that would be too

much information.

"So, lesbians have a type, too?" I joke.

"Of course," she says. "I have a type. Everyone has a type."

I glance at her and meet her stunning gaze. She has a teasing smile on her lips. I feel my heart shake inside my chest.

"I mean, don't you... have a type?" she wonders.

I feel my cheeks heat up and I laugh nervously at her question. There are many girls I find attractive, but none of them significantly stand out. Not like Jamie does. I try to focus on the features I tend to appreciate but can only formulate a picture of the girl sitting beside me.

"I don't know," I answer.

"You don't know?"

"Nope."

"Well, what does your ex look like?"

My ex. God, how the hell am I going to tell Jamie I've never even dated anyone? She wouldn't look at me the same if I tell her that.

"They uh..." I stammer. "Well, the funny thing is, I'm always so busy-"

"You've never had a boyfriend?"

I roll my eyes at the word.

"No, I've never had a boyfriend."

"A *girlfriend?*"

"I've never been in any type of romantic relationship," I confess.

The car falls silent. Like, *dead* silent. I'm massively embarrassed. My face grows hot and I'm too afraid to look at Jamie. She probably thinks I'm such a loser. As I silently burn with humiliation, I pull up to her house.

"I mean, the virgin thing wasn't surprising, but that's..."

I glare at her. "Seriously?"

"You just seem like such a good girl, I'm sorry!" She laughs and throws her hands up in defense. "But I just figured you would've at least *dated* someone."

My body is on fire as my hands squeeze the steering wheel. I can't even look at Jamie anymore.

"But you know, it makes a lot of sense." Jamie unclicks her seatbelt. "You also seem like the kind of girl who doesn't put up with bullshit, and relationships can be *a lot* of bullshit."

I want to tell her the reason I've never been in a relationship is because no one knows I'm attracted to girls. That no one, not even my best friend, knows I'm gay, and that makes it awfully difficult for me to possibly have a chance at dating anyone.

"Yeah," I lie. "I guess that's right."

We fall silent again, but Jamie doesn't move to leave my car. What is she waiting for? And why am I so damn nervous?

"Do you want to come inside?" she asks. "I know it's weird but, I kind of hate being home alone, and mom won't be home for another hour or so."

I just stare at Jamie.

She shrugs. "It's taco night. You can stay for dinner if you want...?"

A chance to be alone with Jamie? This is the opportunity I've been hoping for but was previously too afraid to grasp. Something inside of me quivers with excitement. I unbuckle my own seatbelt.

"Sure," I agree. "I love tacos."

Ten

JAMIE'S ROOM ISN'T AT ALL what I had pictured in my mind. Not that I had pictured it at all. Ever. Because that would be weird. It's a little disheveled, but so is she at times, so that's expected. Her room is also a lot bigger than it seems from the outside of her house.

"Sorry about the mess," she apologizes. "I-I just didn't know... you know, you would be..."

Is she nervous? I can't help but find it endearing.

Her bed, that sits in the corner of her room, is half made with a neutral gray duvet paired with darker gray pillows. There are a few articles of clothing sprawled across her hardwood floors, and in the corner closest to the door is a small desk. Judging by the paint stains, it seems as if its intended use isn't for schoolwork.

"*This* isn't a mess," I assure. "You should've seen my older sister's room when she still lived with us full time."

Jamie throws her gym bag in her closet and her backpack on her desk chair. Then, she plops herself right in the middle of her bed after taking her shoes off.

"Well, now I don't feel so bad."

She's looking up at me with this hopeful smile, and I know exactly what she's doing. After all the negative tension from the back-to-school party and the fact that she probably believes I'm somewhat homophobic, this feels like a test. As if she's waiting to see how I respond to being alone with her.

So, I kick off my own shoes and crawl onto the edge of her bed.

"Why don't you try out for track?" I attempt to break the ice. "You're really fast."

She shrugs. "Not feelin' it."

"So, you just run for fun?" I joke. "Or do you enjoy self-torture?

She laughs to herself. "I used to run track at my old school, but it would just feel wrong if I ran for another team."

"But you run the track like, every day."

"Well, it's therapeutic for me, too."

I want to ask her what's bothering her, but feel it isn't my place. Even though she invited me inside her home, her walls are still sky high. The only thing is, I don't understand *why.* What is she trying so hard to protect?

"That's what art is to me," I confess. "Therapy."

"You don't think this competition is gonna ruin it for you?"

"No."

"Even if you lose?"

I narrow my eyes. "Are you trying to say something?"

"I just think you're very... *competitive.*"

There's a hint of playfulness in her voice, like she's teasing me. I find myself smiling.

"And you're not?" I counter.

"I own my competitiveness." She gives me a heart-throbbing smirk. "*You* try to act like you don't care, but you care. A lot."

I hate that she's right. I hate that she seems to know me better than most! Has my attitude to her and Jacki's relationship shown my true colors?

"You act like you know so much about me," I defend. "But you don't know anything."

"Well, you make it really hard."

Our conversation comes to a halt. I watch her eyes flicker to my lips for just a second before she reluctantly shifts away from me. There's a tension I'm unfamiliar with, but recognize, nonetheless. It makes my heart pound inside my chest.

"You're a very guarded person," Jamie explains. "And I don't get why."

"Well, I can say the same thing about you."

My response seems to strike a nerve. She gives me a dry smile and looks down.

"Feeling unwelcome tends to do that to people."

Her words surprise me like a quick slap to the face. Why does she feel *unwelcome*? Do I make her feel that way? Why does she think that?

"You feel unwelcome?" I ask.

She shrugs. "I'm an outwardly gay person living in a small, conservative town. Of course, I feel unwelcome."

"Who makes you feel like that?"

She just stares at me, then shakes her head.

"Most people here who *don't* identify with the LGBTQ+ community, even if they claim they're "accepting," still say and do things that are offensive," she confesses. "And I know they don't mean to be, but..."

I reflect on her words and wonder if that's why she's glued to Jacki's hip. Not because she wants to be, but because that's where she feels most accepted, even if it comes with toxicity.

"I'm sorry," I whisper. "I wish it were different..."

Jamie gives me a sad smile. "It's okay."

There's a lull in the conversation, and only for a moment do I want to confess everything to Jamie. How trapped I feel in my own skin, how everything everyone knows about me is a lie, how I'm terrified of losing my friends and family, and how much I like her, in so many ways. I want to tell her *so* much.

Then her phone buzzes from her side table, and when

she checks it her eyes roll.

"Your mom again?" I wonder.

"Jacki." She texts back a quick response. "She wants to come over and watch a movie."

My skin grows hot at the information.

"Sounds more like she wants to Netflix and chill," I say.

"Maybe." She laughs before setting her phone back on the table. "I'm just not into Jacki like that."

My anger quickly dissolves. Had Jamie just said... what I think she said? She doesn't like Jacki? It's hard to believe after all the things she's said about her, and *did* with her, in front of me.

"You know she acts like y'all are together, right?"

"Yeah."

I'm so confused. "But you aren't...?"

She shakes her head.

"Why not?"

The question escapes before I can swallow it.

"It feels forced," she admits. "Like she's... *flaunting* me? If that makes any sense. I don't know. She's fun, and beautiful, but just... not what I'm looking for, I guess."

Jamie's gaze locks with mine again and I can't help but feel something different. The fact that she doesn't like Jacki feels like a confession. As if she knows it's been bothering me.

"Jacki tries *really* hard to be the best," I say. "And I guess in her head, having your attention means a lot."

This time she smiles, like *really* smiles, and it lights up the room. I want to tell her that it does mean a lot to have her attention. It means a lot to me. And if I were Jacki, if I were out and proud of who I was, then I would want to flaunt it to. Jamie is unique, but not just because she's from Chicago, or because she's attractive. She's unique because she's Jamie.

She is sweet, and kind, and caring, and passionate. And she's a good person.

I check my phone before getting carried away. "Your mom's fixin' to have a late dinner, huh?"

She rolls her eyes. "Knowing her, she's probably just gonna stop at the little Mexican restaurant down the street and bring home dinner."

I laugh. "I love their food."

"Me too. It tastes a lot better than what my mom cooks."

That's when I hear the front door open, and a feminine voice calls out for Jamie.

"Speaking of..." Jamie climbs off her bed. "Guess we should go help."

I follow her to the kitchen and feel enlightened from our conversation. I know Jamie better, and I'm relieved that she isn't getting involved with Jacki the way I had pictured. I feel awfully comfortable with her now.

And I hope that it's what I need to finally be honest with myself, and eventually, with others.

Eleven

AS THE HEAVY RAIN PUMMELS the Georgia soil outside my window, I find peace in the sound. It's been raining since last night, which I also found grace in because it had granted me an excuse to cancel my plans with student council. It's a rare opportunity for me to be able to relax on a Friday night.

Now, it's high noon on Saturday, and the rain is still going strong. Half of me is still grateful, while the other half is becoming restless. Should I see what my friends are doing?

As if on cue, my phone chimes. It's our group text.

Gibbs: *Perfect day for muddin', am I right?*

Darian: *You're such a hick, Gibbs.*

Gwen: *I JUST washed my hair...*

I laugh at my friends' responses and find slight appeal in the idea of taking out some four-wheelers and riding out in the muddy fields. Call me country, but it's a great stress reliever.

Peyton: *I'm in need of a little fun.*

Then a name I've never seen in our group chat appears. My heart flutters. Who added her?

Jamie: *WTH is "mudding"?*

And then the chat goes wild.

Darian: *LMAOOO*

Gibbs: *Seriously, Chicago... We MUST culture you.*

Gwen: *Guys, don't be rude.*

I can't help but find Jamie's ignorance adorable. We really do need to show her how we manage to have fun in a small town like Branton.

Peyton: *Just wear old clothes. It'll be fun.*

Gibbs: *So... is that a yes?*

Gwen: *Fine! I guess I'll just wash my hair AGAIN.*

Darian: *On my way.*

Jamie: *...Guys, I need a ride to the lake house...*

My blood rushes to the surface as I quickly type a response, attempting not to sound desperate.

Peyton: *I'll pick you up in a few.*

Jamie: *Thanks, P.*

A deep breath escapes through my lips and I smile to myself. Another opportunity to hang out with Jamie. The only thing that has me nervous is the fact that we wouldn't be alone because I'm convinced it is obvious how Jamie makes me feel. I try not to think about it as I throw on an old pair of gym shorts and an old debate club t-shirt.

I all but run out of the house, surprised to find the mid-October day so *hot.* Just one of the many perks of living in the South, I guess. The rain had also slowed to a light drizzle.

Jamie is outside waiting when I pull up. She's also wearing a pair of gym shorts, a faded gray t-shirt, and some dingy looking shoes. Yet, she still looks stunning.

She eagerly climbs into my car and looks at me. I watch her eyes travel over my exposed legs. My face heats up.

"What am I really about to get myself into?" she asks.

I smile. "It's a surprise."

"I don't like surprises."

I give her a side glance.

"You'll like this one," I say. "Promise."

"And if I don't?" she teases.

God, why is she so flirty today? The burning in my cheeks has to be noticeable!

"Then I guess you'll never have to hang out with us again."

My brain tells me to resist looking at her because I know if I do, my eyes will just give me away. Yet, my heart is *begging* for just one glance. I feel Jamie already looking at me, which makes something deep within... *hot.*

"Nah," she replies. "I like hanging out with you too much."

My stomach flips. Had she meant to say "me"? Or did she really mean me and my friends? As much as I want to flirt back, I can't find the courage.

We pull up to the lake house in no time. The rain has now stopped, and the sun is miraculously fighting its way through the clouds. Darian and Gwen pull down the gravel road behind us. We exit our vehicles and expect Gibbs to exit the lake house. He never does. Darian and Gwen approach us.

"I can't believe I'm about to do this," Gwen complains. "Does he know how long it takes me to do my hair?"

"No, but I can tell you he doesn't care." Darian rotates his baseball cap, forcing the bill behind his head. "Chicago, are you ready for this?"

"I'm not really sure what 'this' is," she answers. "I'm kinda scared to be honest."

That's when I hear the roaring of an ATV. Everyone is searching for the source of the noise, and then Gibbs emerges from the tree line on a bright red four-wheeler, popping a wheelie for show.

"Jesus," I whisper.

Gibbs tears through the field, slams on his brakes, and nearly covers us all in mud right away. Luckily, his depth perception is off.

"Hope you guys are ready to get *dirty*," he teases in a sexy voice. "I have two other bikes in the back."

The rest of us make our way around the lake house and spot the two bikes. Gwen climbs onto the back of the ATV

Darian has picked, leaving me with Jamie.

"Have you ever driven one of these before?" I ask.

"Does it *look* like I've driven one before?"

"Touché." I climb onto the bike and rev the engine. "Guess you're riding passenger."

"I'm supposed to get on there with you?" Her hand rests on her chest. "How do I know you're not gonna kill us on that thing?"

Darian and Gwen take off after Gibbs, no longer hanging back. Jamie and I are alone, and I seem to have the upper hand in this situation. The confidence flows through me.

"I guess you'll just have to trust me, then."

Jamie's eyes glow, and she takes my response exactly how I intend. The fact that she gets excited about me flirting back makes me giddy inside. She hesitantly climbs onto the back of the bike.

Her arms snake around my waist and hold me tight. The flame in my stomach grows three sizes. My skin is ablaze, and not from the sun finally coming out from behind the clouds. I take a deep breath.

"You better not kill me," she threatens in my ear.

But instead of responding, I give the bike some gas and take off. Jamie lets out a small yelp and her grip on me tightens even more. I'm so glad she can't see the massive grin that's on my lips.

I catch up with my friends who are waiting for our arrival. Gibbs gives me a big smile when we make it close enough.

"'Bout time," he teases.

"Sorry," I apologize. "Jamie was a little... *hesitant.*"

"You scared, Chicago?" Darian laughs.

Jamie scoffs. "I'm chill."

She's playing it cool, but her grip on me says otherwise.

"Try and keep up!" Gibbs yells as he takes off down a beaten path.

Jamie and I fall behind because I don't want to overdo it on the first run. I want her to have fun, not be completely terrified, because I know riding a four-wheeler for the first time can be very intimidating.

Then, Gibbs tears through a mudhole and sprays mud in all directions. Some of it hits Darian's ATV, but it doesn't bother them. He and Gwen tear right through it as well.

"We're driving *through* the mud?" Jamie panics.

"Why do you think it's called muddin'?" I question.

We hit the mudhole full speed. The sensation of mud and water hitting my legs cools me off from the heat my body is radiating.

"Ugh!" Jamie protests.

I can't help but laugh to myself.

"Don't be such a city girl!"

I speed through the field and after my friends, half wishing Jamie would rest her head against my neck. Just her touch sends me up the wall. I just can't believe one person has me feeling this exhilarated.

After about half an hour, and a few mudholes later, we're taking a break.

"So, Chicago, how're you feelin'?" Gibbs asks.

"Dirty," she answers.

The group erupts with laughter.

Jamie sits on the tail of our bike while I sit at the front. After her holding on to me for so long, I feel cold now that she's not. I'm hoping to start up again soon just so I can have an excuse to be close to her again.

"Peyton?"

I snap out of my trance. "Yeah?"

Jamie's smile melts my heart. "Think you'd feel safe if I drive once?"

I'd be lying if I said yes, but she looks way too excited for me not to agree.

I shrug. "Sure. You can't be as bad a driver as Gibbs."

"Hey!"

Jamie takes the driver's position as I scoot up behind her. I bask in the new sensation as my thighs press against her, sending chills through my body. Our friends start up their bikes and leave us alone, again. I'm grateful for the time alone.

"Okay, so you make sure the gear shift is in neutral..." I instruct as I lean forward to hold the brake and shift gears. "Then once it's in neutral, you can hit the gas."

My chest is pressed tightly against Jamie's back, and I can feel her tense under me. Am I making her nervous?

"O-Okay," she says. "And once it's started?"

"Just shift up."

She follows my directions and before I know it, we're chasing after our friends again. I feel her body relax when I pull back.

We ride in silence for about ten minutes as Jamie tests the waters while hitting a few mudholes and laughing in response. I'm lost basking in the feeling of Jamie's toned stomach while trying not to make it obvious that I'm enjoying it.

"Okay..." Jamie starts. "I can see why you like doing this."

"Right?" I agree. "It's relaxing."

"That's not how I would describe it."

"You're just not comfortable yet."

That's when I feel her lean back into me to press her back against my chest. Something deep within me stirs, *hard*, and my legs tighten against her. My lips are close to her neck, and for a moment I wonder what it would feel like to kiss her skin.

She stops the bike after a while and searches for Darian, Gwen, and Gibbs. We had lost them due to her slower pace, but I can hear their bikes in the distance.

Then they both appear and are racing straight for us.

"What are they doing?" Jamie asks.

"It looks like they're... racing?" I respond.

But when I look around, my heart sinks. I know exactly what my friends are doing. Jamie had stopped right in the middle of a giant mud spot, and my friends were about to absolutely *drench* us.

"Shit," is all I could whisper.

Then, within seconds, Jamie and I are covered in cold, wet mud. It's everywhere. In my hair, on my face, all over my arms and legs...

But when I open my eyes and look at Jamie, I erupt with laughter.

She's covered in mud and only specks of skin show through. Her clothes are ruined, and her hair is matted with chunks of the earthy substance. That, paired with the frown on her face, equals the most hilarious sight I'd seen in months.

"Are you *serious?*" she hisses.

"Now you look like you've had some fun," I tease.

Everyone drives back up in hysterics and I can't help but join. Even though they had played dirty, I know it's because it was Jamie's first time. They had to break her in eventually.

"Sorry Chicago," Darian apologizes.

Gibbs chuckles. "You were lookin' a little too clean."

Jamie doesn't look happy, but there's still a hint of thrill on her face. She may not be comfortable, but at least she's having fun.

"You guys *suck!*" Jamie yells.

Then she reaches down into the mud, grabs a handful, and throws it right at Gibbs' face. This inevitably leads to a mud war between the five of us and ends with everyone literally covered from head to toe.

When everyone is finished, we all just stare at each other.

"Now what?" Jamie asks.

"Now, we go to the lake," Gibbs answers. "Last one there has to skinny dip!"

The five of us take off for the lake that's just over the hill. Jamie and I surpass Gwen, who isn't even really trying. Darian hangs back to make sure she's okay, despite his ability to outrun us both. Gibbs isn't fast. At all. Which leaves Jamie and me racing for the water.

"You're fast," she pants.

"Yeah?"

"You're not gonna win, though."

I know Jamie's a lot faster than me, but she isn't pulling ahead. Is she trying to let me win?

"Don't let me win." My legs pump harder. "You better not let me win."

"You sure?"

"Positive."

"Like I said..." The sound of our bodies moving swiftly fills my ears. "Competitive."

We're almost there. I can feel the cold water already soothing my hot skin. I feel heavy from the mud, but I am not backing down.

"Loser still has to skinny dip?" Jamie teases.

I just scoff at her.

Then she finally leaves me. Her height gives her a great advantage as she shoots in front, my eyes watch her in awe.

But she stops right at the edge of the pier. I smirk to myself.

My feet hit the wooden pier and I glide over it, jump, and feel the cold water of the lake surround me. It only hurts for a second, but once I'm submerged everything in me that had been screaming falls silent.

I pop my head back up.

"I won!" I shout.

"I made it to the water first!" she protests.

"You have to get *in* loser!"

She takes off running over the pier and jumps in right next to me. The cold water splashes my face. I feel excited and just a *little* boastful.

She reemerges without the mud that had once covered her skin. A cute frown grows on her lips.

"I'm not skinny dipping," Jamie refuses.

"But you lost."

"Technically, I came in second."

"You seemed excited about that bet being just between me and you, though."

The sunlight reflects off the water and in her eyes. They're glowing. I watch them flicker back and forth from my gaze to my lips.

"I was only excited because I thought you were gonna lose."

The look on her face tells me she isn't just flirting with me anymore. Does she really mean that? I feel my body tingle at the thought of being naked in front of Jamie.

Then a splash shocks me out of my fantasy. Gibbs,

Darian, and Gwen are now joining us, and the moment comes to an end.

"Looks like Peyton beat you, Chicago," Darian teases.

Jamie just splashes him in response.

We swim for a bit to wash off the mud that had once covered our bodies, and then climb back onto our bikes and ride around until we're fully dry.

Through it all, I can't help but notice that there's been a huge shift within Jamie's and my relationship. It's snowballing, and the more I paid attention, the more aware I became of how she acts specifically around *me*. The flirtatious comments, the staring, the smiling... it was all so exhilarating, yet terrifying.

I'm afraid, because she's tearing down my walls faster than I can rebuild them, and there's nothing I can do about it.

Twelve

AFTER ALMOST A MONTH AND A HALF of sitting on this mural, it feels good to finally start. Now that the wall is taped, primed, and ready to go, working on my idea becomes a lot easier.

I trace over the painted brick with a color pencil, mapping out how big I want my piece to be. The idea had come to me the day I had dinner at Jamie's house, and it had been stuck in my mind ever since. Now I'm determined to bring it to life, but it'll take time because of my tight schedule.

I plan to work on the mural every day during fourth period, but I know it'll most likely take time outside of school as well. Prioritizing the mural this time of year is crucial because of soccer season later on, but if I stay on track, I can finish it on time.

It isn't until I'm about thirty minutes in when I hear footsteps approaching. Excitement overwhelms me at the thought of it being Jamie. I turn around eagerly, only to meet focused, brown eyes that are certainly *not* Jamie's. Jacki studies the wall with a condescending smile on her face. What the hell does she want?

"An artist, too?" she wonders aloud. "Peyton Kelly, you're just a walking talent."

"Do you need something?" I counter.

"I was just hoping to get some before pictures..." She flashes her camera. "Y'know, for yearbook."

Right. Jacki is senior yearbook editor. Suddenly, her visit doesn't seem so random.

"Alright. Sure."

Jacki snaps some pictures of the wall, each from a different angle, and then focuses her attention back on to me.

"Could you keep working on it, for a few action shots?"

I oblige, but her presence has a way of making me feel on edge. There's tension, and it doesn't feel good. I secretly hope that she's almost done.

"That's good," she finishes, studying the pictures she had just taken. "I guess this'll be one more thing to add to your list of accomplishments, huh?"

Her comments are passive aggressive, of course, and I can't help but notice. A part of me wants to engage in the conversation and ask what her problem is, but then another doesn't have the time or energy to even care.

"It'll be an even better accomplishment when I win," I answer before returning to my work.

This gets Jacki to at least stumble and hesitate to find a comeback, which gives Jamie enough time to blindly walk into the conversation. She throws me a smile without even seeing Jacki who is standing ten feet away. Jamie senses the tension and her expression changes, right before she spots Jackie.

"Hey," Jamie greets hesitantly. "Did I walk in at a bad time?"

"Of course, not!" Jacki's overly cheery voice makes me cringe. "I was just bothering Peyton for some pictures for yearbook."

Jamie's gaze meets mine, but she doesn't say a word. There's something about her, Jacki, and me being in the same place that just makes me *so* uncomfortable. I don't like it. My face certainly indicates that.

"Peyton's confident she'll bring home the big prize," Jacki says.

Just the sound of my name coming out of Jacki's mouth makes me roll my eyes to another universe. There's acid on her tongue when she talks about me, and I know she's aware it bothers me.

"I'm confident she will, too," Jamie agrees.

I feel my cheeks heat up from comment. Jamie gives me a smile and a wink, and only for a moment do I forget

Jacki's standing right there. I hear her grunt in disapproval.

"Well, she'll have to make a big statement." Jacki turns to Jamie. "Are we still on for our movie date this weekend?"

Movie... *date*? I thought Jamie and Jacki weren't involved? Jamie sees the shock on my face, but I've caught her, and the blood rushes to her cheeks. She knows better than to reject Jacki. Even I know that much.

"Y-Yeah," she stutters. "Sure."

Jacki smirks before looking at me, as if this means she's somehow won the exchange. I try my best to look indifferent knowing that she and Jamie have a date this weekend, but I have a bad feeling Jacki sees right through it.

"Good luck," she finishes before walking off.

I stay silent after she leaves and return to my work, ignoring Jamie. There's a burning in my chest knowing that she's still spending one-on-one time with Jacki, but I have no right to be angry because it isn't my place. I don't want her to see how upset it makes me either, because that would say too much.

"It's not a date, by the way," Jamie explains. "We're going with other people, and..."

"I don't care," I forcibly blurt.

I realize how harsh my response sounded, so I turn around and shove the anger and pain down to spare myself. Jamie looks hurt but doesn't know how to take my response.

"You can hang out with whoever you want, Jamie," I

clarify. "You don't have to explain yourself to me."

She knows this. I can see it on her face. So why does she feel the need to? Why does she look so... *guilty?*

"I-I know..." She shrugs. "I just don't want anyone getting the wrong idea."

"The only one that seems to have the wrong idea is Jacki," I say. "You might wanna explain yourself to her instead."

Jamie's hurt expression makes me immediately regret saying that. Jesus Peyton, if it wasn't obvious that it bothers you, it sure is now! I mentally slap myself for saying that aloud.

"I guess." Jamie steps away from me. "I'll see you later, Peyton."

She disappears through the doors that lead back into school and I rest my head against the brick wall and squeeze my eyes shut. No matter how hard I try to hide how much hurt I'm in, I always seem to needlessly take it out on her.

It isn't her fault that I'm not out. It isn't her fault that she doesn't know I like her. It isn't her fault that I'm jealous of her and Jacki's relationship. It isn't her fault, but I can't seem to stop acting like it is whenever things like this happen between us.

I feel the tears well in my eyes. The pain seems to bubble and overflow, causing my throat to grow tight. I desperately want to tell someone. I want to tell *Jamie*, but I can't. I can't tell her and not my best friends, or my sister, or my parents. I can't seem to find the courage to release any of this pain, and I'm afraid it's going to kill me.

I look up at what little of the mural I had started. The lines are only half finished, but now I lack the motivation to start up again. Tears roll down my face as I pack up my things and run for the parking lot.

Keeping my sexuality a secret had never been such a problem until now. Ever since Jamie had crashed into my life, things just continued to get harder, and I didn't know how to deal with it.

Thirteen

I SIT IN THE CORNER OF THE CAFETERIA alone, sorting cans of non-perishables and placing them into cardboard boxes. Branton High is in the middle of our annual food drive, but this year is by far our biggest yet. We already have tons of boxes ready to be distributed, and there's still an entire week left to go.

Being so involved has a lot of pros, but it also has just as many cons. One being the fact that I must be the one to stay after school, even when most of the student council committee had already bailed, to make sure we stay on track. Despite the fact, the feeling of helping others always makes it worth it, so I don't mind.

The sound of doors opening pulls me out of my head. I

expect to see David, one of my friends who's been helping haul boxes to the gym, but it isn't him. Instead, I see Jamie being escorted by my English teacher. What the hell?

I stand after noticing that they're walking over to me and I prepare myself. It's been a few days since Jamie and I have talked, courtesy of me ignoring her. Again.

"Peyton, you look like you could use some help," my English teacher says. "Would you mind Jamie joining you?"

"I guess not?" I respond.

"She was in detention with me, but I have a family emergency and need to leave."

Jamie had been in detention? I silently wonder how she had managed to do that.

"Sure," I comply. "That's fine."

Then our teacher leaves us alone in the quiet cafeteria.

"Detention, huh?" I ask.

"It was stupid."

She follows me over to the area that I've been using to sort the supplies but refuses to elaborate on *how* she had ended up in detention. Is she embarrassed?

"How stupid?" I wonder.

"I don't wanna tell you."

Ouch. Okay. I guess I deserved that considering I had said maybe a handful of words to her over the last week.

We work in silence after that and refuse to break the tension that feels like it's choking me. I wonder if she feels the same. She doesn't seem bothered by it, but maybe Jamie is good at hiding her emotions too.

The silence continues on for what feels like forever. It's easy to ignore Jamie whenever I'm not around her, but when I'm in her presence, it becomes impossible.

I reach for a can that Jamie also reaches for and our hands touch. She pulls back casually and allows me to grab it.

"Sorry."

I roll my eyes. God, why does it annoy me that she's icing me out? I had asked for it!

"Y'know, you don't have to stay," I say.

She doesn't even look at me.

"I wouldn't tell if you left," I continue.

"My mom thinks I'm working out," she rejects. "So, I have to be here regardless."

Her response burns me, but I try not to let her see.

"She doesn't know you got detention?"

"Hell no."

The attitude is getting to me. I'm trying my best to be understanding, that I deserve it because I had been a bitch to her over the past week, but she usually doesn't act like this. I want her to forgive me. I want her to *want* to talk to me, but that isn't the case today.

"What? Did you fall asleep during her class? Because I know she hates..."

"Why do you wanna talk to me all of a sudden?" Jamie interrupts.

I fall silent. I hadn't expected her words to cut me like a knife. I can feel the pain ooze from my invisible wounds like blood. My throat tightens and I force myself to look down into my lap. Why do I feel the need to cry?

Instead of furthering the conversation, I give her what she wants and work in silence. The pain in my chest has become almost unbearable over the past few months. It feels like I'm always on edge, like I'm seconds away from combusting because of everything I keep buried inside. I notice it's only completely intolerable around Jamie, which is why I avoid her.

Unfortunately, I find it easier to ignore her and the feelings that I have rather than face her and the truth. It's less painful that way. Everything inside of me feels all fucked up.

"I'm sorry, I didn't mean..." Her sentence falls. "I got detention because Jacki and I skipped first hour together."

I refuse to look up because I don't want Jamie to see how much her comment had hurt me, but I also don't want her to see how annoyed I am at the revelation.

"She wanted to get high before second period..." She shifts uncomfortably. "But then, after about twenty minutes, she starts trying to mess around..."

I feel my blood boil at the image of Jacki's hand on Jamie's skin.

"I told her no, of course, and she got upset, so I left." Jamie rolls a can of beans back and forth. "The gym teacher caught me hiding out in the locker room."

Suddenly, I realize why Jamie hadn't wanted to tell me what happened. I look at her and notice she's red with embarrassment, even when she has no reason to be. The anger I feel at Jacki non-consensually touching Jamie is blinding, but I try to remain level-headed.

"Are you okay?" I ask.

"Yeah." Jamie tries to shrug it off. "It wasn't how you're probably picturing it, but..."

"I'm sorry that happened."

"It was really nothing."

I'm hanging on to every word, hoping she continues to talk because I desperately miss her voice. I miss the flirty conversations and the jokes... I miss it all but am too much of a coward to just *tell her.*

"You act so different when it's just me and you," she reveals.

My skin grows hot at her comment. I can't say anything because I know she's right.

"But as soon as other people are around, you ice me out." She stops playing with the can and looks at me. "I don't like the person you turn into whenever that happens."

It feels like she's so close to saying something else, but she hesitates.

"What kind of person do I turn into?" I ask in a curious whisper.

"I don't know." She shrugs. "You get nervous, and uncomfortable, and when you talk it sounds... *rehearsed.* I just don't get why you feel the need to do that, or why you're so scared of what people think of you..."

I may have everyone else fooled, but Jamie can see

right through it. Maybe it's easy for her because she has an outsider's perspective. That, on top of the fact that I only feel comfortable around her when we're alone, practically makes me transparent.

Jamie isn't stupid, and she's tired of me treating her like she is.

"People expect a lot of me," I answer. "And that's *really* hard."

Jamie gets I'm leaving stuff out, but I feel she knows the truth and just wants to respect my privacy. And if she *doesn't* know, she probably just believes I act different because everyone's eyes are always on me, waiting for me to fuck up.

"Are you afraid..."

Jamie hesitates again. My heart is pounding so hard in my chest it feels like I'm going to drop dead right here. What the hell is she about to say?

"Afraid of...?" I press.

"Are you afraid that people will think you're gay if you're friends with me?"

For just a moment do I want to laugh. She isn't far off, but she's damn close. No, Jamie. I ice you out around other people because I know it's obvious that I like you. I want to scream it, but it feels as if my lips are wired shut.

"I didn't mean to offend you," she defends. "But I remember your sister saying you've never had a gay friend, and you don't like Jacki..."

"I'm sorry," I cut in. "I'm sorry that I ice you out, and

I'm sorry that you have to be here, in a place that's so different from Chicago."

She stops talking and her eyes stay locked on me. I quickly realize this is the first time I've seriously apologized to her.

"I'm sorry that I assumed the worst of you the night after the back-to-school party, I'm sorry that I made you feel unwelcome..." Okay, Peyton, where are you going with this? "I'm just really sorry for being such an asshole, Jamie. You don't deserve it."

The look on her face tells me that she's accepted my apology, even though I haven't answered her last question. The tension disappears, not only from around us, but from inside of me. I can finally breathe a little better.

"It's okay," she assures. "Being raised in a place like this... you don't get much exposure to different. And I can tell you're trying really hard to be open-minded."

God, if you only knew, I think.

Silence falls between us, but it no longer feels hostile. I hate that Jamie and I are constantly on edge because of my insecurities. I hate that I value my reputation so much that I'm willing to sacrifice my happiness for it. I hate it all but still can't find the will to change.

"I'm sorry, too, by the way," she includes. "For snapping at you."

I shrug. "I deserved it."

"No, you didn't."

I look up from whatever can of food I've been

mindlessly staring at and lock eyes with Jamie. My heart flutters at the sight of her studying me. I notice we're closer than we were before. For a moment I feel an extreme amount of courage to lean in and kiss her. Her eyes bounce between my eyes and lips for a second, which causes my cheeks to grow hot.

"I don't know why, but it hurts when I think you're upset with me," she whispers. "It drives me insane, Peyt."

The air leaves my lungs. Is this really happening? I hadn't expected her to say something like that. What does that even mean? And had I instinctively moved closer to her without noticing?

"W-Well..." I stutter nervously. *Jesus, Peyton!* "It's probably best to stay on my good side."

Jamie smiles playfully. "Yeah?"

"Yeah."

I should stop. I should stop encouraging the flirting and the stares and the lip biting. There should be boundaries, but no matter how hard I try, I can't find the will to stop.

"What happens if I get on your bad side?" Jamie teases while leaning in closer.

My words fail me. I'm like a deer in headlights. The intensity of the situation has me dying to kiss Jamie just to shut her up. I'm convinced I've never wanted to kiss someone as bad as I do right now. She tilts her head and allows me to get a good look at her neck. Images of my lips kissing the soft skin makes me hot. I feel as if I have no control over what's happening.

Then, the cafeteria doors open, forcing me to jump away from Jamie in response.

"Anymore boxes, chief?" David calls from the doors.

I try to catch my breath. "J-Just these right here."

I stand and notice my heart is slamming against my chest. What would've happened if David had just waited a few more minutes before interrupting us?

We pick up the remaining boxes, haul them to the gym, and all leave for the day. I don't know what to think about what had just happened between Jamie and me, but I know it'll replay in my head for days.

What am I getting myself into?

Fourteen

THE SOUND OF SOFT RAIN paired with the dull, gray morning makes working on the mural today oddly peaceful. I focus on the rain droplets hitting against the corridor's skylight while my paintbrush traces the white lines I had finally finished yesterday. Everything is quiet, but in a few minutes, I'll have to stop, pack up, and return my art supplies.

I push through the pain of cramping in my hand as I reach the end of another line. The mural is coming out a lot better than I had expected. Of course, the process is slow, but patience is key. I tell myself it will be worth it in the end.

The days pass fast now, and November is quickly

coming to an end. Thanksgiving break is right around the corner, and then, once December arrives, soccer practice will commence. That means even less time to work, so getting ahead now is a good idea.

I check my watch and realize it's time to stop. It saddens me how fast an hour passes whenever I was creating.

As I make my way back to the art classroom to return supplies, I picture Jamie sitting in her usual seat. She'll look up at me and probably give me a teasing smile, like she usually does, and I'll grow hot in response. Maybe she'll hang out with us for lunch today...

Once I reach the classroom, I knock. Familiar hazel eyes meet me at the door as Jamie offers to take some of the supplies from my hands.

"Here," she offers. "Lemme help."

She moves in close and her hands graze mine as she grabs a paint can. Had she been waiting for me to come back? She looks excited to see me. The dismissal bell rings and releases the rest of the student population to lunch. I move farther into the room to put things back where they belong.

"How's it comin' Peyton?" Mr. Z asks from his desk.

"Great," I reply. "I'm really excited about it."

He just gives me a warm smile.

Jamie and I put away the supplies I had used today and head for the door.

"I think it's taco day," I say.

"That means Gibbs and Darian are probably already stuffing their faces."

"Most likely."

Jamie and I leave the safety of the art classroom and slowly make our way toward the cafeteria and, without discussing it, we both decide to take the long way around. As we walk, our hands touch every now and then. My heart is in my throat when she breaks the silence.

"So, am I allowed to know the story behind the mural?" she asks. "You know, whenever it's finished."

I smile. "It depends."

"On?"

My heart squeezes at the thought of telling Jamie the meaning behind my art. In my head I can see it fully finished, the girl's happy expression, the swirls of every color in the rainbow painting her skin, the way her eyes glow with life... and then the mask she's taking off, plain and boring with dull eyes and lips pulled into a noticeably fake smile.

Of course, it should be open to interpretation. Was she taking the mask off? If so, was it because she finally felt comfortable in her own skin to reveal her true self? Or was she putting the mask on, in hopes of covering up her flamboyancy that was too much for the society around her?

Right now, I personally feel like the latter.

"Peyton?"

I snap out of my head and look at Jamie.

"What?"

"You don't wanna explain the meaning behind your art?" she repeats.

I feel a pull in my chest.

"It's meant for interpretation," I dodge. "It should be able to explain itself."

Jamie falls silent and refuses to press me about it. I appreciate the fact that she never pries. She respects the fact that sometimes I didn't want to reveal personal things to her, which inevitably makes me want to anyway.

We're almost to the cafeteria, but it's the last place I want to be. We'll just be surrounded by our peers since no one is outside due to the rain. My friends will ask what the hell took us so long. Jacki would probably intervene somehow...

"I say we ditch taco day..." Jamie suggests, as if she's read my mind. "And go get burgers from the diner down the street."

"Are you telling me you *don't* want stale tortillas, cold shredded cheese, and lukewarm meat?" I tease.

"Well, when you put it *that* way..."

Jamie and I just laugh as we detour for the parking lot. My heart races at the thought of being alone with her, but it's getting easier to manage. Yet, the way our hands and shoulders touch while we pace to my car still makes it hard to keep my composure.

Then, before we're in the clear, Jacki, of all people, quickly rounds the corner.

"Are you two ditching taco day?" she mocks. "Gibbs

and Darian are gonna be hurt."

"They're big boys," I retort.

Jacki just gives me a cheeky smirk.

"Besides," Jamie intervenes. "The tacos aren't *that* great. They'll understand."

"So, you're blowing off our lunch date?" Jacki says.

Jamie tenses, which makes me think she had previously made plans and forgotten about them. Why was Jacki always able to ruin a moment?

"We have a lunch date?" Jamie asks.

"We eat lunch together every Friday." Jacki rolls her eyes. "Jamie, you know this."

There's tension between Jacki and Jamie that I don't quite understand. It seems as if neither of them are on the same page. Jamie just seems confused.

"It's cool," Jacki forces. "No biggie, hun."

Then, out of nowhere, Jacki goes to kiss Jamie, but Jamie pulls back and rejects her. I feel my heart sink in response.

"What the hell?" Jacki spits.

"What?" Jamie asks.

"So you don't wanna kiss me now that Peyton's around?"

My eyes must be the size of golf balls because they're burning from not being able to blink. What the hell is happening?

Jamie's eyes narrow. "What are you even talking about...?"

"I didn't stutter."

Jamie's getting fed up and Jacki is about to crawl out of her skin. I feel as if I'm an innocent passerby caught in the middle of a two-car, head-on collision.

"We're not together Jacki," Jamie reminds. "I'm allowed to hang out with other people, and I'm certainly allowed to tell you no if I don't want you to kiss me!"

I step away from them. As much as I'm enjoying the scene, I can tell Jacki is *pissed*. It almost seems like the first time she's ever been rejected, because for once she's speechless. Her furious brown eyes find mine and there's a hate I've never seen before, but maybe it's because she's embarrassed.

Then she storms off.

It's silent between Jamie and me for a few minutes, as if we're riding the aftershock of an earthquake. I have no idea what to say after that.

"Jeez..." Jamie exhales heavily. "I've been dying to say that... I just didn't mean for it to sound so..."

"Brutal?"

"Exactly."

I take in a deep breath, and then, out of nowhere, begin to laugh. This causes Jamie to laugh along with me, because, let's be honest, Jacki had it coming.

"I've never seen Jacki so angry," I say.

"I'm pretty sure she's gonna kill me now."

"Probably."

"Guess this means I'm officially evicted from the gay

squad." Jamie composes herself. "Jacki's never gonna let any of them talk to me again."

I roll my eyes. "The fact that she can dictate who they talk to is sad, anyway."

"You're totally right."

"Of course, I am."

Jamie looks at me with a teasing smile, and I can tell she isn't upset about it at all. She doesn't care if she loses a group of friends because the relationships are rooted in toxicity anyway. Just because people are gay, just like you, doesn't always make them good people to be around, especially if those people are like Jaqueline Ross.

Manipulative and easily manipulated friends are never good, gay or not.

"Let's go get lunch," I finish. "I think we both deserve shakes after that."

"Absolutely," Jamie replies.

Jamie and I leave, but I have a feeling this won't be the end of whatever battle Jacki thinks she's fighting. There was this look in her eyes that screamed "you'll pay for this," but I wasn't sure if it was just my paranoia showing.

But, for now, I'll just enjoy the freedom of hanging out with Jamie until that downfall came.

Fifteen

THERE'S ONLY BEEN A FEW MOMENTS in my life where I had felt completely crushed. Once, when I was fifteen and had to put my childhood dog, Max, down because of old age. And second, when my grandma died of a sudden heart attack when I was sixteen.

Now, in year seventeen, as I stare up at the words *FAKE BITCH* graffitied across my mural, I can't help but wonder how much shittier high school could get.

The late November cold is rushing in through the broken double doors that had been kicked in when the intruder decided to wreck my work. Usually, I would be shivering, but right now I'm numb.

It's the Monday morning after Thanksgiving break,

and I had wanted to check on my work in hopes of feeling re-inspired, but was met with the principal, Mr. Z, and a janitor instead. The police would be here to investigate the vandalism soon, but first hour will be well underway at that point. I haven't decided whether I wanted to stay at school or not yet.

"Peyton..." a voice says behind me. I hear feet kick broken glass out of the way. "What happened...?"

"What the hell does it look like?" I spit.

The anger and sadness seep from my acidic tongue. I feel betrayed. I feel defeated. I feel so many negative things that I don't know how to speak to anyone at the moment, and the last person I want to see right now is Jamie.

This mural had become very personal to me, and now something that had started to bring me peace and comfort is now covered in darkness.

I pick up my things and go to leave. There are tears on my water line threatening to spill over at the thought of someone hating me enough to ruin the one thing that brought me joy.

"Peyton," Jamie calls out.

But I storm forward and attempt to get past without looking at her. I don't want her to see me cry. Why the hell is she here anyway? She should be in first hour with everyone else. She must've heard the gossip and came to check on me. I hear footsteps follow behind me but refuse to acknowledge her. The tears are falling now, and I'm trying so hard to outwalk her.

"Peyton, you can't outwalk me," she says. "I'm taller and faster than you."

"I can try!" I shout back through the tears.

She groans as I press the unlock button on my keys. If I start running now, I can make it to my car, lock her out, and drive away. Then I could at least cry in peace.

I race to my car. My hand yanks the handle and I throw myself inside, but Jamie is fast. She stops the door from closing as she bravely wedges herself inside. Then, suddenly, I can no longer hold back the pain.

It forces its way out, tearing and scratching through me. I lack the strength to even try to stop it, so I don't. I let it rip through and tear me limb from limb, even in front of Jamie, who probably thinks I'm being dramatic.

For some reason, this has broken me.

"Hey, it's okay…" she comforts me. "It can be fixed…"

The thought of continuing the mural is beyond me. I really just need to get away from Branton High, but I couldn't do that with Jamie blocking my door.

"P-Please j-just…" I stutter through the tears. "J-Just leave me a-alone."

"No," she refuses. "I'm not gonna do that. I'm sorry. Now scoot over."

"W-What…?"

"Scoot," she demands, shoving her way inside of my car and forcing me to the passenger seat.

"Jamie, stop."

"I'm gonna drive," she states.

I just watch her turn on my car and put her seatbelt on. What the hell is she doing?!

"What are you doing?" I ask.

"Leaving school?" she replies with a confused expression. "I thought that's what you wanted?"

"It is!" I shout. "*Without* you!"

"You wouldn't even be able to see the road if you drove right now."

"Jamie, get *out*."

"No."

"Oh my *God*!"

I cross my arms and stare out the passenger window. Who the hell does she think she is?

"Put your seatbelt on," she demands.

"Excuse me?"

Her eyes widen in fear as she thumbs my steering wheel nervously.

"Please, put your seatbelt on, Peyton," she asks calmly.

I want to be mad at the world, but Jamie Kendall makes that hard when she's just so damn cute. I grab the seatbelt and angrily pull it over my torso. We ride in silence after that. I refuse to ask her where she's planning on taking me, considering she has no idea where I even live. The devastation I feel over my mural comes in waves, and every so often my eyes release small tears without consent. Hopefully, Jamie wouldn't take me somewhere public.

But after about fifteen minutes, we're arriving at her house.

"I didn't know where else to go," she explains.

"It's fine," I lie.

I exit the car and follow her inside. There are so many things I want to be angry about, but the fact that Jamie doesn't want me to be alone forces me to feel happy instead.

"Also, I'm sorry I kind of kidnapped you..." She throws her bag on the floor. "But it's for good reason."

I can't help but laugh. This gets her to release a wide smile, resulting in me losing my breath for just a moment. But, just as fast as the moment comes, it leaves.

How on earth will I ever finish the mural now? There's no way. Soccer season is right around the corner, which means practice every day after school. Games and tournaments on the weekends... I'm too far behind to finish it strictly on school time...

Plus, who's to say the vandal wouldn't just ruin it again?

"You okay?" Jamie asks from the edge of her bed.

I shake my head. "I'm not gonna be able to finish the mural."

"Why not?"

"Because..." I force away tears. "I won't have time. I'll have to paint over the vandalism and soccer practice starts soon... I just..."

Jamie studies me in silence, probably waiting for me to break down and start crying again. She knows there are other reasons but waits patiently for me to reveal them.

"I feel absolutely shattered," I confess. "Every time I

look at those words..."

The anger and sadness bubble in my stomach again. *FAKE BITCH* just replays over and over in my head. What the hell made me a fake bitch? And who had the right to call me that? Because I'm positive *everyone* in high school was a fake bitch at some point!

Jamie moves closer. "They're just words, Peyt."

She's right, but I have a feeling I know exactly who's behind this. Jacki is the only one who seems to have the ability to read me through and through. It's why she's able to get to me so easily.

Is it possible that she was the one who broke into school and ruined my work? She doesn't seem like the vandal type, but she could manipulate people to do her dirty work. I've seen it happen before.

But I know why those words get to me so much. It's because they're plastered all over my advocacy of showing the world who one truly is. I'm a hypocrite. Hell, maybe I deserve it after all. And I also believe Jacki knows the truth about me and is just *dying* to find hard proof.

"Is that supposed to make me feel better?" I ask Jamie. "That they're just words?"

She sighs. "No. I'm sorry. That was the wrong thing to say. I just..." She hesitates. "I don't want you to give up."

"I don't *want* to give up," I stress. "But the mural is *ruined*. You know how hard it is to start something all over again. It takes away the initial artistry. It's impossible to relay the same emotions, especially if I have to paint over the words 'fake bitch.'"

She lets me rant without interruption, and then tilts her head in thought.

"You also don't have to do it alone," she reminds.

The sadness seems to dissipate for a moment. Is she...?

"I mean, *if* you decide to continue..." She looks at me. "I could help."

"Are you serious?" I ask.

"Of course, I am."

We just stare at each other. The thought of Jamie helping me with the mural is terrifying but also exciting. Plus, she's a great artist.

"What?" she jokes. "Are you wondering if I'm fit for the job?"

She's teasing me. I'm convinced she knows exactly how to make me melt and she uses her powers at the perfect time. Then she stands from her bed.

"Would you like to see my portfolio?" She floats to her art corner and shuffles through canvases. "This one is my most prized piece. I was offered a whole twenty dollars from my best friend, who is very broke, by the way."

It's an amazing painting, but I can't get past her stupid antics of trying to sell herself for the job. She should know she already has it.

"Or this one..." She pulls another canvas. "My most recent piece that my mother now wants to hang in her bedroom."

I laugh as she turns to shuffle through more paintings.

My own eyes find a stack of canvases and decide to look for the hell of it. I really do enjoy looking at Jamie's work. But when I stumble upon a pair of vibrant brown eyes, my heart stops.

Jamie had painted it about a month ago. The eyes are big and full of life. Hues of yellow and red dance within the gaze. I had seen paintings of eyes before, but never had someone painted brown eyes so... *beautiful.*

"Oh, uh..." Jamie stutters. "That one's good too."

"It's amazing," I whisper.

I couldn't stop staring at the painting, up until I wonder who inspired it and determine it was probably Jacki. I gently set the piece down even though I want to throw it out the window at the thought.

"Anyone in particular inspired that painting?" I ask, flipping through others for distraction.

"No."

I laugh at her defensive response.

"You don't have to lie..." I look up from her paintings. "It was Jacki, wasn't it?"

Jamie rolls her eyes but doesn't say anything right away. I didn't want her to. The thought of Jacki being a muse for her made me hot with jealousy. Is that another reason Jamie enjoyed hanging out with Jacki so much?

"It was you, actually," Jamie informs, pointing at the painting's date. "This was the day after we went mudding at the lake house."

Suddenly, I don't know how to feel. She had painted

my eyes? My eyes aren't anything special. They're brown. The color of dirt. When people compliment me, it's never on my eyes. I find this hard to believe.

"Yeah right." I laugh. "My eyes don't look like that."

"Y-Yeah well you don't see what other people see," Jamie defends. "You don't see how they turn yellow in the sun, almost like they're pools of honey. Or when they give off a tiny hint of red when you're mad... Have you ever seen the way sunlight reflects off hardwood floors? That shits beautiful. A-And..."

I just watch her talk in fascination and tune out every word just to focus on the excitement on her face. No one has ever compared my eyes to honey, or sunlight, or anything other than just brown. No one had made them feel special. No one had made *me* feel special.

"Help me finish the mural," I say.

She stops rambling. "Really?"

I nod.

"Okay, well..." She tries to contain her excitement. "I guess we should start brainstorming."

"I guess we should."

So, we do. We produce about twenty different ideas that morning, and by the afternoon we come to a decision. There's an excitement between us that's electric, and I've found motivation to continue the mural regardless of the incident from this morning.

And at the end of the day, even though my mural was ruined, I still feel as if I've won.

Sixteen

JAMIE AND I START REPAIRING the mural the very next day. I'm surprised at how quickly I find the courage to face the harsh words, but probably only because Jamie is willing to stand next to me. She makes it easier to focus on the task at hand and see the potential for creating something better.

Mr. Z had even prepared to help by buying a large paint roller he had planned to use to cover up the profanity. Luckily, when I told him Jamie would be helping me from now on, he offered it up for us to use, no questions asked.

"So…" Jamie stands up after pouring white paint into a pan. "Would you like to do the honors?"

She holds out the paint roller for me to take. I grasp the wooden handle and place the roller in the paint pan, coating it with white. Then, I press it against the graffiti and begin to cover it up.

I have to admit, I'm still terrified this would all be for nothing. That whoever ruined my work the first time would be back, but hopefully now, with the police involved, they would at least think twice.

Mr. Z told me surveillance had caught someone breaking into the school, but it was impossible to identify them. The figure had been covered up from head to toe, and had one goal the night they broke in, and that was to vandalize my mural.

Of course, they asked me if I had any bad blood with anyone, but I couldn't be honest. I'm senior class president. I'm the *good* guy. Why would I have any enemies? Besides, as much as I believe Jacki was behind it, it was wrong of me to accuse her without any factual proof, because what if it *wasn't* her? So, instead, I just kept my mouth shut.

"Just a few coats of this stuff and you won't even be able to see those words," Jamie states, pulling me out of my head.

"That's all we'll have time for today, anyway," I say.

I set the roller down and sit next to Jamie, who's preparing to play music on her phone. A part of me wants to tell her my theory behind the ruining of the mural, but another part is terrified.

In my head, Jacki had either manipulated or paid someone to do this. I already suspect that she knows I'm in the closet. Hell, she had grown up by my side for seventeen years. So, when Jamie, the cute, new girl from Chicago, blew Jacki off in front of *me*, someone she apparently couldn't stand, it was enough to fuel her to ruin something dear to me.

Motives remain fuzzy, but I figured Jacki was either trying to discourage me from coming out, or she knew I was afraid of such a thing and this was nothing but a threat to out me. I wasn't too afraid of the latter because she had no way to prove it, but if she was trying to discourage me, it was certainly working.

The only thing I had going for me was that every time Jacki tried to do something to hurt me, I still ended up winning, because now I got one-on-one time with Jamie. Every. Single. Day.

"So," Jamie starts. "What are your plans for the weekend?"

"Gibbs wants to have a bonfire," I tell her.

"Oh yeah, he told me about that," Jamie says. "Are you gonna go?"

"Yeah." I shrug. "After this week, soccer's pretty much gonna take up my weekends…"

"So, this bonfire…" She changes the subject. "Should I be prepared to get wasted like we did for the back-to-school bash?"

"No. It's gonna be more chill."

The conversation dies, and I desperately wish I could find something to say. Over time, it never got easier to be around Jamie, I had just gotten used to the constant ball of nerves in my stomach. Today, it feels exceptionally bad.

"Can I ask you something?"

I look at the brunette sitting next to me and study the contours of her face. She's wearing mascara today, and her eyes are unusually green due to the sunlight dancing around in her irises. For a moment I forget she's asked me a question.

"Sure," I whisper.

"Why...?" She hesitates, and then shrugs off the initial question she was going to ask. "W-Why... soccer?"

I narrow my eyes. "That's *not* what you were gonna ask me."

"Yes, it is," she lies.

"No, it wasn't."

"Was too!"

"Jamie."

"Fine." She exhales a deep breath. "I was gonna ask why you've never dated anyone before."

I just study her some more. Where had that question even come from? It seemed completely random.

I pick at my cuticles. "Just never had the time, I guess."

She doesn't seem to buy it, but I decide it doesn't matter. I stand from where we're sitting and pick up the paint roller to put on another coat. Jamie huffs because, apparently, my answer isn't good enough.

"But usually people *make* time," she argues. "If they like someone enough."

"Well, then I guess I've never liked anyone enough to

make time," I finish.

"No one?"

"Nope."

"So, are you saying you've never even felt attracted to anyone?"

I'm *so* glad I'm not currently facing Jamie, because if I were, she would be able to see the blood rushing to my face. There are many girls I had encountered over time who definitely... *solidified* the fact that I am attracted to girls. There was no doubt about that.

"I don't know..." I sigh heavily. "I guess?"

Jamie falls silent as I continue to apply another coat of paint. It would be more annoying that she was asking me this if I didn't like her so much, because let's be honest, it's frowned upon when a straight person did it to a queer person, so what made pressing me okay?

"What about you?" I wonder. "How'd you know you were gay?"

She laughs. "What does that have to do...?"

"What about a girl attracts you?"

There's a look on her face that says she's shocked, but also intrigued, by my question. She leans back against the wall and stares up at me.

"I like girls who are low maintenance," she says. "I love their natural beauty." She shrugs. "I love their voices, and their shapes..."

"Their *shapes*?" I mock.

"I love curves."

I just laugh. Most guys I know went for the girls who were a size zero and could still fit in children's clothing. Not to mention the stigma of staying small when it came to society's standards for young women. Unfortunately, I was never able to fit into a size less than a six due to my curvier figure when I hit puberty.

As I finish the second coat, I wonder if I should end this conversation with Jamie while I'm ahead. I take my place next to her on the wall and look over. She has this look on her face that I can't read, but it screams with arrogance.

"Did that answer your question?"

"Sure." I try to sound indifferent.

She shifts next to me and extends one leg while the other pulls up for an arm to rest on it casually. The posture tells me she's comfortable and that she's enjoying the conversation, which means she isn't going to let it die.

"Do you have any more questions?"

I just give her another shrug even though deep down I have about a million of them. The tension in this room grows thick, and I am sure Jamie knows what that stupid smirk on her lips does to me. I can feel the fire in my body grow at the sight, and I frantically search for a way to extinguish it.

"So, if you like low maintenance, why'd you fool around with Jacki?" I panic.

Jamie doesn't like me mentioning Jacki, but it's the only thing I could think to say to save myself.

"We never fooled around."

"She would literally make out with you all the time."

"So?"

"So...?" I continue. "Why'd you do it if you didn't like it?"

Curious eyes study me, but she hesitates to answer. Again. There's something on the tip of her tongue. *Come on Jamie*, I think. *Just say it.*

"I was just bored, I guess."

It was such an underwhelming answer. I know it isn't the full truth, but it was what she was giving me. I check my watch and decide in about five more minutes I would add the last layer and call it a day.

"That answer sounded really bad," she says.

"Yeah, it did," I agree.

"I just..." She sighs. "Jacki's fun, believe it or not, so I guess she was a good distraction."

"What did you need a distraction from?"

Her eyes seem to accidentally find mine but refuse to hold my gaze. Once again, there seems to be a thought on the tip of her tongue, but she suppresses it.

"Nothing."

I frown but decide not to press her. I begin to paint the last layer while I wonder if there is a girl back in Chicago who Jamie still has feelings for. Was *that* why Jacki had become Jamie's go-to girl? Did she need someone else's attention to mend what she was missing back home?

I finish up the layer and step back. "That should be good, right?"

"Yeah," Jamie agrees while picking up her things. "Guess that's it for today?"

"Yep."

We bring back the supplies in silence, but I can't help but wonder what's on Jamie's mind. Had I unintentionally resurfaced memories she had been ignoring for the sake of her heart?

Then the bell rings and dismisses us for the day.

"See you tomorrow?" I ask.

"Sure," Jamie says, then she walks off without another word.

Suddenly, I have a feeling that Jamie has unchecked feelings for someone, and I had managed to bring them to her attention. It bums me out, because that means I have even less of a chance of grabbing her attention. Not that I believed I really had it at all.

But, as much as I want Jamie, I still couldn't find the will to tell her the truth, which means I never had a chance in the first place.

Seventeen

I'M RELIEVED THAT OUR SATURDAY night bonfire hasn't turned into a huge party, because I was desperate for quality time with my friends. Things were getting hectic, so hanging around the fire and talking is exactly what I need.

"And then Gibbs comes out, dressed in literally nothing but a cowboy hat, cowboy boots, and boxers, holding a half empty bottle of bourbon," Darian finishes.

Everyone is in hysterics from the story, but I feel distracted. Jamie sits across the fire, next to Gibbs and another football player, and has yet to notice my gaze. She's been distant the past few days, but I figure it's the season. Usually, around the holidays, it's hard for people who've recently lost something important. Jamie probably misses her old friends back in Chicago, so I decide not to bother her. Even if her distance really puts a damper on my mood.

We haven't been out here long, maybe about an hour or so, but people are finally starting to get loose. I, on the other hand, haven't been able to catch a buzz. I quickly think about asking to sip on some of Gibbs' whiskey to help it along.

"Peyt," Darian calls out. "You're quiet over there."

I look at my friend and see him and Gwen cuddling in a chair. I throw him a quick smile.

"I'm just chillin'," I deflect.

That's when my gaze finally locks with Jamie's. She throws me a half smile, but there's something there that tells me she too is lost in her thoughts tonight. It kills me that the one night Jacki isn't around to ruin things, we seem to be on different pages.

I stand. "Anybody need a refill?"

"Me," Gwen says, holding up her cup.

I take her empty drink and walk back to the lake house. It isn't until I'm inside that I hear movement behind me. When I turn around, I see Jamie following me into the kitchen.

"Did you need more to drink?" I wonder.

"No, just the restroom."

She disappears into the half-bath while I refill drinks and try to fix my lame mood. I finish around the same time Jamie does.

"Darian's right. You are really quiet tonight," she says. "You okay?"

"Yeah," I lie. "What about you?"

Her lips pull into a tight line. I know that look.

"Could be better."

"Why? What's wrong?"

She leans on the counter and takes in a deep breath. Is she unsure about telling me what's bothering her? And if so, why?

"My ex, uh..." She shakes her head. "She texted me the other day."

I didn't know what to say, but the look on her face tells me things between her and her ex might've ended sour.

"Is that bad...?" I wonder.

"It's not bad, it's just..." She folds her arms. "It brings up old feelings, I guess."

I feel bad that Jamie seems to be so upset over this. I didn't like seeing her hurt. Usually Jamie is upbeat and happy, and it was always contagious. But just like her happiness is contagious, so is her sadness.

"I'm sorry," is all I say.

"It's fine." She shrugs it off. "Let's head back."

She heads out the door and I follow, taking my previous seat across from her around the fire. But, unfortunately, we came back too early, and were now in the middle of a conversation I did not feel safe being a part of.

"I'm just saying, I understand girls being attracted to

girls because well, girls are hot," Darian says. "But guys being attracted to guys... I just don't get it."

"Well, that's because you're not gay," Courtney answers.

"Right," Jamie agrees. "But you know it's not that simple, D."

"Whatchu mean?" Darian wonders.

"I'm saying, some people can be sexually attracted to multiple genders, or not sexually attracted to any gender..." Jamie explains. "It's not just a guy/girl thing."

"Like bisexuals," Gwen includes.

"Or pansexuals." Then Jamie gives me an unsure glance. "They have people that are asexual, too."

"What the hell is an asexual?" Gibbs asks.

"Someone who has no sexual desire for any gender," Jamie answers.

There's a lull in the conversation, but I can tell most of my friends are confused. Hell, I'm even a bit confused. These are terms I've never heard of before.

"I can't imagine not having sexual desires," Darian jokes.

"Same," multiple people around the fire say in unison.

I, of course, make the mistake of not answering, which grabs the attention of one of Gibbs' friends.

"What about you, Peyton?" Cory asks.

"What about me, Cory?" I answer condescendingly.

"Well, correct me if I'm wrong, but I don't think you've ever had a boyfriend," he explains. "Are *you* asexual?"

I roll my eyes. "No, Cory, I'm not asexual."

"So why haven't you dated anyone?"

"Bro..." Gibbs warns.

"Because guys are annoying."

"So, are you asexual?"

"I *just* said I wasn't asexual."

"So then are you a lesbian?"

The question makes me clam up, but my face is on fire. My eyes find Jamie, and then Gwen, who are both looking at me with concerned expressions.

"N-No?" I stutter.

"Have you ever kissed a girl?"

"Well, no, but..."

"So, you *could* be a lesbian."

"Cory," Gibbs warns again. "Enough."

The only people who don't think this is funny are my three best friends and Jamie. Everyone else has smirks on their faces, as if they're waiting for Cory to nag me into confessing.

"I'm sure Jamie wouldn't mind a little experimentation," Cory jokes as he sips his drink.

"Actually, I would mind," Jamie defends.

I feel as if I'm being pushed into a corner. All eyes are on me, waiting for me to break down and admit the truth. In return, this just causes me to grow defensive.

"Well, I don't think you've had an actual relationship since freshmen year, Cory," I counter. "Are *you* gay now?"

This causes Cory to grow angry. So, I guess he can't

take his own medicine.

"It was just a joke, Peyton. Chill out," he deflects.

"Have you ever kissed a guy?" I jab.

"Fuck no!"

"Then how do you know *you're* not gay?!"

"Because at least I've slept with girls," he hisses. "So, either you're a prude or you're gay."

I can't take it anymore. I stand suddenly and knock over the folding chair I had been sitting in. This is bullshit and I didn't deserve to be cornered like this. Jamie, Gibbs, and Gwen stand as well.

"Peyt," Gibbs calls.

"Thanks for the backup guys," I hiss defensively. "I really appreciate it."

I stalk to the lake and away from the fire. I shiver even though I'm hot with rage and embarrassment. Who the hell does Cory think he is?

What a dick, I think.

I stand on the pier and wonder what was going on back at the fire. If I'm lucky, my friends are defending me and convincing everyone else that I'm not gay, regardless of my reaction.

"Peyton?" I hear behind me. "Are you okay?"

I laugh to myself. "Peachy."

Gwen walks closer. "That was really uncalled for on Cory's part."

I didn't have anything else to say to her, so instead I just sit on the cold pier and stare out at the lake. Minutes of silence pass as I find my head and regain my composure, but what comes after this?

Should I just come out to Gwen? She should be the first one to know the truth about me. It was only right. We knew everything about each other, but there were obvious fears holding me back.

"Peyton..." she starts again, grabbing my attention. "You know... if you ever need to talk, I'm here..."

It sounds as if she's coaxing me to admit the truth. Does she know? I wouldn't be surprised, regardless of all the meaningless conversations we had about guys. Gwen isn't stupid.

"I know," I whisper with a tight throat.

"And... if you *are* gay..."

"I'm not fucking gay, Gwen!" I snap.

All goes silent. I swear my voice echoes for an entire minute as Gwen just stares out at the lake. I can tell my response cuts her deep. We never raised our voices at each other. Hell, we barely ever disagreed. Suddenly, I feel overwhelmingly sad.

Tears choke me. Why the hell am I so scared of tainting my image with the truth? Why am I so afraid of people treating me different? I shouldn't care. I should want the fake people out of my life, even if it is one of my best friends. I should want to be honest with everyone, but fear has me by the throat.

And no matter how much I want to be honest, I couldn't make myself do it. I just wasn't ready.

"Please, just leave me alone," I beg. "I need to calm down."

"Yeah," she whispers.

Then she leaves me on the pier.

I feel the pain bubble over and force tears from my eyes. It hurts so much. It feels like something is trying to climb out of my chest, ripping me apart from the inside out. I'm not a liar. I'm honest in all areas of my life...

All areas but my sexuality, and it's killing me. I'm sure of it. And I'm not sure how much longer I could hide the truth.

Eighteen

WEEKS HAVE PASSED SINCE THE BONFIRE at Gibbs'
place, and to me, things just feel different now. In my head,
everyone around me is secretly talking about me. Even
being around my friends makes me uncomfortable, which
has a way of making me feel a dangerous type of darkness.
A darkness that, on most days, leaves me sick with anxiety
and nerves that have me jumpy and distant, especially
around the people I care most about.

And I've never felt so alone.

Over the past few weeks, I've basically avoided
everyone as best as I could. Soccer now takes up my time
after school and on the weekends, I bail on the mural during
art and blame it on having to study for finals, and I skip out

on lunch most days. I know that my friends have noticed my changed behavior, but they refuse to acknowledge it, which somehow makes me feel relieved and even more depressed at the same time.

And on top of it all, I just couldn't seem to find enough courage to face Jamie.

The fear that what happened that night had been spread by gossip throughout the entire school was debilitating. I was on edge every second of every day, waiting for someone to bring it up. Whether it be a student or teacher. The anxiety of believing everyone knew the truth had a way of screwing with my mind, and it was driving me insane.

"Peyt," I hear.

I snap out of it and realize I had been having lunch with my friends for the first time in a while. The sound of cafeteria chatter fills my ears.

"Hmm?" I answer.

"Don't you agree that Gibbs should cut his hair?" Gwen asks, remaining oblivious to my weird behavior.

"Whatever he wants," I say hollowly.

"See." Gibbs leans back into his chair with a smile. "Whatever *I* want."

The conversation continues as if I'm not even here. I don't mind. Everything feels forced and fake anyway. And if they're playing dumb on purpose, well, then it only makes it worse. I stand, which causes the attention of my three friends to fall on me.

"I'll see you guys later," I say. "I've gotta study."

"Awe, come on Peyt, you know you'll pass calc with flying colors," Gibbs pleads. "Hang out for a bit."

"Yeah, I'm sure I will pass with flying colors," I agree. "If I *study*."

Then I give them a forced smile and leave, heading for the door. I walk outside and let the frigid air hit me, sending shivers through my body. It's exceptionally cold today, and I can faintly see my breath as I exhale from my mouth.

I make it to the corridor I hadn't been to in weeks, reveal the key I had been granted and let myself in.

Ever since the mural had been ruined, the two entryways had been locked, for safety. The principal had granted me a key to access it, which meant that no one could get into the room unless you were him, a janitor, or myself.

But it also meant Jamie couldn't work on the mural without me.

I slump against the wall across from the mural and stare up at the nearly blank canvas. We're so far behind at this point that it would be a miracle if we ever finished, but I couldn't seem to find the motivation or courage to work on it anymore. I pull out my calculus book and start going over our final study guide.

It takes all but five minutes for someone to interrupt me.

"You can't tell me studying math is more fun than painting," Jamie teases.

"It isn't," I reply without looking up from my book. "But my art skills won't get me into college."

"Says who?"

"Says my mom," I finish.

I hadn't meant to stiffen the mood, but hey, I wasn't lying. My mom expects a lot of me, but my art was never one of them. It was always the grades, or the sports, or the clubs... Every one of those had a specific way to do it *right*. There was a way to measure perfection.

Art, well, that was nothing more than a hobby to her.

"Well, I disagree." Jamie slides down next to me. "If that's something you'd ever want to do, of course."

I remain silent. I had thought about it, but my mom would never let me study art. I wasn't even sure if I wanted to. I enjoy creating without the restrictions of grades and deadlines. The mural is an exception, of course.

"You've been MIA," Jamie continues.

"I've been busy."

"Sure..." Jamie crosses her legs. "But you still find time for things that are important to you."

"Okay."

"And this mural is very important to you."

"A lot of things are important to me, Jamie."

My tone is walking the thin line between annoyed and straight up mean. I didn't want to be mean to Jamie, but I had come here for a reason. To be alone. And that meant I didn't want anyone around. *Especially* her. She just made the ache in my chest worse.

Jamie is silent for a minute. Maybe she's regretting her decision to come and find me. Maybe she's fed up with my crazy mood swings just as much as everyone else.

"What's wrong, Peyton?" she asks.

It's such a loaded question. It's the question that I could usually answer with "nothing, just tired," but today that isn't the case. Today it's the question that opens the flood gates. Pain squeezes my heart and forces tears from my eyes. I try to suppress as much as I can but find the more I hold back, the harder it becomes to breathe. As much as I want to tell Jamie, I can't because of the knot in my throat.

She doesn't say anything. She doesn't respond to me crying, or continuously press me to answer her out of worry. She just scoots closer and pulls me into her chest.

I sob into her shirt and wonder if she cares that my tears would ruin it. The fact that she was the only one to come and check on me makes everything I feel even worse. Why hadn't any of my best friends cared enough to do the same?

"I don't know what's going on," Jamie says. "But I need you to know it's gonna be okay."

Her chest is warm against me. Any other day I would be besides myself, being this close to her, but today is clearly different. I quickly realize what's happening and recognize I'm not okay with Jamie seeing me like this. I pull back.

"Sorry," I mumble as I wipe my tears.

"Don't be sorry," she states. "It's okay to cry every now

and then."

I laugh cynically. "Not for me."

"Why not?"

"Because..." I lean against the wall. "I'm supposed to be the happy one. The one that helps other people."

"You're not superhuman," she argues. "You have your own shit just like everyone else."

I fall silent. She's right, but it doesn't make anything different for me. I still feel like I have to be strong. That I have to keep my act up. I wonder if that would *ever* change for me.

"You know, I felt the same way once," Jamie says. "About having to stay strong."

I study the contour of her jaw as she stares up at the unfinished mural. She seems to go to a different place.

"My dad left when I was ten," she reveals. "I'm not sure why, my mom never gave me a straight answer, but I think it's because she doesn't really know either."

I watch the sadness wrap around Jamie as she tells her story.

"It crushed my mom." She looks down into her lap. "And ten-year-old me felt the need to always be happy to make her feel better, but... my dad leaving crushed me too."

She falls silent then, probably remembering the time in her life where she had felt most vulnerable. Maybe, in a twisted way, her dad walking out granted Jamie the strength to come out and be herself, because hiding would've been too painful.

I once again find myself admiring her.

"I hurt in silence for years," she confesses. "And I can tell you it doesn't make things better. It just makes you cold."

We're still close, and I hadn't realized up until now that my hand is still resting on her knee. I feel a different type of closeness to Jamie now, but I don't know how to respond to her monologue. I fear I'll say the wrong thing.

Then she looks at me, and it feels like she's studying my soul. I feel exposed and vulnerable, but somehow okay. Jamie is one of the few people who *could* see past it all, and maybe that's why I had such a bad habit of pushing her away. It frightens me that she can see things others couldn't.

Suddenly the bell rings and signals the end of lunch. I move away from Jamie even though inside I'm just dying for a few more minutes.

"I'll meet you here tomorrow," she demands with a smile. "We've gotta mural competition to win."

I just smile in return. There's a small sense of comfort after the conversation, but I wonder how long it would last. Things had a way of breaking me down easier nowadays.

But there are just a few more days until Christmas break, and if I could make it there, then hopefully things would be okay.

Nineteen

I HAVEN'T SEEN MY FRIENDS IN WEEKS. Since Christmas break started, I had avoided virtually everyone except for my family. The guilt of reality was eating me from the inside out, but for some reason I just wanted to be... *alone.*

Now, as I sit in the safety of my car after days and days of isolation, I would soon come face to face with most of my peers for this New Years Eve party.

I stare at my ceiling fan and continue to watch the blades as they rotate in a painfully slow circular motion. Post dinner has me feeling mentally exhausted because Alyssa is home from college, and when she's home, conversations consist of political talk and bickering.

Lately, I just couldn't find the will to leave my bed.

Small vibrations pull me out of my head. I frown when I realize someone is calling me. I roll over and check my phone. It's Jamie. My heart races as I sit up. Why is she calling me? I hadn't seen her since the last day before Christmas break. I hover my finger over the answer command prompt before I exhale a deep breath and slide.

"Hello?" I say.

"Hey," Jamie answers. "What are you doing right now?"

Don't tell her you've been lying in bed for an hour, *my mind demands.*

I search for a quick lie. "I, uh, I just got back from having dinner with the fam." Lame. "Why?"

"Well, Gwen said she couldn't get in touch with you..." *She sighs.* "But uh, there's a party tonight."

"Yeah, I forgot to get back to her," I lie. "I don't know if I'm feeling another party, though."

"You should come," *she suggests.*

"Yeah? Why's that?"

"Because it's New Year's Eve and we haven't seen you all break."

I know she's right. I know that I've avoided everyone and every text I had received to hang out. I know it and still don't feel inspired to leave my room.

"I just figured y'all needed a break from me," *I let slip.*

"What?"

I mentally facepalm myself. "I didn't mean it like that. I just, you know, we see each other all the time..."

Jamie is silent on the other end of the line. I know how my comment sounded, and I know exactly how she's going to take it, but I really hadn't meant it like that. Had I?

"Well, I miss..." She stops. "We miss you. A lot. So, you should come out."

Only for a moment does the gray surrounding me flash with color. Had Jamie meant to say she missed me?

"I'll think about it."

"I'll text you the address."

Then more silence. For a moment, I think she's hung up. I pull back to look at my phone, but realize she hasn't, and then I press it back to my ear.

"Jamie...?"

My phone buzzes from a text.

"Please, just come over," she begs. "I... I really miss you, Peyt."

She sounds desperate, which makes me feel even guiltier than I already do. I look at the clock and sit up.

"Fine. I'll come."

I check my phone. It's already eleven thirty. I should go in now. Everyone is probably already plastered.

After exiting my car, I pace up to the front door. There are a few people already making out on the porch, but I ignore them and make my way into the house. Bass rattles the walls as I'm greeted by a handful of people. None of them are Jamie or my friends. I say my "hellos" and continue to search for them, but figure they are in the heart of the action.

I round the corner in the process of shimmying out of my coat, only to run into Jacki. She's accompanied by three of her friends, and when she sees me her arms cross, a smirk stretching on her lips.

"Oh my God, Peyton, I'm so glad you could *finally* join us!" she teases.

"I bet you are, Jacki."

I hadn't meant to sound so bitchy. Or had I? At this point, I blame it on the sadness.

"Where've you been?" she continues. "Giving out food to the homeless? Donating blood?" This has everyone around her snickering. I feel my body heat up. "Oh, *I know...* you were working hard on that mural, I bet."

I refuse to answer her this time. We exchange glares and I hope she can see that I know she was the one behind the vandalism. She doesn't seem intimidated at all. I turn away from her quickly. I should just leave and go home. No one really wants me here. Jamie just feels bad for me. None of my friends had even called to invite me like she had.

But before I can make it to the door, I hear my name.

"Peyton Kelly," Jamie calls out. "Where are you going?"

I turn and lock eyes with her. The ache in my chest disappears for only a short moment. I hadn't realized how much I had missed her up until now, and the pull to fall into her is insanely strong. It's always stronger after avoiding her for a while. I try to hide the burning in my cheeks.

"I was just looking for you," I lie. She smiles. "To bitch you out for making me leave my house."

Her smile falls to a frown. She crosses her arms and sways from imbalance, giving away the fact that she's probably a little tipsy.

"Really?"

"No," I joke.

She sighs in relief and studies me. I become self-conscious, which is weird because usually I enjoy Jamie's attention.

"Y'know, usually people gain weight over the holidays..." She tilts her head. "You look thinner."

"It's just because you haven't seen me in a while," I lie again, fully aware that I haven't been eating regularly.

She wants to argue but also doesn't want to ruin the moment. Then, without much warning, she grabs my hand.

"Well, let's go and say hi," she suggests. "Everyone's waiting-"

"Can I get a drink first?" I ignore the heat on my skin from the contact. "Everyone else is already drunk."

She looks back and studies me some more. The worry on her face is clear, but why does she care if I drink? Everyone else is. I deserve a drink, probably more than anyone here.

"Fine," she agrees.

I settle on beer and allow her to drag me to my friends, who are in the main room awaiting midnight.

"Peyton?" Gwen expresses.

"Look who finally decided to show!" Darian calls out excitedly.

I cringe at the attention but hug my friends and force myself to stick around for meaningless chat. The clock winds down as the Ball-Drop ceremony in NYC plays on the big screen. It all feels so forced that it manages to make me sick, but I'm here now, so I might as well suck it up. I chug the rest of my beer and watch the minutes tick away. That is, until I hear my peers talking about who they're kissing at midnight.

"I've got my kiss," Darian says as he pulls Gwen into him.

"Yeah, well, Courtney is ignoring me," Gibbs mumbles.

"One minute 'til midnight!" someone shouts.

I roll my eyes at the chaos. People scramble to find their significant others or random people just so they wouldn't be considered lame for *not* having a kiss. Then Jacki and her crew make it into the same room as us. I watch her walk up to Jamie and feel the defeat already taking over.

"Do you have a New Year's kiss, Chicago?" Jacki asks.

"No," Jamie deadpans.

"Do you want one?"

"Y'know what?" Jamie shrugs. "I'm good, Jacki."

I tense at the exchange, but luckily their conversation is covered up by chaotic noise, so Jacki doesn't feel *too* humiliated. She just rolls her eyes and moves on. That's when I feel a soft hand grab my own. I look up at Jamie.

"Let's go outside," she suggests.

I don't have much motivation to resist, so I just allow her to pull me into the backyard. You can still hear the chaos inside the house even after she shuts the door behind us.

"I don't know why people put so much importance on a New Year's kiss," Jamie complains. "It's stupid."

I want to agree with her. I want to say that I don't care that I didn't have someone to kiss, but it wouldn't be the truth. Truth is, I want *her* to be my New Year's kiss. But I'm just so sad. It's why I've avoided everyone for weeks. I believe my sadness is contagious, like a disease you could catch just by being around me. I'm afraid that if I even *touch* Jamie, all the color she feels would turn gray. Her body would go numb and cold, and she would feel just like I do.

I can't fathom the thought.

"Yeah, it is stupid," I reply.

She reveals her phone just in time to see the numbers change to midnight. Her gaze falls onto me, but I can't even hold eye contact with her for longer than a few seconds.

"Happy New Year," she whispers through the dark.

"Happy New Year," I respond, trying not to let my voice shake.

That's when an array of fireworks illuminate the night. Colors of red and green and yellow paint the black sky. It's as if all the houses around us are professionally synchronizing their fireworks to put on the best show possible.

Then I finally allow myself to look at Jamie who seems to be mesmerized by them. The colors flash in her eyes, and even though she's part of the reason I'm so torn up inside, I can't help but think she's absolutely beautiful.

She had crashed into my life without warning, completely unaware of the effects she would have on me. Like a summertime hurricane, I had made it through the first wave of destruction. But, right now, in this very moment, I seem to have made it to the eye of the storm, where things are calm and quiet. Where I was able to observe the damage.

Debris is scattered throughout my streets, houses are missing shingles, snakes of electrical lines are exposed, while abandoned cars and flood water line the roads... but somehow, I'm still standing.

"I thought I was gonna celebrate the New Year with my friends back home in Chicago," she claims. "Like I have for years..."

I feel my heart shudder in pain. She isn't happy to be here?

"But this isn't half bad either."

My smile breaks free and exposes itself on my lips. For some reason, the comment heals some of my pain, even though it only lasts a moment.

"Thanks for coming, Peyton," Jamie finishes. "I would've been miserable if you hadn't."

My heart squeezes at her comment. Does she really mean that? I want to believe her comment means more, that she wants me here because she likes me, but why would she? After everything I had made her believe about me. I refuse to get in my head, so I watch the last of the fireworks instead.

"Thanks for making me come out," I respond.

I bite my lip at the sentence.

Then, as if Jamie knows what I need, she grabs my hand and holds it. It's like she's the light and I'm the dark. The black ink that swirls around inside of me drains, only to expose the color that had been covered up. We don't say anything. We just stand there and enjoy each other's company while the fireworks start to die down.

The storm's destruction is plentiful, and I know it isn't over. Not yet. There's still a lot of pain and struggle to come, but right now that doesn't seem to matter.

Jamie isn't just the storm that's tearing through my life, she's also the sunlight that would warm the streets after it's all said and done.

Twenty

THE PAIN IN MY BODY GROWS as I push myself to run this play just *one* more time. If my teammates screw it up again, I'm surely going to lose it.

The ball is passed to me and I dribble it between my feet while dodging a defender. Then I pass, just like I had done three times already, and watch the ball go untouched, an opposing player picking it up. I throw my hands up in frustration and place them on my head, attempting not to lose my cool.

"Guys," I state. "How many times are we gonna have to run this play before we get it?"

We're a week out from our first match, and it isn't looking good. Not if we played like we practiced.

"Sorry," one of my teammates apologizes. "I'm just not in it today."

"We have a week," I reiterate. "A week to prepare and we're not anywhere near where we need to be."

"Maybe we can just take a break..."

"We'll take a break when we get this play right," I say.

We run the play again, nearly perfect this time, and I allow the girls to take a water break. I hate being the bad guy, but as team captain, it's my job. Plus, there aren't many upperclassmen on the team anymore to take the lead.

The water break ends, and Coach decides to have us run a few more scoring plays to end the day. I ready myself on the field and wait for my time to work. The black and white ball travels over to midfield, allowing me to perform alongside my teammates. I pump my legs and pass the ball to a forward, then relax for a minute.

"You should totally do it," one girl, Brittany, says to Lora.

"I just don't know if she and Jackie are still...?" Lora answers cautiously. "Because if Jackie is still interested..."

"She'll bite your head off."

I find my annoyance growing, and not just because they weren't focused on practice.

"I don't know..." Lora pants while jogging.

"What?" Brittany laughs. "Are you actually *scared* of Jacki?"

"No!"

I roll my eyes at the conversation. *Why* do they feel the need to talk about this right in front of me?

"But Jamie's just so... *hot.*"

Ugh!

"Guys. Focus," I order, trying not to give away my jealousy.

My teammates fall silent and I try not to get too worked up over what I had just heard. Is Lora planning to ask Jamie out? Are they friends? Why the hell do I care so much? It's not like Jamie and I are ever going to date.

I allow my anger and jealousy to turn into motivation during the last few minutes of practice. At least on the field I could release everything I've been holding in for months.

Practice ends and I head home with many things on my mind. I have a lot to do this week, and no motivation to do any of it. But one thing I have *absolutely* no motivation for is my mom asking me a million questions as soon as I walk through the door.

"Something came in the mail." She sits at the small island in the kitchen. "A university in Tennessee?"

I freeze. I had meant to keep my applications to myself until I couldn't anymore, but being the only child living here, it's nearly impossible to get things past mom.

"They had recruiters come to school," I lie.

My mom grunts in disapproval.

"TSU has really great programs, and Nashville's a cool city..."

"I thought you were set on Georgia State?"

There was a threatening tone in her voice, but I should've expected this. My mom is overbearing and controlling. She had been that way with Alyssa, but Alyssa had barely made it into college to begin with. I'm not Alyssa, and I wish she wouldn't treat me as such, but I attempt to do some damage control anyway.

"I really just applied for fun," I lie. "I didn't think they would actually accept me so quickly."

My mom buys it.

"Honey, colleges are going to fight over you," she boasts. "You're very bright and talented."

The defeat in my heart grows.

"But I just think GSU is a perfect fit for you. Not too far from home, plenty of great programs..."

What my mom is saying just fades into the distance. I sigh in defeat.

"Yeah," I voice. "Right."

I go up to my room and throw my things on the floor in frustration. How am I supposed to tell my mom that I was deliberately applying out of state because I want to get away from Branton? That the *last* place I want to go for school was only an hour away from home.

Maybe there were things I was missing about her adamantly wanting me to attend GSU, like out-of-state tuition, or maybe she would just miss me too much? I roll my eyes at the thought. More like miss nagging and controlling every day of my life.

I love my family, don't get me wrong, they just have

their ideas and beliefs that would probably never match mine. I see it in my older sister. It kills her every time she comes home and is forced to deal with the bigotry and ignorance. The difference between Alyssa and me was that she's very vocal about her beliefs.

I feel a heavy pressure settle on my chest. Unless I somehow manage to get a full ride, or at least a decent scholarship, it's looking like GSU is in my future. A future that would be too similar to my past.

But I wouldn't allow it. I was getting out of Branton, Georgia, no matter what.

● ● ●

The sound of soft pop music fills the corridor where Jamie and I work on the mural. It's particularly quiet at the moment since we're both focused, but thankfully it's still a comfortable silence.

It's beginning to take form, but we still have a long way to go. At the turn of February, we still have quite a bit of ground to cover, and it makes me anxious as soccer season approaches.

"You're quiet," Jamie says. "Are you okay?"

"Just focused," I reply.

Jamie chuckles to herself. "You know, I can tell when you're lying."

I continue to work on the mural in silence and hope Jamie doesn't continue to press me. I'm in a weird mood.

My mother confronting me yesterday has me feeling a deep sense of dread that I can't shake.

"So, what's really wrong?"

I carefully trace another line, finish, and then exhale the breath I was holding. Then, I allow my gaze to meet Jamie's.

"I just..." I wipe my brow. "I feel like I'm gonna be trapped in this town forever."

"Why's that?"

"Because..."

My sentence falls away. Do I really want to tell her my family problems? Mom always had this weird thing about seeming perfect from the outside. Telling strangers about our disagreements was none of their business.

Jamie just leans against the wall and waits.

"My mom thinks I'm set on going to GSU," I reveal. "But that's the last place I wanna go to for college."

"Why?"

"Because it's too close."

Jamie falls silent in thought, probably debating whether she wants to get into this conversation with me.

"Too close to...?"

"To Branton, to home..."

She nods. "I get that."

I know there's nothing Jamie can do about it. Hell, she's probably in the same situation as I am. To my knowledge, she's the only child of a single mother. I couldn't imagine her mom being okay with Jamie moving somewhere else.

"Not trying to invalidate your struggles, but..." She looks at me. "At least you have a plan to get out."

I give her a confused look.

"College doesn't seem to be in my future," she confesses. "So right now, it's looking like I'll be staying here after graduation to help mom with her own business."

"Really?" I ask.

She just nods somberly. "I don't have the grades."

"Well, do you want to go to college? Because I can help tutor you..."

"Nah," she cuts off. "College is for doctors and teachers and such... plus, it's just too expensive. So, unless I miraculously get a scholarship, it's just not happening."

"And your mom's okay with that?"

"Sure." She continues painting. "She was never the kind of mother to force me into things, anyway."

I feel envious again. It sounds like Jamie has a hell of a lot of freedom on top of the opportunity to be out in her household. I bet if Jamie wanted to move back to Chicago after graduation her mom would help her do so.

"Do you wanna leave Branton?" I ask.

She sighs heavily, as if attempting to release some of the sadness sitting on her chest.

"Yes and no," she answers. "I mean, most of my family is here. My mom and my grandparents..." Jamie steps back from the mural. "But I don't think I can stay in this town longer than another year."

"Have you thought about moving to Atlanna?"

She forces a smile. "Yeah."

It doesn't seem like that's what she wants. Does she want to go back to Chicago? Or somewhere completely different? Or is she possibly upset that I plan on leaving the first chance I get?

"Well..." I decide to break the serious tone. "If I do end up at GSU, like everyone else, you should definitely move there."

She gives me a teasing smirk. "You only want me to move there if you do?"

"Yeah." I shrug. "If I don't, well, go where you feel you need to be."

Jamie laughs. Her lips pull back and expose her amazing smile. Nowadays, I seem to crave it. My body heats up with a warmth I rarely found outside of art and Jamie.

"Fine," she agrees. "I'll move to Atlanta if you do. You know, to make it more bearable."

Then she sticks out her hand, as if she's waiting for me to shake it. I stare at her dumbly.

"What?" I ask.

"Are we making a deal, or not?"

I stare at her hand. I don't want to go to GSU, but if Jamie agrees to follow me there... that could change. I take her hand.

"It's a deal, Jamie Kendall."

Twenty-One

THE MONDAY MORNING CHILL makes me shiver on this gloomy February day. I'm already dreading this week, and not just because I have a ton of things to do, but because Valentine's Day is in a few days, and I absolutely *hate* the holiday.

If Valentine's Day falls on a weekday, Branton High's student council conducts a rose giveaway. We're in charge of keeping track and collecting the money, which means I get to see everyone else get sent roses while I usually receive none. And this year, I *really* don't want to witness all the roses Jamie is most likely going to receive.

I spot Gwen hiding out with Gibbs and Darian in the cafeteria through the window, waiting for the bell to signal them to class. Then Jamie meets up with me on the way.

"Morning," she greets.

"Good morning." I look up at her. "How was your weekend?"

"Insignificant."

To my knowledge, Jamie had hung out with Lora this weekend, according to Lora's Instagram story. It looked like they had a good time, but maybe Jamie just wasn't impressed. Or maybe she didn't want me to know she was potentially seeing her.

I refuse to ask her about it.

We walk up to our friends who are now hovering over Gwen's shoulder, staring at her phone.

"What are you guys looking at?" I ask.

"That stupid blog." Gwen shakes her head. "You know, *The Branton Buzz.*"

"The one run by Jacki and her yearbook minions?" I roll my eyes. "Why do y'all still give that thing attention?"

"We don't *really* know if Jacki is the one running it," Gwen says. "But check this out."

She turns her phone toward Jamie and me, only to reveal a semi-disturbing picture taken in the girl's locker room. The headline reads: *Lost and Found¸* and below the headline is a picture of a pregnancy test sitting on the locker room floor.

And to make things even juicier, the test is positive.

I take the phone from Gwen and begin to scroll. I hadn't looked at this in forever because I think it's the stupidest and most disturbing idea ever. Jacki, or *whoever* is running the damn thing, just seems hellbent on starting drama and gossip here at Branton, and I couldn't support something like that.

"Wait, go back," Jamie says. "That looked like..."

It was an old post, but it wasn't that old because the haunting words I had covered up months ago were now staring me in the face.

"Branton High vandal on the loose?" Jamie reads.

Below the headline is not one, but two pictures. The old mural idea was there, with no one else in the picture, and next to it is a picture literally *right after* it had been ruined.

Well, I think. *And here I thought we had kept the gossip about the mural to a minimum.*

I hand the phone back to Gwen. "So y'all weren't gonna tell me they posted about the vandalism?"

Gibbs sighs. "Peyt, you were already really upset about it."

"Yeah," Darian agrees. "And bringing it up again felt wrong because we didn't wanna make you feel worse."

In the middle of their explanation, a *bing!* comes from Gwen's phone. It must've been another post on the blog, and judging by the look on Gibbs' face, he isn't at all happy about what he's looking at.

"Lemme see," I order.

Gwen hands me her phone.

This headline reads: *Don't forget a rose for your crush*

this Valentine's Day!

Below is a picture of a single rose, and a guy and girl kissing in the background, except whoever posted it didn't bother to blur them out for a reason, because it's Courtney Wilcox and David Lowell.

I look at Gibbs, but I can tell he's trying to hide the pain on his face. He and Courtney were never officially together, but he always claimed it was because neither of them wanted a relationship. Judging by his expression, that wasn't entirely true on Gibbs' part.

"Bro." Darian reaches over to comfort him.

The bell rings for first hour.

"Whatever, man." Gibbs stands and slings his backpack over his shoulder. "It doesn't matter."

Then he leaves us without another word. I look at Jamie, only to see her angry and confused over everything she had just learned about this "blog." Gwen and Darian leave together for first hour, but I feel the need to confront someone about this. That picture had been posted on purpose, to openly expose Courtney and hurt Gibbs. It was to start drama, because everyone knows Gibbs and Courtney had been on and off forever.

"That's pretty horrible," Jamie fumes. "Whoever manages this blog is messed up."

"Yeah," I agree. "They are."

We walk together in silence while I continue to be angry about Gibbs being affected by the blog's latest post. It isn't fair that it was a thing, but for some reason students kept quiet about it, even if it is borderline bullying.

The sound of obnoxious laughter pulls me out of my thoughts. It's Jacki and a few others, laughing over *something* that's apparently hilarious, even this early in the morning. A part of me believes it's over the latest post, which starts a fire in me. I find myself storming over to her.

"That picture was uncalled for," I say.

Jacki rolls her eyes as she pulls her gaze up from her phone. "What picture?"

"On the blog."

She scoffs. "Are you accusing me of something?"

"I know you're involved somehow."

"I didn't post the picture." Jacki looks down at her phone and smirks. "But I kinda wish I had."

"Because you're a bitch?"

Everyone falls silent. I hadn't meant to use the harsh language. It isn't expected from me, but lately my patience has been running low, especially when it comes to Jacki.

"*I'm* a bitch?" She tilts her head and steps into my personal space. "I provide the truth, Peyton, when *fake bitches* like you lie about who they really are when people aren't looking."

That was it. That's Jacki's blatant confession to ruining my mural, yet only her and I seem to catch it. The condescending smile on her face infuriates, and mildly intimidates, me. I step back.

"That was also uncalled for." Jamie steps between us and grabs my arm. "C'mon."

I allow Jamie to pull me away from Jacki before I could give her a real reason to hate me. Fighting isn't something I ever felt compelled to do, but lately it's becoming harder *not* to hit Jacki in her left tit. Her passive-aggressive threats and subtle comments that hint at knowing I'm hiding something low-key scares the hell out of me.

Why would she *want* to out me? She, of all people, should know how important it is for people to come out on their own terms. It shouldn't be forced, and should be as natural as possible, because if it *isn't*, it could be traumatizing. But Jacki seems dead set on ruining my life any way she can, and I couldn't let her take away the one thing I'm so dearly holding onto.

● ● ●

It's last call to buy roses and people are scrambling. Everyone usually waits until the last minute, which makes this morning a busy one for student council. I take my last payment before closing the safety box and look around for stragglers.

"Are we done?" David asks.

"Yeah, looks like it," I confirm, refusing to ask David about the picture posted on *The Branton Buzz* a few days ago.

Luckily, senior student council isn't responsible for handing out the roses to people. That was a sophomore job. I find great relief in this.

I make my way to my first class and watch the time pass in a blur. My mind is elsewhere with the thought of the mural's progress and my soccer tournament this weekend. The stress weighs heavy on my chest, but I keep telling myself the school year is almost over. Just a few more months, and then I will hopefully escape Branton for good.

I just have to make it past my mom first.

Eventually fourth hour comes, and Jamie meets me in the art room to collect the supplies to work on the mural. To my surprise, she's empty handed.

So, *no one* had gotten her a rose?

"Looks like we're the only two in Branton High that didn't get a rose," she says. "I'm kinda happy about that, actually."

I smile, but silently wish I had gotten her one, and vice versa.

We make it to the room where the mural waits for us. There's still so much to be done. I'm afraid we won't be able to finish it in time at this pace, but we're aiming for perfection.

"Stop looking at it like that," Jamie orders. "We're gonna finish it in time."

"We only have two and a half months left," I inform her. "And if we continue at this pace..." I shake my head. "There's no way we'll finish it."

"We will." Jamie picks up a brush. "I promise."

I give her a trusting smile and hope that she's right.

We have a lot riding on this, especially since the *entire* school apparently knows about the vandalism that occurred. We have to finish, because Jacki *couldn't* win.

We begin working on the mural and make conversation to fill the silence. This goes on for about twenty minutes until an underclassman knocks on the door to grab our attention.

"I have a delivery," he says, revealing two roses. "Two for Jamie Kendall, from Lora and Jacki."

I roll my eyes at the names. I should've figured Jacki would send one to Jamie to spite both of us, so I don't take it to heart. As for Lora, well, she's certainly making it known that she's interested.

Jamie accepts her roses. "Thanks."

I continue to work on the mural and pretend not to care, even though I'm annoyed that Jamie had received not one, but *two*, while I still sat empty handed. God, she probably thinks I'm such a loser.

"And one rose for Peyton Kelly," the delivery boy claims.

I turn around in shock.

"From Quinton Peterson."

Twenty-Two

QUINTON PETERSON? THE SWEETHEART JOCK who every girl, and maybe even some guys, literally swoon over? The guy who gave me a ride home one time after a party and expected nothing out of it? My longtime friend from second grade, Quinton Peterson?

Jamie and I just stare at each other for a moment as the silence settles around us. I believe we've both been caught off guard with the roses, but I'm beyond surprised about mine.

"Quinton Peterson, huh?" Jamie sets her roses down and continues to paint. "You've never mentioned him."

"He's uh... he's a friend," I explain through my confusion.

"Seems like he may want more than friendship."

I set my rose down and wonder why she seems so... shocked? I mean, don't get me wrong, I'm shocked myself, but is the thought of someone being interested in me that surprising to her?

"Or maybe he's just being nice," I finish.

Jamie laughs to herself, but it doesn't sound humorous. If I didn't know better, I'd think she was jealous, but that couldn't be. Right?

"Are you still talking to Jackie?"

Jamie frowns. "No. She's just relentless."

"And probably found out about you and Lora."

The conversation is seeping with passive-aggressive jealousy, even though it shouldn't be. I should be over it by now. Jamie and I aren't going to happen. I'm too afraid to come out and she isn't going to put herself out there for someone who claims to be straight. It's just logic.

"How'd you know about me and Lora?" she asks skeptically.

"Her Insta story," I reveal.

"Oh."

She turns away from me to hide her embarrassment, probably for assuming I had stalked her social media or gossiped about her when that wasn't the case. Trust me, if I could be blind to Jamie's love life, I would. It hurts too much to watch.

We remain silent until the end of fourth and return our supplies before the bell rings. I decide to skip lunch when I spot Quinton walking to the cafeteria alone.

"I'll uh, see you tomorrow," I say to Jamie. "I wanna talk to Quinton."

"Sure."

Then Jamie leaves my side in a hurry. I find her behavior weird but pin it on the fact that I had caught her trying to keep the whole Lora thing from me. Which I don't understand, anyway. Why wouldn't she just tell me about it?

I pace up to Quinton Peterson. He's our starting pitcher for our varsity baseball team and isn't nearly as obnoxious as most of our male athletes. He's not an AP student like me but will certainly score an athletic scholarship by the end of this year. He stands at around six-foot with smooth, mahogany skin and dark curls that sit atop his head. He's hands down one of the most attractive guys at Branton High.

We've known each other since second grade when his parents moved here, and Quinton desperately needed a friend. We stayed close, but our relationship never extended past occasional tutoring sessions and friendly glances in the hallway. I had never suspected Quinton could like me, but was the rose a confession? And why now?

"Quinton," I call out.

He turns with a huge smile, and then his cheeks turn deep red at the sight of me. His shoulders tense as he shoves his hands into his pockets.

"Hey, Peyton."

I just hold up the rose with a confused expression.

He laughs nervously and scratches the back of his neck. Then, he says, "Happy Valentine's Day?"

I just lift a brow.

His smile fades when he realizes I want an explanation. "I'm sorry it was so random. I just wasn't sure if you were seein' anyone, and I mentioned sending you a rose to my friends, so they made sure I followed through..."

"Since when?" I ask.

He tilts his head and lifts a brow. Why is he looking at me like that?

"You want the truth?"

My heartbeat speeds up. "Y-Yes?"

"Probably since sophomore year..." He shrugs. "Maybe before that? I don't know. I've always liked you, it's just..."

All I can do is stare up at him in disbelief.

"You're you and I've never had the guts to just ask," he reveals.

"I'm... me?"

"Y'know..." He waves his hands in the air. "Peyton Kelly. Overachiever, president of like...*everything*."

"Not *everything*."

He just gives me a smile and a "seriously?" look.

I cross my arms. "Well, I'm not?"

He finally finds an ounce of confidence and steps closer to me.

"And you're one of the prettiest girls I've ever met."

Is this really happening? I mean, it feels like a scene

out of a movie, except... I'm *gay*! What the hell am I supposed to say?

"Thank you," I force. "I uh...it was sweet of you..."

"It doesn't have to mean anything if you don't want it to, Peyton," he explains. "But now, you know where I stand."

God, *why* can't I feel anything?! It's so frustrating! Why am I gay? WHY?!

I sigh. "Thank you, again. It made my day."

He just gives me a kind smile before leaving the conversation and disappearing into the cafeteria. My heart is racing. What does this mean? I know I don't like him romantically, right? I mean, maybe I could, with time? I've never been in this kind of situation. God, I sound so *pathetic* right now...

"Peyt!" I hear behind me.

I turn to see Gibbs making his way over.

"Hey," I say. "Are you getting lunch?"

"Well, we were thinking about burgers instead." He looks past me to wave someone over. Probably Darian and Gwen. My hunch is proven right when I turn to see them walking over.

Then I see Jamie talking to Lora, and my heart sinks.

"B-Burgers sound good." I turn back to Gibbs, who is looking at my rose.

"You got a rose?"

"Yeah."

"From?"

"Quinton Peterson."

"Quinton Peterson?" Gwen says as she walks up. "That's... random."

"You're telling me?" I ask.

We head for the parking lot and I silently hope that when we pass Jamie, she doesn't look at me. I'm a complete mess with the thought of her and Lora possibly dating.

"Chicago!" Darian calls.

Darian, shut up!

"You comin' to get burgers or what?" he asks.

"Uh, I don't know..."

"Come," Gibbs urges. "You can ride with Peyton and Gwen."

The pressure to make a decision shows on her face. I don't expect her to blow Lora off, because, well, they look like they're having an intense conversation.

C'mon, just say no Jamie. They'll get over it.

"Sure," she agrees.

Seriously?

She falls into stride with us, conversing with everyone while I remain silent. A part of me wants to know what she and Lora had been talking about, while the other part wishes I didn't care at all.

Gwen, Jamie, and I pile into my car and head for the diner. I hope no one brings up the roses they've received today.

"So, Jamie, who are your roses from?" Gwen questions.

Gwen. I love you, but seriously, shut up. Please.

"Jacki and Lora."

"Jacki's persistent," Gwen claims. "But Lora's cool. She's on the soccer team with Peyton."

The car falls silent as we pull up to our destination. Thankfully, it isn't a far drive from Branton High. I escape the conversation quickly. We choose a round booth that can fit all five of us and chatter erupts as soon as we're all settled in.

"So, Q Peterson, huh?" Darian teases. "I like him."

"You two *would* be pretty cute together," Gwen agrees with her boyfriend.

I can't help but look at Jamie, who's all but hiding behind her menu. Why is she acting so strange about this? Does she know something I don't about Quinton? Hell, she's been friends with Jacki, and Jacki knows dirty things about nearly everyone.

"I don't know if I even feel that way about him," I lie. "I mean, I had no idea he was even interested. And I'm swamped with soccer and school and the mural... Besides, why would I even pursue a relationship when I'm about to graduate?"

My friends just look around at each other. Then Jamie looks up from behind her menu.

"Peyt, you've never been in a relationship though," Darian says.

"Thanks for the reminder," I respond. "I totally forgot."

"What he's saying is..." Gwen interjects. "This could be good for you."

I sigh. No, it really wouldn't be. I would get myself into a meaningless relationship knowing deep down, I wouldn't feel anything other than platonic attraction for Quinton. All I would do is lead him on. Then, eventually, I would have to break it off because I couldn't stand lying to him anymore, and then possibly hurt a good guy for absolutely no reason.

"I'll think about it," I finish.

My friends drop the subject and look at each other nervously. They know pushing me to pursue a relationship is a bad idea, and I appreciate that. The only person who had refused to give any input at all was, of course, Jamie. I find her silence on the subject odd. Usually, she has a lot to say.

We eat lunch together while I drift away into my own thoughts. Despite knowing that I wouldn't feel anything for Quinton, even if I tried really hard, there is *one* benefit to possibly pursuing a relationship.

It would certainly look good.

And not just aesthetically. It would look good to the administration. It would look good to my peers. And it would look good to Jacki, who seems convinced she knows that I'm gay.

Would I go through with it? Probably not, because it would be out of character for me to lie further about who I am. But it was only a matter of time before people started seeing through the growing cracks in my mask.

Twenty-Three

THE LAST MONDAY OF FEBRUARY is a cold one. On my usual trek to my art class, the frigid air initiates a shiver that seems to rip through my entire body.

This past weekend felt like some sort of a turning point. The vividness of every little thing that had happened at the lake house this past Friday plays in my head over and over, and I wonder if there would be any backlash over it.

I grab the cart of paints and head over to the mural without Jamie. She's late. Or maybe she isn't even here today, I have no clue. I hadn't seen her this morning before first hour, so it's likely she's just absent.

After unlocking the door and setting up the paints, Jamie finally shows up. She shuts the door behind her.

"Hey," I greet.

"Hi."

I turn to look at her. Why does she look so... *annoyed?*

"Listen," she continues. "I'm gonna head out a little early today..." She finally locks eyes with me. "I'm going over to Lora's."

Lora's? She going over to her *house?* For what? Then I suddenly remember, they had grown awfully close over the past week. Hell, they might even be dating for all I know.

Jamie refuses to tell me anything about it, though.

"Okay," I respond.

We fall into our normal work rhythm, except now there's this negative tension between us. What the hell is that about? Had I done something to piss her off? I can't put my finger on it... Had I said something or done something at the party? I try to distract my brain from the feeling, but only find my curiosity over Lora and her escalating in response.

"Are you and Lora dating now?" I blurt.

Peyton, what the hell are you doing?

Jamie shrugs. "Maybe. That's what we're gonna talk about today, actually."

Something in my heart quivers with pain. God, why the hell does it still hurt? I saw this coming from miles away! *Especially* after this past weekend.

The lake house is packed. More packed than usual, but this is because of the wind outside. Gibbs and Darian had extinguished the bonfire not too long ago. They had been worried it would spread and start a problem they couldn't lie to the cops about. So, now we're confined to the inside, and even though the lake house is spacious, having almost every senior in here makes it a bit cramped.

I squeeze through the kitchen with my new drink and search for my friends. They're here somewhere, probably at the beer pong table, so I head there. When I arrive, all I see is Jamie and Lora killing the game, together. Jamie makes a shot. Lora pulls her in for a well-deserved kiss. The bile rises in my stomach at the sight.

"Nice job, babe!" Lora shouts.

Babe, I think. They're on a pet-name basis now?

They pull apart just in time for Jamie's gaze to lock with mine. I hope the jealousy isn't blatantly written on my face. I look away, but not before I catch the hint of a smirk on Jamie's lips.

"Me and Peyt get next round!" Gibbs shouts.

Then, Jamie and Lora both end the game as winners.

Jamie leans on the table arrogantly and looks at me first, as if she's silently taunting me. What the hell?

"Well, I hope you brought your a-game, Peyt."

We ended up winning, Gibbs and I, and successfully dethroned Lora and Jamie. The only bad part was that we *kept* winning, which meant I ended up getting way too drunk. This obviously didn't help when I saw Jamie and Lora getting cozy on the couch.

"*Shit,*" I say. "*I didn't expect to win that much.*"

"*We're a good team.*" Gibbs belches. "*You should've expected it.*"

I just laugh as I search for Gwen and Darian, who are standing around in the living room. They look as if they're having an intense conversation. Intense enough to discourage Gibbs and me from walking up to them. Then I see Jamie and Lora talking it up on the couch. This time, Jamie's hand is on Lora's thigh, inching its way up with every joke told. Lora doesn't seem to mind. I mean, why would she?

I turn away from them and look at Gibbs, but the image is still burned into my brain, and my imagination escalates. Jamie makes a joke. Lora laughs. Jamie finds the courage to lean in and, before you know it, they're making out. People stare, but try not to make it too obvious, but who could blame them? They're both hot, and Jamie's probably a really good *kisser.*

"*You okay?*" Gibbs asks.

"*Sure.*"

It's a robotic response. I know that. What else can I do? My heart hurts. It's been hurting for months. I feel more dead inside every day. It probably wouldn't be long until I couldn't feel anything at all.

Then, out of nowhere, a third party joins us.

"*Hey, Peyton.*"

I look up at Quinton. He's wearing a cologne that really compliments him. God, I desperately wish I could feel *something. I really do. For him. He's such a good guy, and I deserve a relationship. I deserve a meaningful kiss. I just wish it could be with a familiar Chicago native instead...*

"Hey, Quinton."

The silence is killing me. Why is Jamie so quiet? She's usually talking about deep and meaningful topics, or about Chicago, or asking me a million questions about my life.

"What about you and Quinton?" she asks.

I can't help but notice the bitterness in her tone.

"What about us?" I counter.

"Well, I mean, the last time I saw you, you and Quinton were making out." She refuses to look at me. "Figured things between you two were progressing."

"Do you wanna go upstairs?" Quinton shouts over the noise of the party. "To talk?"

Upstairs? We could just go to the kitchen, or outside... but hell, what do I have to lose? We're having a decent conversation, and I have to pee really bad.

"Sure!"

He follows me upstairs and into a guest room. I disappear into the bathroom and relieve myself. Then I'm staring at myself through a mirror.

You're drunk, I think. Like, really drunk.

I wash my hands and exit the bathroom. Quinton is circling his thumbs against his plastic cup while he nervously sits on the bed. He really is a cute boy. If I were straight, he would be my first pick, for sure.

"We're not sleeping together," I blurt. "I just wanna clarify..."

He just laughs. "I know."

I join him on the bed and sit close, but not too close. The heat radiates from his body. Is he nervous? Am I nervous?

"Can I ask you something?" he wonders.

My heart speeds up. I hate that question. The asking of permission. As if it's a disclaimer that the next question will probably hit me like a punch to the gut.

"I guess."

He finally quits staring at his hands and looks at me. His expression manages to make my stomach sink to my knees.

"Is there a reason..." He stops. "Like, I've noticed you really haven't dated..."

God, just spit it out! I know you just want to know if I'm gay. Just ask. I'm going to lie about it anyway. I raise my brow in annoyed anticipation.

"There's just this rumor going around that you might be a lesbian," he finally says.

Ah, there it is. The confirmation I need to prove all of my worst fears right. See? My paranoia wasn't all for nothing, now was it?

I laugh. "Of course, there is."

Then I down the rest of my drink.

"I don't care if you are!" he defends. "I mean, I care because, well, I like you a lot, but I've known you forever, and you're a great person. And there's nothing wrong with being gay..."

"Quinton," I interrupt his rambling. "Stop."

He falls silent.

I study him. Like, really study him, as if looking at him hard enough would somehow trigger some sort of attraction. I imagine him kissing me, my fingers running through his hair, his hands gliding over my thighs... but nothing. There's nothing there. No excitement, no desire... Somewhere, deep down, it makes me feel broken.

Yet, maybe actually doing it would be different.

"I didn't mean to upset you," he apologizes. "I'm sorry."

I shake my head. "No one knows who I am, but me. Let's just leave it at that."

I watch his eyes fall onto my lips for a split second. He wants to kiss me. I can see it, plain as day. I could let him. It's just a kiss. And maybe, if I did, a miracle would occur, and I would feel something other than numbness.

"I really wanna kiss you," he confesses.

Why did he have to be so goddamn sweet? He's making this harder than it has to be. If he had been an arrogant douche, I wouldn't have a problem hurting his inflated ego. But that isn't Quinton.

"So, kiss me."

It could be the alcohol. Or the loneliness. Or the unnerving knowledge that everyone is, in fact, talking behind my back about possibly being a lesbian. It could've been the stress from lying to my mom about applying to out-of-state colleges, or the pressure to finish high school with perfect grades, perfect relationships, and winning this goddamn mural contest.

Or, maybe, I just didn't care anymore because I'm now coming to terms with the fact that I've somehow completely fallen for Jamie, and she's now with someone else.

Quinton's kiss is gentle, and his lips are soft. His hand cups my cheek and pulls me into him. I close my eyes and allow my lips to connect with his. It isn't bad. It isn't rushed. It's nice...

Unfortunately, it also isn't anything special.

Our lips move together, and I try hard to feel something for his sake, but instead find myself fighting off images of Jamie. I can feel her long hair tickling the sides of my face, her delicate fingers tracing my jaw... Our noses touch, and the nose ring I always thought was kind of hot grazes my skin. Then, her tongue glides over my bottom lip, which causes my stomach to clench in response...

Then, out of nowhere, the bedroom door swings open, causing me to jerk away from Quinton.

"Peyton? Jacki said..." Jamie stops at the sight. "Oh. Sorry. I didn't mean..."

The look on her face is blurry from the alcohol. Why is she here? Why had she been looking for me? And why is Jacki somehow involved? Then, she shuts the door just as fast as she had opened it. Quinton and I sit in silence. What had just happened?

"I-I'm sorry, I uh..." I stand abruptly. "I should see what that was about."

Quinton nods sadly. "It's fine, Peyton."

But when I make it downstairs, I see Lora and Jamie walking out the door, together.

"It was just one kiss," I reply. "And why were you even looking for me in the first place?"

Jamie finishes the section she had been working on before she sets her brush down on the cart. She looks as if she's getting ready to leave. I need answers before she does.

"Jacki said you went upstairs 'cause you got sick," she reveals. "I was worried, so I went looking for you. But I should've figured Jacki had other motives."

Motives? What exactly could be her reasoning behind making sure Jamie saw Quinton and me making out?

She throws her backpack over her shoulder.

"I'm gonna head out," she says. "I'll see you tomorrow."

Then, before I can even get a goodbye in, she's out the door. The confusion of the situation is disorienting, but at least now I could analyze everything in peace.

Jamie's face the night she had caught Quinton and I together... well, it had never left my mind. She had looked so... *shocked.* Or hurt? But why would that make any sense? And why the hell would Jacki insist on sending Jamie after me, fully aware that I had gone upstairs with Quinton. Had she wanted Jamie to see? And for what?

Deep down, I already know the truth.

Jacki is constantly in competition with me. Every one-up she could get was a small win, but the one thing she seems to desperately want is... Jamie. So, if she wanted Jamie to see Quinton and me, alone, that meant she knew it would upset Jamie.

Which means Jacki not only knows that I'm lying about being a lesbian. She also knows Jamie likes me, and I had, once again, completely ruined it.

Twenty-Four

JAMIE LIKES ME? JAMIE KENDALL, the girl who is hands down one of the most amazing and interesting people I've ever met... likes *me*? Suddenly it all makes sense. The wanting to help with the mural, the looks, the flirtatious comments, the touches... I had written them off as Jamie just being flirty, because how could someone like her like someone like me, but *God* how could I have been so blind?

It could've been because of her involvement with Jacki, or me icing her out the majority of the time. Not to mention how she's now getting close to Lora. Hell, she's probably about to define the relationship with her!

I step toward the door, ready to yell for Jamie. The adrenaline rushes through me. I couldn't let her date Lora because that meant we wouldn't...

Wait.

I stop. My hand sits on the door, but I make no sudden movement to open it. Jamie is out, and I'm sure has no intention of hiding it. I'm in the closet and still can't imagine coming out. I literally hadn't been able to see the most obvious of attractions because of that!

So, even if I told Jamie I like her too, what would happen after that? We could possibly date in secret, but how could I ask Jamie to put herself in that situation? I didn't want to hold her down because I'm still struggling with the idea of being out. That would be beyond unfair and completely selfish.

I step back from the door. The pain of the truth only makes my bones ache in response. God, if I came out now, I feel everything would be jeopardized. Teachers would look at me differently and I might even receive a lot of backlash from student council... Hell, coming out might encourage the judging committee to discriminate against me for the mural competition. This town is *filled* with silent homophobes.

My back presses against the wall and I slide down in defeat. What the hell am I supposed to do now? I couldn't even confirm if Jamie really likes me unless I ask her, and I know she won't admit that unless she's sure there's even a slim chance of reciprocation.

So, come out to Jamie.

Could I really come out to Jamie, and not to my three

best friends? They might feel disrespected and lied to. *Especially* Gwen.

And what about my parents? Oh God, telling them would be the absolute *worst*. I can already hear my mom, yelling some bullshit about how it's a disgrace and how she doesn't believe her baby girl could ever be a *lesbian*.

The truth of it all develops a pain that's able to squeeze tears from my eyes without even trying. I wipe quickly, but there's no stopping it. Fuck. I had literally made out with Quinton three days ago! How could I ever be honest with Jamie when I can barely be honest with myself?

I stare up at the half-finished mural and try to compose myself. It feels as if the stress of it all is literally going to crush me. My breathing quickens, and suddenly I need to get out of here. I need to go home.

So, I return the art supplies and leave school before anyone can see me break down.

● ● ●

I collapse in the locker room from defeat. We had been so close to winning. God, I'm embarrassed because, honestly, as a team, we had played like crap. I begin removing my uniform as I try not to blame Lora and Brittany for our loss today.

Lora and Brittany are our starting forwards because they work great together. When they were on, we could easily crush most of our opponents. *Unfortunately,*

Brittany and Lora had been recently benched because of their slacking grades, resulting in two underclassmen taking their place.

I want to blame my rage over the loss on Lora and Brittany, but really, I know I'm misplacing my emotions. I know that I resent Lora because she and Jamie are... *kinda* dating, I guess? They aren't "official" official, but they're exclusively talking to each other now. This had resulted in Jamie hanging out with Lora more and me and my friends less.

I would see them walking to class together or hanging out in the cafeteria for lunch. Hell, Jamie even showed up to a soccer game for Lora before she was benched.

It made me sick with jealousy.

After becoming aware that Jamie was – or *had* been – interested in me, every memory we had together is now skewed. The day I went to her house, the painting, the conversations, the day we went mudding... it was all so blatantly obvious that I had literally started to hate myself.

She had been so upfront with her feelings, and I was afraid I had missed my chance for good.

Then, I suddenly receive a text. I look down to see Gibbs' name.

Gibbs: *How was the game?*

Peyton: *Lost by one.*

Gibbs: *Damn. I'm sorry, P.*

I change into other clothes and shove my uniform into my athletic bag. Honestly, I didn't feel like talking to anyone, including Gibbs. Even if he is the only one checking in on me nowadays.

But my phone buzzes again.

Gibbs: *Wanna come over?*

Peyton: *Not really. Kinda tired and I have homework.*

Gibbs: *... It's Friday, tho*

Gibbs, out of all my friends, knows when I'm spouting bullshit regardless of what I did. I blame this on the fact that we had literally grown up together, since pre-k days. We're practically brother and sister. So, hiding my moods from him is near impossible.

Peyton: *Maybe some other time. I'm not feeling it today.*

Gibbs: *Then how about Sunday afternoon. We can fish at the lake...*

I can't help but smile. At least he's considerate and cares enough to get me out of my house on the weekends. Darian and Gwen are stuck up each other's you-know-what's, which left little time for me. And Jamie is now with Lora and blatantly ignoring me.

I throw my stuff into my car and climb into the driver's seat, inevitably deciding to take Gibbs up on his offer. Maybe a little quality time with my best friend would be good for me.

"*Fine, I'll come over Sunday,*" I type.

Twenty-Five

THIS MID-MARCH SUNDAY IS PERFECT. The sky is clear and as blue as ever. The wind is just cool enough to keep the heat at bay, and I've convinced myself that this is a sign that I'm supposed to be outside with Gibbs today.

I find him by the lake, already casting his line into the water. He sits on the pier, his legs dangling and skimming the surface.

"You know," I start, mildly startling my friend. "I could've been a psycho murderer and you would've been completely unaware."

He laughs. "Too bad you're too small to be a good murderer."

I just roll my eyes.

He leans back and hands me a fishing rod, allowing me to take my place next to him on the pier. It's silent as I ready the bait on my hook. Then, once I cast into the water, our conversation starts.

"So, have any new colleges tried to win your hand?" he jokes.

Gibbs knows I'm desperate to leave Branton. He's also constantly encouraging of the idea.

"MTSU," I reveal. "Over in Tennessee. And UNC in Asheville."

"Nice." He slowly reels in his line and recasts. "Have you found one worth the struggle?"

"MTSU offered me a full ride." My bobber bounces, signaling a bite. I tug, but nothing. "But I'm not so sure about it."

"Well, it's only March. You still have a month or two. Plus, you might get an even better offer if you hold out," he says. "I'm more impressed by how you're successfully keeping it from your mom."

My mom. Right. The biggest obstacle I would have to face once I decided to pick a school. She hadn't found out yet because I left school just in time to check the mail before she got home. The last thing I needed her to do was open more of my mail and see the truth.

"Honestly, I am too."

We laugh at the thought of me sneaking behind my parents' backs, but I feel a sadness grow between us. Maybe Gibbs would miss having days like this. I know I would.

"So..." Gibbs starts. "I'm not sure if there's a right or wrong way to say this, so I'm just gonna say it."

I look up at him in confusion.

"Do you trust me?"

All I can do is stare at my friend. His eyes are soft with sympathy, but I have no idea what he's about to say. All I know is that it feels bad.

"Yes," I whisper as fear bubbles in my stomach.

"I've known you the longest out of our group of friends," he continues. "Since pre-k. And you know you're like family to me, so uh, it's hard not to notice..."

He pauses again. The fear of saying the wrong thing is wrapped around his throat. Deep down I have a feeling I know exactly what's coming.

"I know, uh..." He swallows nervously. "I know you haven't been yourself for a while..."

"What are you about to say?" I ask sternly.

"I-I just... Quinton told me that he mentioned the rumor going around..."

"The rumor going around that I'm *gay?*" I fume.

The look on his face lets me know that's *exactly* what he's about to bring up. Suddenly, I feel cornered. Why is everyone so determined to make me admit the truth?! Why couldn't they just mind their own business!?

I stand abruptly. The anger must be radiating from me because Gibbs looks completely terrified.

"Oh my *God!*" I shout. "Everyone is so *fucking* nosy!"

I turn to leave and throw down the fishing rod in the

process. My own best friends are cornering me now. Who can I even trust? Then, I feel his strong hand grab my wrist, refusing to let me leave.

"Peyton," he calmly says. "Stop."

I try to yank away from him, but it does nothing.

"Let me go," I demand.

"No." He continues to hold me hostage. "I'm not letting you run away. Not from me."

The fear of admitting the truth infects every cell of my body. It feels as if it's burning me from the inside out. Tears well in my eyes at the thought of my best friend pushing me to come out. I'm not ready! I'm just *not*!

Then I break. The tears come in one giant wave, as if they had been building up for years and years. And, in all honesty, they kind of had. I would've collapsed to the ground had Gibbs' strong arms not wrapped around me. My face buries itself in his chest and soaks the front of his t-shirt as all the pain escapes through my eyes.

"It's okay," he whispers. "It's okay, Peyt. I promise."

He gently guides both of us into a sitting position on the wooden pier. His strong arms never let me go, as if he's afraid I would literally fall apart if he did.

I cry for about ten minutes before I feel the pain let up. Luckily, I hadn't worn makeup today, so at least his shirt wouldn't be completely ruined. But even when I finally stop sobbing, he continues to hold me.

"You know what's crazy? I remember meeting you in pre-k back when I was *five* years old," he says. "And you know I have the memory of a goldfish, right?"

A laugh involuntarily escapes my lips.

"I remember because even when half the class was crying because their parents left, you were trying to comfort them."

This time, I allow him to comfort me.

"You were always so happy," he continues. "Every single first day of school, you were the happiest kid ever. You even won that title back in like, what, fourth grade?"

I laugh again. God, when is he going to rip the bandage off?

"Voted *Happiest Fourth Grader*," I confirm. "You were voted *Most Friendly*."

"But things changed in high school." He gazes out on the lake. "Somewhere you kind of lost your light, and this was before your grandma passed away, so don't try to say that's it."

My grandma's passing certainly hadn't helped my situation, but he's right. This pain had started long before.

"I know you're gay."

There it is. The truth. He had even said it so confidently, as if there wasn't an ounce of doubt in his mind about it.

"I've known for a while," he confesses. "And I'm sorry I waited until it got this bad to talk to you. I just..." He sighs heavily. "I just wanted you to come out on your own, but you wouldn't, and I can see that it's killing you. I couldn't just stand around and keep watching..."

His sentence stops. I feel a drop of water fall on my head. Is he crying? I didn't want to look, but I know exactly what he's trying to say.

Gibbs isn't just one of three boys. There had been another brother, Matthew. He was older and had joined the military when Gibbs was just ten years old. He did three years in Iraq.

I remember when Matthew came back too, and he wasn't the same as before he left. He had come back with a darkness in his eyes I had never seen before. A darkness that had driven him into a sadness he couldn't escape.

"I see the same sadness in your eyes that I saw in Matthew's," he whispers. "I see the pain and the loneliness, and I can't just watch what happened to my brother happen to you."

I'm crying again because now I remember how Matthew's death had affected Gibbs. I remember the funeral, and the painful cries of Gibbs' mother, and how Gibbs had basically died a little with his brother. He hasn't been the same since.

"Listen, I don't care if you like girls," he says. "I don't care if you don't come out to Gwen or Darian. I won't tell anyone. But I couldn't watch this pain kill you anymore, because you should feel safe talking about anything with me."

I'm beyond terrified now that the truth is out, but I trust Gibbs. I trust him the most because he and I had been through a lot as friends. My tears stop flowing as I feel the weight rise from my chest. I take in a deep breath.

"I'll never see you as anyone other than Peyton, my amazing best friend that makes sure I pass my classes and keeps me out of trouble," he explains. "And I'm sorry if I ever said things that made you feel otherwise."

"I'm sorry I blew up," I apologize.

"Don't apologize," he says. "I came on strong."

"But I needed that, I think."

Then I sit up. There isn't much more to say after that, is there? That's it. The truth is out in the open and all we can do is move on from it.

"Now pick up your pole," he demands. "You promised me a fishin' buddy today."

I cast my line into the water and feel lucky this time. There's a warmth in my chest I haven't felt in awhile. A sense of relief that had the ability to make me smile on the inside.

Then my bobber disappears, which means I have a taker. I reel it in with a smile.

Twenty-Six

THE LAST TWO WEEKS OF MARCH were a whirlwind. So many things were happening, and I was struggling to keep up. Not to mention me staying on top of the college packages coming in through the mail. It was getting more and more difficult to hide them from my parents, and that provided enough stress to make me go crazy. Soccer season was progressing, even when two of our starters were benched, and we just weren't doing all that great.

Gibbs and I kept the conversation we had a few weekends ago to ourselves, which I appreciated more than I could express, but I still wanted to tell Gwen and Darian. It felt unfair to have them on the outside, and after it going so well with Gibbs, I felt confident enough to tell them. I just wasn't sure *when* that was going to happen.

Another thing I had confessed not only to myself, but to Gibbs as well, was how I felt about Jamie. He wasn't shocked, which was predictable, because if I were being honest, my feelings were probably blatantly obvious.

Or just obvious to everyone *but* Jamie.

Now we were nearing the end of spring break and hanging out at the lake house. The first week of April had been a good one, I just hoped I could finish this school year strong.

"Oh! I got one!" Gwen yells and startles everyone.

She... *clumsily...* attempts to reel in her fish and seems to struggle. I look at Darian who is looking at his girlfriend with disappointment.

"Judging by the way you're reeling it in..." Darian starts. "It should be impressive."

I can't help but laugh. Gibbs casts his line as I lean back on the pier, enjoying the company. It feels like old times again. After telling Gibbs the truth, the weight that had previously been crushing me, had since lifted. I could finally face my friends again without feeling trapped in a box, knowing someone was on my side.

But I have a goal today, and that is coming out to Darian and Gwen.

Eventually Gwen tugs her fish out of the water, but the size of it is underwhelming.

"Oh my God, wow," she says.

Gibbs, Darian, and I give each other funny looks.

"Good job, babe." Darian kisses her head. "Now take it off the hook."

"Hell no." She passes the line over to her boyfriend. "That's your job."

"But you caught it?"

"So? It's slimy and gross…" Gwen whines. "And I just got my nails done."

"Oh, my God." Darian takes the fish in his hands. "You're somethin' else."

There's a lull in the conversation, and I feel as if I need to break the news now. It still scares me. Coming out to Gibbs had been involuntary, but much needed. Besides, he had known the truth already, so it wasn't a shock when I didn't fight the accusation. I wasn't so sure if Darian and Gwen knew. They *could* know, but could be playing dumb…

"So, I need to tell you guys something…"

"Chicago!"

My heart stops in my chest. Of *all* the times she could crash the party, why now?

Darian notices my annoyance.

"What?" he asks.

I shake my head. "Nothing."

"I invited her last minute," he confesses. "I felt bad for leaving her out."

Gibbs pats my back, but I can't find the strength to start up the conversation again. Maybe it isn't the right time. Maybe there would be another window of opportunity because I didn't want to come out to Jamie. Not yet, anyway.

Besides, the knowledge that she and Lora are still seeing each other bothers me.

"So, how was the Windy City?" Darian wonders.

Jamie smiles as she walks up in a pair of blue jean shorts and a band t-shirt. She has a lightness to her step again. I hadn't seen her look so happy in a while. Then again, I hadn't seen her much during the month of March because she had made it a habit to skip art, probably to hang out with Lora. I had been on my own with the mural and it was starting to show in my progress.

"It was great," she says as she sits on the pier. "I got to see my old friends, go to my favorite restaurants..."

The conversation continues but I tune her out. I silently wonder if she had met up with her ex who had been texting her a few months ago. Oh, how Lora would have a fit with that one...

"... And I told her I couldn't do it anymore," Jamie finishes.

I quickly tune back in at the confession.

"What happened?" Gwen asks.

"She's too controlling." Jamie gazes over the lake. "And she was texting me nonstop the entire time I was in Chicago. It was just too much. Lora's sweet but... I don't know."

Wait. So, they *aren't* exclusive anymore?

"Did you guys know we only have *thirty* more days left

of senior year?" Gibbs casts his line. "I've started a countdown."

That also means we only have thirty days to finish the mural.

I stare at Jamie in annoyance. On one hand, I'm glad she and Lora are done. On the other, I'm pissed because she's avoided me for a month because of it, which meant she had avoided working on the mural that she promised to help me with!

But maybe I just need to talk to her about it. Maybe there needs to be some sort of confrontation, and then things will hopefully go back to normal.

One thing is for sure, there's still *a lot* to do. Finish the mural, tell Gwen and Darian the truth, organize senior prom, pick a college, take finals, tell my parents... The overwhelming sensation of anxiety creeps up. There's so much I need to do, but all I could really think about is making it through all of it without losing my mind.

And how that feels completely impossible.

● ● ●

I pace quickly to the art room, eager to make it to the mural and get to work. Now that spring is well underway, the Georgia heat is also making its grand return. Sweat forms on my brow as I make it into my familiar art classroom. There's still a lot to be done, and there's absolutely no time to waste.

Because Jamie is still avoiding you and the promise she made to help with the mural...

I roll my eyes at the thought.

After pushing the paint cart to the room in which the mural stands, I start setting up, but there's a truth to my previous thought. Jamie had *promised* to help me, and now she isn't. Why? Because of Lora? That apparently isn't the case because they aren't even talking anymore, so what is it?

The unanswered questions swarm my brain, causing my anger to grow. Why the hell is she still avoiding me? Because of the Quinton thing? That isn't even fair! Not when she was involved with Lora way before that!

By this time, she would either be walking to the parking lot or in the girl's locker room changing to work out. I decide it's time for her to stop avoiding me.

I make my way toward the gym, but don't find her there, which means she's currently on her way home. My legs instinctively carry me to the parking lot in a hurry.

Luckily, I spot her soon enough to call out to her.

"Jamie!" I yell.

She stops walking, but she must've recognized my voice because then she starts again. I find my anger flare up in response.

"Jamie!" I yell again as I run up to her.

She slows her pace, either out of pity or because she's tired of trying to outwalk me. I finally catch up and stand my ground in front of her.

"Where are you going?" I ask.

"Home."

"Why?"

"Because school is over?"

I shake my head. "It's not over? You're still scheduled art, remember?"

I hadn't meant to say it in a condescending way, but that's how it had come out. Shit. I probably sound like a snitch, and not someone who is trying to rekindle the fire Jamie had felt before every stupid thing I did had managed to dim it.

She frowns. "So, what? Are you gonna rat me out now?"

There's this look on her face that makes me uneasy. I hate that she thinks of me this way now, instead of a friend, or something more. I take a step back and take in a breath. I need to do this right if I want it to work.

"You promised to help me with this mural," I say. "After it was ruined, you told me you would help me finish."

She doesn't say anything, but there's another look that crosses her expression. It says, "that was before you took my heart and smashed it against the wall." Is she expecting an explanation? Or an apology? God. I didn't know how to read her!

"I said I was only gonna continue if you helped," I confess. "And you're not honoring your promise."

Stoic. That's what she is right now. Unreadable, stone-faced, and still upset with me. But why is she upset? Is she upset that I had caught her skipping or because I haven't gotten to the point? What does she want? I didn't know! I didn't know how to make her see me halfway!

"I-I..." *Goddammit Peyton, just say it!* "I need you, Jamie."

The sentence takes a lot out of me. My heart races and my knees shake. She's going to walk away from me. That's what I expect, no matter what I say, but I *need* to be honest, at least about the mural. It's important that I am. Even if it drains me.

"I need you," I repeat. "I need your help, I need you to finish this mural, just like you promised. I can't do this without you."

That's when her stone demeanor shatters. I see through the cracks. It's all there for me to see, her feelings, her angst, her pain... It's all there and I had been too blind to see it. God, how stupid I've been...

"And I'm sorry if I made you feel like I didn't," I finish.

She looks stunned, like she isn't sure what to say to my confession. I take this as a good sign.

"Please, just..." I look down at my fidgeting hands. "Just help me."

I didn't know what I had said that caused her to change her mind, but I can see it on her face. I had somehow won her back.

She nods. "You're right."

I sigh in relief.

"You're right, and I'm sorry," she apologizes. "I've been an idiot."

I smile. "Me too."

We stare at each other for a minute, as if we have more to say, but nothing comes out. I'm disappointed, but not for long. I had gained Jamie's trust, even if it's only a little bit, and that means everything in the world to me.

Then, without any more hesitation, we start making our way back to the mural, where we can hopefully mend things and pick back up where we had left off.

Twenty-Seven

MUSIC FILLS THE ROOM as I work next to Jamie on the mural. After the confrontation, I feel as if we've made progress and that we could move forward, but even after my apology, there still isn't much coming out of Jamie's mouth. I expect questions and conversation but instead get nothing. Am I still missing something?

"I think we need to put in more time," I say. "We're never gonna finish at this pace."

She takes in a deep breath. "I agree."

I step back from the wall and study it. The mural now extends past the minimum requirement and is now taking up nearly the entire wall. It would look absolutely fantastic once it was finished, but that's *if* we finished it.

"How about we stay a few extra hours every Monday?" I ask. "Neither of us have classes after art, plus it's the only day I'm free from soccer."

"That sounds good." She returns to work. "Would you mind bringing me home after?"

"Not at all."

She glances at me and I feel my heart squeeze at the sight. We're walking on this tightrope, as if we're dancing around another disagreement or something. I don't understand it. What am I missing? I had addressed the mural, I had apologized...

Quinton. I hadn't addressed the Quinton thing.

I take in a deep breath and know that I should explain the night at the lake house when she had caught me making out with him. It had been the turning point.

"We need to talk about the night at the lake house," I claim. "I need you to know what happened with Quinton."

She continues to paint. "That's none of my business."

Jamie may have agreed to work on the mural with me, but I know her walls are still sky high on the friendship field. I understand why. God, it's just so hard, though. She isn't making any of this easier.

"I care what you think," I admit.

She finally gives me her full attention.

"I care what you think about me, so I wanna tell you what happened."

We both face each other. The pounding in my chest quickens at the sight. There's this look on Jamie's face that wants to say she's grateful we're having this talk, but another is telling her not to trust me. It's there, plain as day. God, I must've really hurt her...

"We were talking, and the house was just unbearably loud, so he offered to move the conversation upstairs," I explain. "We were both kinda drunk, and..."

Jamie doesn't seem impressed. I'm aware that I am leaving out a lot but telling her is *hard*. Why is she looking at me like that?

"He brought up the rumors," I confess. "About me being gay. He didn't ask me for the truth. He didn't ask me for anything..." I feel the emotion tighten around my throat. "But Jamie... I was just so desperate to *feel* something."

Her hard expression softens.

"Gwen and Darian said it would look nice." I shake my head. "And I feel like everyone is watching me, waiting for me to do *something* to confirm what they've heard... and I just..."

I feel myself breaking. I could feel the angst and anxiety bubbling in my stomach. The aching in my limbs returns. I hate that I can't control or contain it. I'm usually better at this...

"I told him to kiss me." My heart shudders in pain. "I told him to, but I didn't feel *anything*, and that's all it was. It was just me trying to feel something, and now it's over."

I try to see if she's relieved, or mad, or *anything*, but there's nothing. No emotion at all. Maybe she's keeping me out because she doesn't want me to see how angry she had been that night. Or maybe she didn't want me to see how happy she is that Quinton and I aren't a thing, regardless of what she may have heard.

"No one else knows," I confess. "Just me, Quinton, and now, you."

We study each other for a good minute. She carries herself differently now, or maybe that's just around me. She's way more guarded than before and is no longer happy and cheery to see me. Maybe I had lost my chance for good. Maybe I had been too blind for too long.

Maybe I deserve to miss the opportunity to be with Jamie.

She looks down at her feet and then picks up her brush. Is she going to ignore me more? What else could I possibly do?!

"You've gotta stop trying to please people, Peyt," she answers. "You've gotta live for you, and only you."

"I know," I whisper.

I watch her paintbrush stroke a line of color on the wall. Then she lets it fall as her eyes meet mine again.

"Thank you." A small smile forms on her lips. "For telling me about Quinton."

It's a silent confession. She is thanking me for the clarity. For the honesty. I haven't officially come out to Jamie, but I realize I don't need to. She knows. She *has* to know. But she isn't going to push me. She knows what it's like to come out on your own terms, so she would respect my silence.

Then the weight lifts. I take in a massive breath and smile. I realize this must be what it feels like to be honest with myself and with others.

● ● ●

Jamie and I work on the mural until the end of school and then we grab food afterwards. Staying late was a fantastic idea because we had made so much progress, and honestly, it had helped me get out of my head about things.

Everything feels like it's slowly falling back into place again, and I couldn't wait to go back to school tomorrow.

I walk into my house with a lightness to my step. The excitement I feel from spending so much authentic time with Jamie has me buzzing. I'm convinced nothing can bring me down.

"Peyton!" I hear mom call from the kitchen.

"Yeah?" I answer.

"Could you come to the kitchen for a minute?"

I start toward her voice, unaware of what she wants to talk about. Maybe she wants to ask me what I would like for dinner. I wasn't hungry, I mean I had a late lunch with Jamie so...

Then I see it, on the coffee table in the living room. A college packet to Penn State. Oh. My. *God.* I had totally forgotten about the reason I came home after fourth period every day! It was to specifically hide this from my mom! And I hadn't even *applied* to Penn State!

My heart races. I know what's coming, and I'm not ready for it. I'm not ready for the war. Not with my mom. Not today.

"I'm actually uh, really tired," I lie. "I had a long day. I'm just gonna go up to my room..."

"Peyton." My mom's tone stiffens. "Kitchen. *Now*."

Shit. Okay. This is happening. I need to be strong. I need to stand my ground and make her see that this is *good* for me, regardless of what she thinks!

My shaking legs carry me to the kitchen where I see my mom prepping for dinner. She looks calm, but I know better. She's fuming inside.

"Sit," she demands.

I do as I'm told.

"What do you wanna talk about...?"

"You said you weren't applying out of state." She continues to chop up a bell pepper. "Was that a lie?"

I'm a deer in headlights, completely stunned and unaware of what to say. I try to calm my heart and steady my voice.

"W-Well, I didn't apply to Penn State-"

"Did you, or did you not, apply to TSU?"

"I did, but..."

Then she reaches under the counter and throws out my MTSU packet, and then UNC, then FSU... They keep coming, which means she had raided my room after the Penn State packet had come in.

"Wanna explain?" She leans on the counter. "Because I

thought we had settled on GSU."

We? *We* had settled on GSU? It's more like *she* had settled on GSU. The anger revolving around college seems to tear through my veins. My skin grows hot. Today had been *so good,* and now it's all going down the drain, all because my mom wants to control my future.

I stand. "*I* didn't settle on *anything* yet."

She looks up.

"Mom, I don't *want* to go to Georgia State."

I watch her clench her teeth and set her knife down, and probably for good reason.

"You said..."

"I didn't say anything!" I shout. "I never wanted to go to GSU! Mom, these colleges are sending *me* packets! They're asking for me!"

"Watch your tone..."

"If you would just *listen* to me..."

"GSU is a great fit, you'll be there with your sister and your friends. You'll only be an hour from home!"

"That's exactly why I don't want to go!"

Silence. It's so silent that I can hear the clock ticking on the wall. I could also hear my heavy breathing. The anger is nearly bursting from my veins at this point.

"I don't want to be close to home," I confess. "I don't want to be anywhere *near* Branton, Georgia, mom."

Mom lifts her head at the statement, but I can tell she's no longer listening, if she ever was in the first place. She isn't hearing what I'm saying. She doesn't *see* that this isn't what I want for myself. She doesn't care.

"Well, good luck getting there without the help from me and your father," she finishes.

I feel my heart shatter. Is this how she wants to do this? Is this how she wants to treat me?

"I'm not Alyssa, mom," I plea as tears form in my eyes. "Please, don't treat me like her!"

"Go to your room," she orders. "Dinner will be ready in an hour."

Everything feels like it's on fire. It's like my world is crumbling under me. Is this it? Is this the end of the discussion? I was going to go to GSU, just like everyone back home. I would fall into the patterns of my parents, settle for mediocrity, and probably *never* feel comfortable being who I am.

I was trapped.

"I won't be hungry," I counter before storming up to my room.

I want to slam my bedroom door so hard that the pictures on my wall rattle, but I know better. Instead, I calmly close it and rest my head against the cold wood. The anxiety returns as I lock myself away and cry silently against the door, my head pressing so hard against it that it starts to hurt. Eventually I move to my bed as the tears flow. Then I release a painful scream into my pillow.

This isn't happening. Not to me. I'm not meant to be trapped in Georgia my entire life, but I don't have the money to move away. I'm turning eighteen in a week, and if they disown me, I'm officially on my own.

Could I do this on my own?

The pain rips through my body as I cry alone in my room. Everything had been fine just ten minutes ago, and now I'm in pieces again. How am I ever going to escape?

Eventually, I cry long enough to put myself to sleep, and no one bothers to knock on my door to check on me.

Twenty-Eight

THE REST OF THE WEEK I spend as a drone. Numb is all I feel after the conversation with my mom, and I had refused to talk to her since. I desperately wish my sister would come home, but I can't blame her for not doing so. At least she has some sense of freedom.

"So, a small get-together," Gwen says. "That's manageable."

I just nod in agreement.

"Oh, c'mon Peyt. You're gonna be eighteen!" She wraps an arm around my waist. "Be excited!"

"I know, I'm sorry," I apologize. "I just have a lot going on right now."

"Well, we'll have fun tomorrow night," she promises.

"You just have to get through today, okay?"

"Okay," I agree. "See you later."

"Later hun!"

Then I'm alone, slowly walking to art class. I honestly don't even have the energy for a small get-together, but Gwen wouldn't let me be alone for my birthday. No way in hell.

So, we settled on small instead. Gwen, Darian, Gibbs, Jamie, and me at the lake house. We would drink, eat pizza, and play some board games or something. It would be low-key, and it would allow me to be away from home for at least twenty-four hours.

Jamie meets me in the art class, ready to push our paint cart to the mural. We had made massive progress Monday, and it really started a domino effect throughout the week. We were nearing the end, but there is still a lot to perfect before the deadline.

"Hey, Peyt," she greets me.

"Hi."

I follow her without another word, unable to get out of my own head. She must've noticed because she can't help but ask.

"What's wrong?"

"Nothing," I lie. "Uh, so my birthday is tomorrow and we're getting together at the lake house around eight if you wanna come."

She studies me, but eventually agrees.

"Sure, sounds fun."

We work on the mural without saying much else to each other. It's hard not opening up and talking to her, but I just feel like Jamie doesn't want to be involved in all of my problems. I didn't want her to see how bad I'm hurting or that I feel trapped in Branton when she pretty much is too.

It would be selfish to unload on her, so I don't.

After fourth hour ends, we part, and I bury the pain and turmoil I'm feeling deep inside. We would be together tomorrow, and maybe hanging out with my friends would make me feel better about staying in Georgia.

And maybe I would get the opportunity to finally be honest with them, after so long of pretending to be someone else.

● ● ●

As my car slowly creeps closer to the lake house, I silently prepare myself. This could be the night that I finally come out to the rest of my best friends and Jamie. It feels overwhelming, but I'm not as scared as I used to be, which means progress, right?

Besides, Gibbs already knows, and I'm convinced that Jamie does as well.

I park and fix my hair. Luckily, my mom had granted me *permission* to have fun tonight, even though it's *my birthday*! God, I do so much for school! I had taken all AP classes, was in a *ton* of extra curriculars, captain of the goddamn soccer team, and she expects me to go to school one *hour* from home?!

I laugh cynically to myself before exiting my car. This is the last thing I should be thinking about. It's my birthday. I should just focus on hanging out with my friends and having a good time.

My legs carry me up to the front door and I quickly let myself in. I see my four friends sitting on the couch already, which confuses me. Why are they looking at me like that?

"Hey guys-?"

"SURPRISE!"

People jump up from behind furniture, come out from the kitchen, and pop out from other hiding places. I jump in response.

Initially, I'm pissed. This wasn't the plan *at all*, and for good reason. This was supposed to be my night, and I had asked for a small get-together. I had asked for nothing special, and they decided to respond this way?

But I can't be upset. Everyone is here for me, even if it isn't what I want.

I fake a laugh as everyone begins to greet me and wish me a happy birthday. Pretending to be happy is the easy part. God knows I've been getting a lot of practice lately. Then once I greet everyone, I turn to my friends.

Gwen gives me a nervous smile. "Listen, I know you asked for low-key, but I planned this like a week ago, and I had already paid Gibbs' brothers for the keg."

"You got a *keg*?" I ask. "Gwen, what the hell?"

"She didn't know, Peyt," Darian includes. "But in me

and Gibbs' defense, we didn't know you requested small, either."

Gwen scoffs at Darian. "So, you're pinning this all on me?"

"Babe, chill..."

"It's fine," I mediate. "It'll be fine. We'll have fun. Please, just..." Jamie's worried expression levels my head. "Just show me where the keg is."

Gwen folds her arms across her chest while Darian tries to console her. Jamie and Gibbs guide me toward the beer.

Sure, she has a reason to be upset. I probably seem ungrateful, but there is a *reason* I had asked for low-key. I wanted it to be a special night. I wanted it to be just us five, because I needed quality time with my friends. I did *not* need to get plastered and put on a show for everyone. This, on top of the stress I feel over my mom blatantly controlling my life, had practically sent me over the edge.

So, *sue* me for being pissed off.

"Here," Jamie offers me a beer. "Happy birthday, by the way."

"Thanks."

Then I take a huge gulp.

"Are you okay...?"

"I'm fine," I blurt out. "Please, just don't ask me that question tonight, okay?"

Jamie tilts her head. She looks majorly concerned, but it's my birthday, and she wants to give me what I want. It's a one-night-only thing, I believe, but it's good enough for me.

I chug the rest of my beer and hold it out to Jamie.

"Fill me up?" I ask.

She raises a nervous brow. "That's how you want tonight to go?"

"Pretty much."

She sighs heavily before picking up the tap to the keg to fill up my cup again. Then she fixes herself a drink. I hadn't eaten much today, which means I'm already feeling the alcohol enter my blood. It causes a quick burst of courage. Tonight should've been the night I finally came out to my friends, but Gwen ruined it.

So, instead of worrying about it, I decide it's my night to have fun regardless of what everyone thinks about me. I grab Jamie's hand, which causes her to look at me with a shocked expression.

"I wanna dance," I state.

She smiles. "Well, then let's dance."

●　●　●

A few hours and rounds of beer pong later, I'm officially wasted. I had done it to myself, and for good reason, but now the room is spinning, and I can't find the strength to sober up.

I continue to avoid Gwen because, now that I'm drunk, it's likely that I'll put my foot in my mouth and accidentally come out to her. I want to come out. Don't get me wrong. I just don't want it to be while I'm plastered.

"Man, I can't stay here," Jamie claims as she leans casually into the couch. "There's like, no way."

Gibbs laughs. "So, what? You're gonna move back to Chicago after graduation?"

"Maybe."

I take a big gulp of my beer at the revelation. Looks like we aren't going to Atlanta together after all.

"An old friend said she has a place for me if I do," Jamie says.

"Old friend?" I wonder.

Jamie looks at me but doesn't elaborate right away. Could this "old friend" possibly be her ex? I doubt that when she had gone all the way to Chicago during spring break that she hadn't met up with her at some point.

"My ex," she confirms. "But it's not like that anymore, and the rent would be cheap."

Fan*tastic*.

I stand abruptly and the room spins. I probably look super suspicious, but I don't care anymore. My feet carry me to the backdoor, and I let myself outside. I shouldn't be this upset. I had lost my chance with Jamie a long time ago, and now she has an opportunity to get the hell out of Branton. I can't be mad at her for wanting to take it.

But I *am* mad, and it hurts like hell.

I lean on the porch railing and try to sober up, but I'm too far gone. God, I'm probably going to regret this in the morning...

"Peyton?" I hear behind me. "Are you okay?"

"I thought I told you not to ask me that?"

Shit. I couldn't help but take my anger out on Jamie. It's such a bad habit. I really need to stop.

"I'm sorry," she apologizes. "I just wanted to make sure you weren't getting sick."

I hear the backdoor open again, meaning she's going back inside. I whip around and look at her.

"Jamie, wait," I call.

She stops and turns around. We're alone, and the party inside is still going strong. No one would come looking for us out here, except maybe my best friends, but they all seem occupied.

Jamie takes a few steps toward me and leans on the railing. The spring air whips around us. The buzzing of bugs in the surrounding trees and brush fill the silence. There are so many things I want to say but feel like it's already too late.

"I guess I won't see you in Atlanna this fall?" I wonder.

Her head drops. "I don't know yet."

"My mom, uh, she found my out-of-state college packets." I sigh. "She's never gonna let me leave Georgia."

Jamie looks at me, but I continue to stare out into the dark. I feel so numb that I'm convinced I'm incapable of feeling anything other than anger now.

"I'm sorry," she whispers. "That's... *beyond* unfair."

"Yeah."

Silence. Again. It's driving me insane. I need to tell her. I need to tell her I like her. I need to tell her that I didn't want her to move, but not because I want her to suffer with me. I just didn't want her to move back in with her ex. It just seems like a bad idea. She has to know that, right?

"God, Jamie I'm such an idiot," I blurt.

Okay, that's not *what you were supposed to say.*

"You're not an idiot, Peyton," she responds.

The tears are already forming on my waterline. It's becoming too much. The irony of it all is breaking me apart.

"Four years," I start. "Four years of pretending to be perfect, taking heavy loads of classes, doing all this... *bullshit...* For what? To go to college an hour away from where I grew up?" The tears roll down my cheeks as Jamie turns to face me. "I've wasted my high school years by caring about what people thought of me and sacrificed my happiness for absolutely nothing."

Jamie probably thinks I'm crazy, or drunk. Either way, she looks confused.

"And I'm *so* fucking jealous of you, Jamie Kendall," I finish.

The silence settles. Okay, I shouldn't have said that either. That sounded *really* bad. Jamie shifts uncomfortably next to me.

"Jealous of me?" she asks.

I finally turn to face her. I'm doing this so wrong and I know that, but I can't help it anymore. The alcohol is giving me the courage I need to be honest, but it's making me reckless. Then again, what does it matter, anyway?

"You're everything I've ever wanted to be," I confess. "But I cared too much about what people thought to ever be that."

It's a lame way to come out, but it's all I could think up. I am wasted, and finding the right words are impossible. They were impossible even when I was *sober*.

"Peyton." Jamie moves closer. "Everyone loves you. Your friends love you. Your teachers love you. Your parents *love* you." She grabs my hands and my heart throbs. "Whatever you're feeling will not change that."

I force my eyes to look up at her. It's so hard. I know I probably look like shit. My makeup is probably running, even though I have tried to control the tears. I didn't want her to see me like this.

"I'm sorry," I apologize. "For making you feel unwelcome, for lying, and for letting my insecurities hurt you, for everything..."

"Stop." She grabs my shoulders. "Peyton, stop blaming yourself."

I want to kiss her. This would probably be the only opportunity, but I'm terrified. It can go either way. I don't know, and uncertainty scares me. But at this point, I honestly couldn't find a care to give.

I grab her face and bring my lips to hers. We're both stunned at the initial contact, but suddenly I understand. *This* is what it's supposed to feel like!

It's like flying, or falling, or walking out into the

sunlight after being in a cold room for a long time. It's the rush of getting a standing ovation after a perfect speech. It's scoring the winning goal in overtime. It's everything all at once. It isn't enough but too much at the same time.

Then it ends.

"Stop." Jamie lightly pushes me away from her. "What are you doing?"

I shake my head in confusion.

"I-I uh..." I stutter.

"I'm not okay being an experiment for you," Jamie states.

"You're not!" I plead. "Jamie, you're not..."

"And you can't just *kiss* me to make yourself feel better," she continues.

The rage of misunderstanding is blinding. I know I pursued this the hard way, but how can she not see? How could she still have her walls up after everything I had confessed?

"You're not an experiment!" I cry. "Jamie, please believe me."

She wants to. I can see it. She wants to believe that I'm not using her, but she's scared. She is scared to be involved with someone like me because it's dangerous.

"I've never done this," I say. "You know that. And I'm so scared, but please don't think that this is just me using you, because it's not."

She's still guarded, but I can tell she's trying.

"Do you remember when I told you I've never felt

strong enough feelings for someone to find time for them?" I ask.

"Yeah, but..."

"That was true," I interrupt. "That was true until I met you, okay?"

She just stares at me in disbelief, but I know deep down she's known all along.

"And it doesn't have to mean anything," I say. "I kissed you because I know I like you. It wasn't just because I was trying to feel something, because you've made me feel so much already, way before I ever kissed you."

I can tell by the look on her face that I had said the right things. She relaxes and steps closer to me. I don't know what this means, but I'm just relieved now that everything is out in the open.

Then she grabs my hands, letting me know that we are *finally* on the same page.

Twenty-Nine

IF I HAD TO DESCRIBE THE REST of Saturday night in one word it would be... *surreal.* It had honestly felt like a dream. The only reason I know it *hadn't* been a dream was because, in a disgustingly hungover state, I had woken up next to Jamie and brought her home the next morning.

"So..." Jamie steps closer to me. "Was that your first kiss with a girl?"

The blood rushes to my cheeks. Luckily, it's dark enough outside to prevent her from seeing.

"Yes."

A small smile emerges on her lips. Her lips. My lips are still tingling even though it had been a good five minutes since I kissed her. My entire body is buzzing from the interaction, and I find myself craving more of it. I had been starved of this feeling for eighteen years. I wanted it, over and over again. Could I tell her that?

"Well, how was it?"

Jamie's being audaciously smug right now, but I can't find a reason to blame her. I'm on cloud nine. Images are flying through my mind of things I want to do with her. Just a quick kiss had been phenomenal, I could only imagine what it would feel like to go further.

I laugh. "Um, it was..."

A warm wave washes through my stomach as Jamie moves closer. She's so close. I can smell the scent of alcohol and perfume dancing together. Does she want this as much as I do? Had the kiss awakened the same hunger in Jamie as it had for me?

"Good enough to..." she whispers. "...wanna do it, again?"

"Yes," I state without hesitation.

Jamie smiles before taking the lead, and I willingly let her. Her steady hands cradle my face as our lips connect again. It's slow and controlled and nothing like the kiss I had initiated. My hands are shaking at my sides from the adrenaline, and I need to find some stability. They grab Jamie's slim hips in a desperate attempt to pull her closer if it's at all possible.

The second kiss is so much better. It's softer. It's more intimate. It's sensual. It is everything I had imagined a kiss should feel like, and more.

Breathe, Peyton.

We pull apart for a second to compose ourselves and catch our breath, but I didn't want to stop. Not yet. I reconnect our lips, afraid that it'll end too soon, and I won't get another moment like this. Jamie's tongue glides over my bottom lip and another wave of warmth washes over me. It feels like I'm freefalling and all I can do is hold on to her.

Then the opening of the backdoor startles us apart.

"Gwen's leaving with Courtney," Gibbs says. "Sorry, to uh... interrupt."

Jamie looks worried, but my expression tells her it's fine. Gibbs wouldn't tell anyone.

"Why is she leaving?" I ask.

"I don't know." He shrugs. "She's been in a weird mood all night. She asked Darian to bring her home, but he's too drunk."

We all go inside, but Gwen is long gone by the time I find Courtney's car driving away from us. I know why she had been in a weird mood, but it was her own fault. I had told her I didn't want a large gathering, so she couldn't be mad that I had practically avoided the festivities.

But I text her anyway.

Peyton: Text me when you get home?

I give her about twenty minutes, but nothing. An hour goes by, and still no response. I find this weird but try not to worry. Except when she doesn't text me back to let me know she's at least safe, the worry starts getting to me. I find Darian in the diminishing crowd of people.

"Have you heard from Gwen?" I ask him. "Is she home?"

"Yeah, she's home," he answers me. "Has she not texted you?"

I just shake my head.

It doesn't matter. All that matters is that she's home safe. We would talk either tomorrow or Monday at school, and things would be fine. I'm not even angry over the party anymore because it's practically over and it's not even midnight. It had ended early in comparison to our other parties, and I'm soon curling up in a guest bedroom bed.

Then the door opening forces me awake as I watch Jamie enter with a small bag in her hand. When she turns around, my presence startles her.

"Sorry, I didn't think you were in here," she confesses. "I'll just sleep on the couch..."

"Stay," I say. "You can sleep in here, if you want?"

She just stares at me from the door. There's a desperation in my expression, I'm sure of it, but I want her to sleep next to me.

"You don't think that'll be too much?" she whispers.

"No."

She's still nervous, but so am I.

"Okay," she agrees. "Do you mind if I change?"

I want to laugh because I think she's joking, but then soon realize she isn't. I shake my head nervously.

She sets her overnight bag on the bed and removes a t-shirt and a pair of shorts. I watch her hands fumble with the buttons on her shirt before I recognize that I'm literally watching her undress. I turn my attention away and wait.

"Are you sure this isn't uncomfortable...?"

"It's not," I blurt, my eyes instinctively look at her. "I-I just..."

I'm just really attracted to you.

My face must've said it because another smug grin stretches across her lips. She's having so much fun with this, and I can't decide if I love or hate her for it.

I catch a glimpse of her toned stomach right before she slips her overnight shirt on and finally climbs into bed with me. My heart has never pounded so hard. I'm convinced it's going to break my sternum. Jamie has to be able to hear it.

"Have you heard from Gwen?" she asks.

"No," I answer. "She's upset, but we'll just talk later."

It falls silent. I study the contours of Jamie's face that are slightly noticeable from the dim lighting of the bedside lamp. I want to reach out and touch her. I want to feel that connection I had felt outside on the porch again.

"What are you thinking?"

God, what am I thinking? I'm thinking loads of things. Why is Gwen mad at me? Had anyone seen Jamie and me kissing outside? Am I still drunk or just buzzing from the hangover caused by Jamie's lips? Is there a possibility of going further? Am I even ready for that?

"I'm thinking you can probably hear my heartbeat

right now," I confess.

She smiles. *"I can't."*

I reach out and grab her right hand, then place it on my chest. Hazel eyes light up at the interaction, but probably only because her hands are literally right on top of my boobs. I find myself grinning at the thought,

"What?" she asks. *"Why are you smiling?"*

"Your face when I did that."

"What about it?"

"You just looked surprised."

She laughs. *"Can you blame me?"*

Is this really happening? Are Jamie and I really in the same bed, inches apart from each other? I never would've thought I'd be in this position, especially not with her. We settle into a silence, but I can tell neither of us are tired anymore. The excitement of our closeness had released more adrenaline, and now I'm wide awake.

"How long have you known?" Jamie wonders.

"Known?"

"That you're gay," she clarifies.

I sigh. *"For a while. I knew for sure by the end of my freshmen year."*

"And you never once thought about trying to be with a girl?"

I just shake my head as Jamie studies me in awe.

"All eyes were always on me," I explain. *"They still are, and I've let that dictate my high school experience. I regret it, and I feel like I've missed out, but I can't undo it."*

"What do you think you've missed out on?"

"You know..." I feel my cheeks burn. "Going to school dances with my girlfriend. Double dates and holding hands in the hallway..." The reality causes me to feel sad. "I've missed out on being myself." I watch Jamie frown. "That's why I wanna get away from here. I wanna start over, somewhere no one knows me, and finally figure out who I am. Without any restrictions."

"Well..." She scoots even closer to me. "I really hope you get to do that."

The pull is so strong I can barely breathe.

"Even if that means I have to leave?" I whisper.

She eyes my lips. "We don't have to think about that right now."

I move in and connect our lips again. I can't seem to get enough. It's like morphine to pain. What I feel when I kiss Jamie completely overshadows the stress and fear I have of the unknown. It distracts me from the anxiety caused from my mother's stubbornness to see my side of things. It does the same for the worry I have over Gwen ignoring me or my peers finding out the rumors are true.

None of those things matter when I'm kissing Jamie, and maybe that's another reason I had avoided this in the first place.

Because it's dangerous.

I return to school Monday in a daze. Twenty-five days, and then I am officially free. I just have to get through finals and graduation. The end is approaching fast, and I couldn't be happier.

I still haven't talked to Gwen since Saturday, which is weird, but Jamie and I have never been better. The memory of waking up in her arms the morning after my party is still thoroughly burned into my brain. I intend to hold on to it for as long as possible because I'm not sure if I'll ever get another night like that again.

After swinging my backpack over my shoulder, I head for the quad. The morning is absolutely beautiful and not too hot. This means everyone will be congregating outside enjoying the weather before classes start. It's going to be a good day. I can just feel it!

That's until my phone starts blowing up.

It all unravels so quickly that there's really no sense to any of it. It just kind of... happens, and suddenly, my promising Monday turns into a complete nightmare that spirals out of control.

Darian: *Peyt, what the hell?*

Gibbs: *Where are you? & It's bad.*

Jamie: *Peyton. Something's happened. Are you at school yet?*

And about fifty other texts, all from people I know. I understand exactly what's happening, courtesy of a few keywords in the alarmed texts, but I'm too stunned to move. The quad is in sight, but I have tunnel vision. Kids watch, their gazes locked on me, waiting for some type of reaction. Everyone knows. They all know the truth.

I'm completely paralyzed until Gwen manages to find

me.

"Peyton," she panics. "I'm so sorry. God I'm so sorry! I didn't mean to do this. I messed up..."

I look at her in my dazed state and she stops rambling. What the hell is she apologizing for? This isn't what I need from her right now. The last thing I'm thinking about is our disagreement over my birthday party!

"What the fuck is going on?" I ask.

Her shoulders shrink in defeat. She looks appalled, but with herself. Gwen hesitates. The anger and fear start to escalate at the realization that something bad is happening, and I'm no longer in control.

Then she shows me the blog.

There it is. A picture of Jamie and me kissing on the porch this past Saturday. It had been taken through open blinds, which skews the image, but you can see exactly who it is if you look close enough. There's no mistaking it. Under the picture reads, *Birthday girl gets the best surprise of them all!"*

My heart wants to climb out of my throat at the sight.

"I'm so sorry," Gwen starts again. "I was drunk, and mad, and I was so confused..."

I back away from her. "You did this?"

She falls silent. The look on her face answers my question, and tears quickly form on her waterline. This is a whole new type of betrayal. I can't even stand the sight of Gwen anymore, so I turn away. She tries to follow but I yell something horrendous that manages to keep her away from me. I don't feel bad, either.

My feet carry me away from everyone. I need to get out of here, but I don't know where to go.

"Peyton," I hear through the pounding in my head. "Peyton, wait!"

The tears cloud my vision as I storm away from the familiar voice and to my car. I need to get the hell away from Branton High. God, if only these tears would stop until I could successfully escape!

My hands fumble with my keys and I struggle to stop shaking. Delicate hands take them from me.

"Get in, I'll drive."

Am I having a panic attack? The weight on my chest is heavier than ever before. Like a ton of pressure is crushing me. Fuck. What's going to happen? How will I go to school tomorrow? How will I tell my parents?

"Oh my God," I cry into my hands. "It was Gwen."

"It's gonna be okay," Jamie comforts. "Let's just get out of here."

We end up at my house, where I collapse onto my bed and allow Jamie to hold me until the storm in my heart fades into sleep.

Thirty

HAD IT ALL JUST BEEN A NIGHTMARE? Was any of it real? The grogginess from waking up makes me feel like I'm in an alternate reality. I can hear my name being called from the front door.

Maybe it had been a dream. Maybe I'm just late for school and my mom is coming upstairs to tell me I had overslept. Maybe none of it had happened in the first place.

"Peyton!" I hear. "Are you home?"

Alyssa?

I sit up and look at Jamie, who's on the phone.

"I'll talk to you later," she says. "Bye mom."

Then she hangs up just in time for Alyssa to barge into my room. My sister's eyes find mine and then Jamie's. She instantly reacts.

"Who the hell are you?" Alyssa fumes.

"Uh," Jamie stutters in confusion. "I'm..."

"Well, you can leave now," Alyssa orders.

"Alyssa, chill," I say back. "You've met Jamie."

She stares at my friend for a second before realizing I'm right.

"Shit, sorry," she apologizes. "It's been a while."

Then Alyssa joins me on my bed, which reminds me that what happened is real, and a lot of damage control needs to be done.

"Why are you home?" I wonder.

"One of my friends texted me the post," she explains.

The post. It had even reached GSU? God. Everyone in Branton would know by the end of the day. What the *hell* am I going to do?

The tears well up again as I bury my face in my hands. I'm not ready for this. I'm not ready to face my peers tomorrow. I'm not ready for the whole town to know I'm gay. And I'm sure as hell not ready to tell my parents.

"Hey, it's okay." Alyssa pulls me into her. "It's gonna be okay, Peyt."

Jamie seems out of place, but I don't know how to tell her that I'll be okay. My sister is here. That's all I really need. That's when I hear a car pull up in our driveway outside.

"I'm gonna head back to school," Jamie says. "Text me if you need anything, okay?"

"Thank you," I answer.

Jamie gives me a sad smile. I can tell she feels bad for me, which I usually hate, but I can't blame her for it right now. She, of all people, knows the importance of what's been taken from me.

Jamie disappears from my room and leaves Alyssa and me alone. It's silent for a few minutes as I attempt to pull myself together.

"This means I have to come out to mom and dad doesn't it?" I whisper.

"Yeah." Alyssa exhales a heavy breath. "Because if you don't, they'll hear about it from someone else."

I want to bury myself alive. Nothing feels right anymore. My best friend had somehow helped with outing me and my parents are going to freak once I tell them the truth. I feel as if I'm going to lose everything today.

"I'll be with you every second," Alyssa says. "I promise."

"But you're gonna miss all your classes."

"Peyton, I don't know if you know this, but my classes aren't my top priority right now." Alyssa tilts her head. "My little sister needs me today, and that's all that matters."

I can't help but admire Alyssa even more. She's the most self-aware and compassionate person I know. She doesn't care about trivial things like I do. She'll be the only good thing about attending GSU in the fall.

I pull back and wipe my face in a sad attempt to compose myself.

"Did you know already?" I question.

"I kinda had a feeling. But it wasn't until you introduced me to Jamie at homecoming that I knew for sure." Alyssa smirks. "You two had some serious tension, even back then."

I can't help but laugh. "Yet, you couldn't remember her today?"

"It's been months since then!" she defends. "I have a shitty memory, okay?"

The joking banter serves as a good distraction, but it isn't enough. I feel dead. Like a part of me has been ripped from my body. How was Gwen involved in outing me? And *why*? Why would she do such a thing? I need to know the whole story, but the pain of betrayal prevents me from answering my phone, which hasn't stopped blowing up.

"So, who did it?" Alyssa asks. "Who posted the picture? Actually, who *took* the picture? Because fuck them, first off..."

"It was Gwen," I interrupt.

Silence settles between us. Shock doesn't seem to be a good enough description for what my sister and I feel at the revelation.

"Gwen?" Alyssa repeats. "As in Gwen, your best friend, Gwen?"

"I think so." I reach for my phone. "The picture was taken at my party this weekend. She tried explaining herself to me this morning when I got to school, but... I basically told her to fuck off."

Alyssa frowns. She doesn't know what to say. I want to believe that's the reason Gwen had been freaking out this morning, because why else would she feel the need to apologize?

"Has she texted you?" Alyssa wonders.

"Only about a million times." I throw my phone back onto my bed after skimming through all the messages. "I don't wanna talk to her. I don't wanna talk to anyone."

"Well, maybe you need to."

I look at my sister.

"Need to what?"

"Talk to Gwen."

"Are you kidding me?" I fume.

Alyssa climbs back onto my bed and sits in front of me.

"I'm not saying forgive her," she says. "I'm saying *talk*. To get the full story, 'cause I've already reported the blog for cyberbullying. They're gonna take one look at those posts, and everyone who took part is gonna be in serious trouble. Including Gwen."

Alyssa's right. Branton has zero tolerance for bullying, and people have nearly been expelled for it in the past. I didn't want Gwen to get *expelled*. Even if I am really upset with her. I know Gwen. There must be reasoning behind whatever she did, even if she had been really drunk.

"That blog should've been reported a long time ago," I state. "*I* should've reported it. If I had..."

If I had reported it, we wouldn't be here. Everyone knows that now.

It's all fun and games until it was you up there on the pedestal for everyone to see. Given, most posts on the blog weren't nearly as bad as the one about me, but all were still embarrassing. We should've done something about it sooner.

I should've done something about it sooner.

"What's done is done," Alyssa says. "You need to talk to Gwen. That's step one. Step two is, well, tell mom and dad before they hear it from someone else."

"Any more *steps* that I should take?" I ask cynically.

"Listen, you like steps. It gives you structure," she explains. "And step three is gonna be harder than step one and two. I'm just building you up to it."

"What the hell could be harder than coming out to mom and dad?" I whine.

Just the thought of sitting down to talk about this makes my stomach turn inside out. Mom and I are already on edge about the college thing, this was just going to blow everything out the water. She's going to lose her mind.

"Step three..." Alyssa takes in a deep breath. "... is going to school tomorrow and *owning* who you really are."

The heaviness on my chest grows. I want to cry again, but I'm convinced I had cried all the tears I had in my body. I'm scared. No. More like *petrified* of what could happen after I come out to mom and dad. What if they tell me I could no longer be a part of this family?

As much as I hate some of my family's ways, by no means do I want to lose them. I love my mom and dad. They love me. I know that. They just get lost in the small mindset of this small town. They can grow. They're good people.

I'm a good person. That means they have to be as well, right? My sister's hands grip my shoulders. My heavy eyes look up.

"How am I gonna do this?" I whisper.

"Like you do everything else," Alyssa answers. "You're still Peyton. You're still their unbelievably smart, talented, kind-hearted, *favorite* child."

I laugh at Alyssa's face at the word "favorite."

"Being gay will just add some..." Alyssa smirks. "*Spice.*"

I shove her. "I hate you."

My sister picks up my phone from the foot of my bed and hands it to me. I know what she's asking me to do, and I know I really don't have a choice anymore.

"Now text Gwen back."

● ● ●

Gwen tells me she'll come over as soon as fourth hour ends. Alyssa stays with me and attempts to distract my mind from the fact that my whole life will be different from now on. The truth is out, and now I have to learn to live with it. My worst nightmare has manifested, but I'm successfully dodging it for now. Soon, I won't be able to anymore.

I check my phone for the time as Alyssa and I sit

outside. Gwen would be here any minute now. I can only imagine what is currently being said at school. Do I even want to know? I don't think so. I don't want to hear it. I refuse to let myself care. I don't want any of it.

"I have some weed in my car," Alyssa reveals. "If you want some help relaxing."

"Alyssa!" I scold. "Since when?!"

"Since *high school*, like everyone else." She laughs until she sees the shock on my face. "Everyone but you, apparently."

That's when Gwen's car pulls around the corner. My heart slams against my chest, but the blinding anger is still there. I stand from my sitting position and cross my arms over my chest. She parks and exits her car with this dreadful look on her face. Alyssa shifts next to me.

"I'm gonna let you two talk," she says.

Then, she goes back inside, leaving Gwen and me alone.

"Peyton, I'm *so* sorry..."

"What the *fuck*, Gwen?" I blurt. "You're supposed to be my best friend!"

"I know, I know...!"

"I told you I didn't want a huge party!"

"I know."

"And I *told you* that because I wanted to come out to you and Darian!"

"I'm sorry...!" Gwen looks up. "Wait, what about Gibbs?"

I hesitate. "He already knows."

Gwen's face contorts with confusion. "You told him?"

"I didn't necessarily tell him..."

"Jesus, Peyton!" she yells. "Yes, I was drunk, and yes, I made a really shitty mistake, but *I'm* your best friend. You just said that! So why was I the last to know?!"

Maybe this is why...

"I was gonna tell you..."

"You've been ignoring me for *months*," Gwen continues. "And you fucking yelled in my face when I tried to give you the chance to be honest!"

My anger boils to the top and I feel like combusting.

"How could I tell you?!" I shout over her.

Gwen blinks in shock at my outburst.

"What-?"

"*How* could I possibly tell you the truth after the things I heard you say about Jamie?" I explain. "How could I ever find the courage to come out to you after that?"

"Because you're supposed to *trust* me." Tears well in her eyes. "You're practically my sister, Peyton. And I didn't mean – I *regret* what I said about Jamie. And yes, when I saw you kissing her, it fucking hurt me. But not because you're gay!"

I can feel tears welling in my own eyes at the sight of Gwen sobbing in front of me. There's an undeniable tear in our relationship now, and I'm not sure if it's repairable.

"The thing that hurt the most was that you didn't feel safe enough to tell me," she cries. "And I was drunk and upset that I had pissed you off on your birthday, and you avoided me *all night!*"

The pain Gwen is feeling is palpable. Even I can feel it. She feels just as betrayed as I. And yes, outing me had been an intention fueled by what she had felt that night, but at least I can see the regret. I can see the fear of losing me. I can see it all, and it breaks my heart.

"I should've told you," I answer. "I should've, but I didn't, and that's my bad, but I wasn't ready, and kissing Jamie wasn't the plan. None of what happened Saturday was the plan, Gwen."

"God." Gwen lifts her hand to her head. "I fucked up, but I felt like I was losing the only sister I've ever had, and all the pain I had bottled up just exploded. I saw you kissing Jamie and realized all the rumors were true, and I was mad at myself for ignoring them and defending you behind your back only to be blindsided. I felt so fucking *stupid*, Peyton, and I was just so mad and drunk that I didn't know how to handle it. I don't even remember sending the picture to Jacki..."

"Wait," I interrupt. "You sent a picture to *Jacki?*"

"Yes." She exhales and closes her eyes. "But the next morning, when I sobered up, I literally went to her house and begged her to delete it. I *begged* Jacki to delete the picture, Peyton."

Jacki had posted the picture. It all makes sense now. Gwen had taken the picture and enabled the opportunity to out me, but she had only *outed* me to Jacki. It was still an obviously shitty thing to do, but the blog post was *all* Jacki, and now she'll go down for it.

"Alyssa reported the blog," I inform.

"Yeah, well..." Gwen nods in acceptance. "I deserve whatever comes after this."

Silence settles between us. I don't know where to go from here because I still feel betrayed, but I also want to know why Gwen had even taken the picture in the first place.

"Why'd you even take the picture?" I ask.

Red tints her cheeks.

"Darian and I had a bet." She shakes her head with shame. "We had a bet on how many girls Jamie would get involved with. It was stupid. Then I saw her making out with this girl outside, so I pulled out my phone and took a picture. Except after I took it, I realized she was kissing you."

The embarrassment I feel is plentiful.

"I didn't know how to react after that," she confesses.

Now that everything is out in the open, I don't know how to react either. There's a lot on our plates to digest, but at least I know the truth. At least I know that Gwen regretted doing what she did, but I couldn't forgive her. At least, not right now.

"Thanks for the honesty," I deadpan. "I guess."

She knows I'm shutting it down, and the look on her face turns to panic.

"Peyton, listen." She steps closer. "I don't care if you're

gay. I love you. You're my sister regardless, but I can't take any of this back no matter how much I wish I could."

The cold pain in my heart makes me shiver.

"I will be there for you tomorrow at school if you come," she promises. "I will punch every person in the face that makes a stupid comment about you. I'm never gonna be able to make up for what I did, but I'm gonna try. I *am* sorry. For everything."

I just stare at her and wonder if we would ever recover from this.

"And I'll understand if you never talk to me again," she finishes.

She chokes on her last sentence as tears escape her eyes. My heart pulls at the sight, but forgiveness doesn't even fall in the realm of possibility right now. I'm positive I've never been wronged so badly in my life by someone as close to me as Gwen.

I watch her climb into her car and drive away, but I stand outside for a few minutes afterwards in numbing pain. I'm still in shock. Did I have enough strength in me to forgive Gwen for what she had done? Could I look past it? God knows I'll need support tomorrow at school, especially if I was going to be questioned about the blog.

The front door opens behind me.

"That sounded... intense." Alyssa pulls me into a hug as I begin to cry again. "It's not over, Peyt."

"I know."

I cry into my sister's shoulder and try to find the

strength to stop, but I can't. Wave number two is here and maybe I just need to let it rip through me. Maybe letting the pain completely destroy me will grant me the ability to build myself back up after it's all said and done.

But I still have to talk to my parents, and God knows I need all the strength I can get for that.

Thirty-One

IT FEELS AS IF I'M ONE CRACK away from completely snapping in half. Avoiding everyone and everything today had allowed me to fool myself into thinking I was safe when I am anything but. The illusion had allowed me to keep myself together, for the most part, but that's all about to change.

"Peyton," Alyssa says. "It's gonna be okay."

"You don't know that."

I watch the clock in the kitchen tick away in silence. Mom and dad will be getting home from the office any minute now and I can feel my stomach caving in on itself. My hands shake and my legs bounce nervously. I literally feel like I'll combust as soon as I see them.

Then I hear the slamming of car doors outside. My heart jumps to my throat.

"They're gonna be pissed you're not at school," I tell Alyssa.

"I'll just lie and say they canceled class."

My foot taps nervously against the barstool I currently sit on. I lean forward and try to gather my thoughts. How will I start this conversation? What if they've already heard? What if they're *pissed?* What if...

"Alyssa?" mom calls. "Why are you not at school?"

"Classes were canceled."

"All three of them?" dad wonders.

I roll my eyes at my sister. Of course, they know her schedule!

"I just needed a mental health day, I guess."

I take in an angsty breath at my sister's response. Out of all the times she feels the need to be a smartass, why now?

My dad sets his bag on the kitchen island and locks eyes with me. There's something there, in his expression, that tells me he knows something. He gives me a sad smile. Does he know what's about to happen? Is he as nervous as I am?

Alyssa shifts on the couch to face us and watch things unfold. Problem is, I can't find the strength to start the conversation.

"Peyton, I think we need to talk," my mom starts.

My heart sinks. They know. They know everything

already and my world is about to collapse around me. I'm convinced I had just lost my best friend. Next: my parents.

No, no, no. Keep it together, Peyton.

But I can't. The stress and pain of it all seems to rip me apart from the inside out. The tears come from the depths of my soul as I try to control my sobbing. I can't even look at my mom and dad because I'm so ashamed of how all of this had played out.

"I-I'm s-sorry," I force. "I-I wanted t-to tell you..."

Another sob cuts off my sentence as I force my eyes shut. This pain is going to kill me. I feel my breathing stagger.

"Honey," I hear. Arms surround me. "What's wrong?"

But I can't respond. My mind has turned to mush as I continue to sob into my mother's shirt. When was the last time we had embraced like this? I can't remember.

"Peyton, why are you crying?" My dad also rushes to my side. "Your mother and I just wanna talk about college."

"It's okay, honey," my mom comforts me. "I know you've been stressed, and I'm sorry for making that worse."

College? They want to talk about college? They haven't heard about the blog?! I quickly wipe my eyes and try to compose myself. They don't know the truth yet! I can tell them the right way! I still have *some* control over this!

Once I gather myself, I'm able to look into the worried eyes of my parents. They both pull up a chair and sit in front of me. Alyssa gets up from the couch and joins us.

"W-What about college?" I stutter.

My mom looks sad. My dad has a similar expression, but there's a glimmer of pride when he locks eyes with me. He remains silent so my mom can speak.

"Peyton, you're so talented," my mom compliments. "You know that. Me and your father know that. And all of these colleges you're applying to know that."

I watch my father slide his hand into my mother's for support.

"But you're still my little girl," mom continues, fighting back tears. "And I never thought you would want to move so far away from me...from *us*...but I should've prepared myself for that because it's so clear that you're meant for great things."

Tears start forming again, but I try my best not to cry.

"I'm sorry for making you think I wouldn't support your dreams." Mom wipes the tears pooling under her eyes. "And I'm sorry for allowing my fear to control your future."

Another sob breaks free at the apology. In all honesty, the ongoing fight with my mom about college had been the most stressful thing this year. So, her apology had lifted a weight that's been suffocating me for a very long time.

My father reaches over and grabs my hand.

"We are going to support you no matter what college you decide to attend," he adds with a smile. "As long as you promise to visit for the holidays."

I laugh through my crying, but the reality of still having to come out keeps me shackled to the pain. Would me coming out only ruin what they had just proposed?

"Thank you," I whisper.

They both give me a smile, but I can tell they haven't forgotten about my breakdown before this. They're still worried. I had never cried like that in front of them before.

I look at Alyssa and silently ask "*Should I still do this?*" She just gives me a stiff nod.

"College isn't the only thing I've been stressed about," I force. "There's a lot going on that I haven't told you."

My parents study me. They show plenty of concern on their faces. I can only imagine what they're thinking.

"I-I uh..."

I can't even stand to look at them because I'm sick with anxiety. My body trembles with fear as I try to swallow the knot in my throat

"I-I'm um," I stutter again. "I'm gay. And the reason Alyssa's here is because I was outed to the entire school this morning."

They just stare at me in silence. My dad's eyes fall to our conjoined hands, but he doesn't retract. He holds mine tighter. Mom's in shock, like she's seen a ghost. Then, streams of tears fall from both eyes as she closes them in pain. This causes my own tears to reemerge.

"Oh, Peyton," my mom cries.

I start to panic. This isn't exactly the reaction I had expected, but I can't say it's worse. I had expected my mother to grow angry and throw blame. I expected a fit of rage. I expected *more*.

But all she does is cry.

"I've wanted to tell y'all for a long time," I reveal. "But I wasn't ready to come out. I wasn't ready to tell everyone, but I didn't want you to hear it from anyone else."

I sob more at the sight of my own mother breaking down in front of me. Is me being gay that painful to her? Does it really feel *that* bad?

I stand from the chair as my mom continues to cry and ignore me. My father releases my hand as my legs drag me up to my room. After collapsing onto my bed, I sob hard into my pillow. The image of my crying mother fuels the sadness as I weep uncontrollably.

I feel dead inside. I'm convinced my mother will never love me the same after this. Like I'm broken and had lost my value.

How will I ever be able to survive outside of the box my mother had put me in?

Thirty-Two

I WAKE UP THE NEXT MORNING alone in my bed. After crying myself to sleep following the talk with mom and dad, I had basically locked myself in my room. Alyssa had stayed to make sure I was okay and that I ate dinner, and then had to head back to Atlanta. I couldn't expect her to babysit me forever. But the worst is over, right?

Now, all I have to do is show up at school and attempt to hold my head up high. Alyssa had told me exactly how to go about it, but could I pull it off?

I take a deep breath and study my tired brown eyes in my mirror. Everything else about me looks normal. So, why do I feel so different?

I can do this. I can show up to school. I can show that

this hasn't broken me and refuse to let this define my story. I can be who I've always wanted to be.

I just have to get past mom first. So, I grab my keys and bolt to the front door.

"Peyton?" mom calls. "Peyton, wait..."

"Can't," I yell back. "I'm gonna be late."

The door slams behind me as I climb into my car and quickly pull out of the driveway. Okay. Step three: Own it. Just act like Peyton. That's all you have to do. No need to be scared. There's nothing wrong with being gay. Besides, people lie about many things on a daily basis, and being straight is a very common one.

My usual ten-minute drive feels like ten seconds instead. I know it's because I'm nervous. The pumping in my chest is intense. I can feel the blood rushing through my veins as I park my car and turn off the engine. I close my eyes and take a deep breath.

"You can do this," I whisper to myself.

One shaky hand reaches for the door handle while the other reaches for my school bag. I open the door and try not to lock eyes with anyone. Not yet. I need a second to gather my thoughts. I just need a second...

"Good morning," Gibbs greets as one of his heavy arms falls over my shoulders.

"Good morning?" I answer in shock.

Jamie joins us. "Hey."

"Listen, we know today is gonna be hard," Gibbs admits. "But we're here for you."

I settle down and allow Gibbs to talk me down.

"Did Gwen tell you...?"

"Yep." Gibbs nods his head. "I bitched her out. Darian bitched her out too, *after* he got over his initial shock."

I wanted to feel bad for Gwen, but she deserved it. I have the right to hate her, but I still couldn't decide if I wanted to forgive her. Then again, I'm sure that decision would take longer than twenty-four hours.

"I came out to my parents," I reveal.

Gibbs and Jamie stop walking to stare at me. Apparently, this is major news to them.

"How'd that go?" Jamie asks.

I sigh heavily at the vivid memory of my mom crying in the kitchen. The pain resurfaces, but I shake my head to rid myself of the picture.

"Not well, but better than expected."

"That's... good?" Gibbs wonders. "Right?"

"I don't know." I continue to walk toward the quad. "I'm ignoring them for now."

My friends fall silent after that. The intensity of what I feel is alarming. My blood is pulsing through my body like I'm running a marathon. What are people going to do? Are they going to treat me differently? Are my teachers no longer going to trust me? How will I react once I see Jacki?

Jacki. I'm going to have to face Jacki.

I stop walking.

"What's wrong?" Gibbs asks.

"I can't do this," I say.

"Yes, you can," he counters.

I shake my head. "I can't face Jacki."

Jamie and Gibbs just stare at me.

"Jacki's gonna get what's comin', Peyt." Gibbs gives me a smile. "But you can't let her think she's won."

He's right. She hasn't won. All she's done is dig a hole for herself. I will come out on top if I refuse to hide from her. I need to walk into the quad with my head held high.

I have to show her. I have to show *everyone*.

"Okay," I agree.

We continue to walk. I can see the crowd of people approaching. Some of them are already looking at us. At me. Oh God, I can't take it. No. Yes, I can. I can do this. I can do this. I can *do this*.

Only about ten more steps. Nine, eight, seven, six... Breathe in. Five, four, three, two... Breathe out.

One.

I had been looking down at my feet the whole time, but once we arrive at the bench Darian and his friends are sitting at, I try to relax. I look up to see Gwen hanging out with her cheer friends, which is unusual in the morning, but she probably figures I need space.

David, a friendly face in the group, looks at me with a sympathetic expression.

"I saw the post," he declares. "My brother was outed in high school, too. I'm sorry that happened to you."

I give him a grateful smile.

"Peyt." Darian stands. "You could've told me." Then his

strong arms wrap around my shoulders and pull me in for an embrace. I bury my face in his chest.

"I'm sorry I didn't," I apologize.

He pulls back. "And *I'm* sorry that I called Jamie the coolest lesbian at this school. You're *definitely* the coolest."

"Hey!" Jamie objects.

Darian shrugs and pulls me closer. "Sorry, Chicago."

The bell for first hour rings and tells us to head to class. The weight and anxiety of showing my face lifts as everyone realizes I'm not going to start any drama. Maybe they expected more of a reaction from me, but they weren't going to get it.

I part from everyone except for Jamie, who seems to be walking me to first hour.

"You're brave," she claims. "You know that, right?"

"I'm not brave. I'm just prideful." I laugh at myself. "If I were brave, I would've come out a long time ago."

"Just because you didn't come out as soon as you knew doesn't mean you're not brave," she disagrees. "You're brave just by being here and talking about it."

"Maybe," I say.

"Now you get to be who you wanna be," she continues. "And experience what you've missed out on."

I look at her just in time to feel her hand slip into mine. It takes everything I have not to pull away immediately.

"W-What are you doing?" I whisper frantically.

"You said you've always wanted to hold hands in the hallway," she explains.

I can't hide the smile on my face. The happiness I feel overshadows the fear of judgement as Jamie and I walk hand-in-hand to class. She doesn't release me until we're standing outside my classroom.

"I'll see you in fourth?"

"Of course."

Then, before anything else can happen, the principal's voice comes over the intercom.

"*Peyton Kelly, please report to the principal's office, immediately.*"

I sigh. "They're not wasting any time with this."

Jamie looks worried. "What are you talking about?"

"Alyssa reported the blog," I inform. "They're probably trying to find out who's behind it."

I start to turn away but realize I'm probably not the only one who will get questioned. Everyone is fair game at this point.

"Don't be surprised if they call you in too," I warn Jamie.

Then, I turn away from her and make my way to the office. I'm nervous, but my mantra for the day is that "I can do this." Whatever *this* is. So far, I've made it through the stares of my peers, but what will happen after the adults who had once trusted me fully start finding out about my sexuality? Will I lose their respect?

When I make it to the office, I'm ordered to wait outside for a few minutes. Then the door opens, and I'm summoned inside.

I've only been to the principal's office a handful of times, but never for bad reason. It had always been a positive experience. Unfortunately, that's no longer true.

"Peyton," the principal greets. "Good morning."

"Morning," I answer nervously.

I force myself to take a seat.

"I'm sorry to start your day off like this, but it's come to our attention that there was a certain... *picture* posted of you yesterday morning and we'd like to get your side of the story." He folds his hands and leans forward on his desk. "Would you like to talk about it?"

Would I *like* to talk about it? No, not really. *Should* I talk about it? Probably.

I sigh. "Well, what exactly do you want to know?"

He never breaks eye contact with me, which allows me to see the disappointment. Is he disappointed that I'm gay? It's known that I was one of his favorites in my class. Homophobia can very well be tangled in his judgement, and I'm nervous to find out.

"Whoever is running this blog is in serious trouble," he explains. "And the post involving you is a clear case of cyberbullying that we must address now that it's been brought to our attention."

He wants names. He wants to know who could be behind this and the other controversial posts on the blog. I can give him names. I can give him *so many names...*

"The picture was taken this past Saturday night. It was my eighteenth birthday party, and..." *Gwen Richardson took the picture.* "And uh, someone took a picture of me and Jamie... kissing."

He jots down notes.

"Jamie Kendall, correct?"

"Yes sir."

He stops writing and looks at me.

"Do you know who took the picture?"

Gwen, my best friend.

The pain chokes me.

"U-Um..." I look down at my hands. "I know who posted the picture."

He sighs. Why is it so hard for me to tell the truth? Yes, I'm mad at Gwen. And yes, she had done me wrong, but if I tell him that Gwen took the picture, she can get into serious trouble. What if she gets expelled?

"Peyton," the principal starts. "I know this may be difficult. It's only been twenty-four hours since the incident, but the faster you work with me, the faster we can get this over with."

Gwen did me wrong, and she knows there will be consequences. I have to stand up to Jacki, and that means I have to tell my story. The *entire* story.

"The picture was taken by Gwen Richardson," I reveal. "Then she sent it to Jaqueline Ross. Gwen told me this herself Monday morning."

He jots more notes down and then looks up with a sad smile.

"Is there anything else you want to tell me?" he

continues. "About the blog? Or anything else you think I should know?"

All I can do is shake my head.

"Thank you, Peyton," he says. "You can go back to class now."

I grab my things and leave the office. This is just the beginning, but I know a lot of people are going to get in trouble. I *didn't* know how serious the consequences would be, but I have a feeling I need to warn Gwen. She's definitely getting called in for questioning.

I enter my English class and feel multiple pairs of eyes watching me. Everyone except Gwen, of course. I take my seat and try not to let it get to me as I watch the clock hands move.

Once class is over, Gwen bolts, but I decide to be the bigger person.

"Gwen," I call.

She stops pacing away from me and turns around.

"The principal asked me questions about the blog," I reveal to her. "I told him you took the picture and sent it to Jacki."

She looks down with shame but nods her head in acceptance.

"He's probably gonna call you in to confirm, but I don't think they're taking this lightly," I state.

This gets her to at least look at me. "Do you think they're gonna expel me?"

I hope not, but I don't know for sure. I just shrug.

"Figured I'd warn you," I finish.

As I turn away, I hear her call my name.

"Peyton." I force myself to look at her. "I really am sorry. I wasn't thinking when I did it. I wasn't sober..."

"That doesn't excuse anything, Gwen."

"I know."

A short moment of silence passes between us. I check my watch and decide I should leave, otherwise I would be late for my next class.

"What will help you forgive me?" she asks.

"I don't know," I confess. "But you can start by telling the truth."

Then I leave her in the hallway, knowing that if Gwen *does* admit to taking the picture, she's essentially admitting to being a part of the blog. If she does, that means she'll lead them to the main problem, which is Jacki, but she'll certainly face *some* sort of consequence.

And if she lies to save herself, then I guess she had never been my best friend to begin with.

Thirty-Three

THE TRUTH ABOUT THE BLOG came out within forty-eight hours. Gwen had been questioned, along with Jamie, Jacki, and all of Jacki's close friends. I hadn't talked to Gwen about her interview, but Jamie said she had been asked to confirm that she was the one in the picture and describe her perspective of Jacki's and my relationship.

It seemed as if we were on the path to justice, but the problem was I hadn't heard of any sort of punishment yet. What was the point of interviewing students and shutting down the blog if there would be absolutely no repercussions?

It's now Friday afternoon and I'm currently working on the mural while I wait for Jamie to join me. She had texted me to let me know she would be running late due to being held after third hour.

Then I hear the double doors open.

Jamie joins me in the room and throws her bag down next to mine. She gives me a soft smile.

"We're almost done," Jamie says. "We *might* even finish with time to spare."

"Don't get too excited," I warn. "It's not over yet."

She starts working next to me. I don't expect conversation because we're both finishing up our last big piece of the mural. After this, we'll perfect the background and clean it up. I am beyond excited.

"Have you heard about the suspensions?" she asks.

"Suspensions?" I wonder. "For the blog?"

She nods. "Gwen and a few other people got a two-day suspension for affiliation."

Damn. Gwen's parents are going to *freak* when they find out why she got suspended for two days. Especially if she tells them she was drunk when she did it. I can only imagine what would take place in her household.

"What about Jacki?" I ask.

"She's suspended all next week," Jamie informs me. "She's no longer senior editor for yearbook, she's not allowed to attend senior prom or walk across the stage for commencement."

A part of me wants to pity Jacki because senior prom and graduation is a big deal, and we've all looked forward to it throughout high school. Not to mention her yearbook status. That's her proudest achievement.

But she had outed me and bullied many others. She had taken away something important, and I need to remember that. What if my parents hadn't reacted decently? What if they'd kicked me out? She would've been responsible for that. Outing someone was dangerous!

So, I refuse to pity her. She could've gotten a lot worse, like being expelled. A suspension and a slap on the wrist seems light now that I think about it.

"Well." I sigh heavily. "I guess karma really is a bitch."

Then the conversation dies. It's over with. I'm out and Jacki had taken the fall for the blog. It just sucks because a lot of people had been affected beforehand. We should've said something sooner, when we first learned about the blog, but we didn't. We hadn't said anything, and it had taken something like outing me for someone to finally step up and do something about it.

But maybe we've all learned our lesson. And maybe, just *maybe*, we can find closure and move on with our lives.

Thirty-Four

THE WEEK THAT JACKI WAS SUSPENDED, I felt as if I could finally breathe normally again. All the tension I had felt prior to the suspension lifted, and I was able to enjoy walking through the halls of Branton High without being suffocated by Jacki's presence.

Gwen had done her suspension time as well and had been grounded by her parents on top of it all. She could've lied to the principal to save herself, considering her parents are *super* religious and absolutely condemn drinking, and a lot of other things, but she hadn't. She had told the truth because she knew if she didn't, I would've never forgiven her. She also knew that if she had lied about taking the picture, it could've made things a whole lot messier. In a way, I feel bad for her, because I know how her parents are and know it couldn't have been easy.

A part of me was starting to forgive Gwen, but I know it would be a long time, if *ever*, for us to return to normal. But one day at a time, I guess.

Another thing that had developed over the last week of April was an undying curiosity to know *why* Jacki did what she did. There had never been an explanation, and as spiteful and egocentric as Jacki is, I had a feeling there was something I didn't know. Something only Jacki herself could tell me.

So, discovering the truth became the goal of the first week of May, even if it meant cornering Jacki and forcing it out of her.

"Am I supposed to be excited for senior prom?" Gibbs wonders. "Because I'm not."

"Me neither," Darian agrees. "I don't think Gwen's parents are even gonna let her go."

The blog thing had really screwed up the ending of our senior year, but I want my friends to have a good time. *I* want to have a good time. I believe we all deserve it after this year.

The bell rings and signals the beginning of our Monday. Okay, so senior prom is this Saturday. I have to make sure *all* of my friends are guaranteed a good time.

First hour progresses as Gwen and I sit side-by-side but ignore each other. I haven't talked to her in days, which had allowed me to see things from a clearer perspective.

Yes, Gwen had taken a picture of Jamie kissing me because she had been sloppy drunk and out of her right mind. Did that excuse her behavior? Of course not. *But* Gwen was dealing with the consequences. Had she meant to out me? Yes, to *Jacki*. I really couldn't believe she had meant to out me to the entire school. She had gone over to Jacki's the very next day and begged her to delete the picture. Gwen probably hadn't even been aware of how deeply rooted Jacki's hatred for me was.

Hell, *I* hadn't even been aware that Jacki hated me enough to literally out me to the entire school. How could Gwen have known Jacki would post the picture on the blog? Especially since none of us had known for sure who ran the stupid thing in the first place.

None of it is right, but it also isn't black and white. It's complex. So, I can sit here and hold a grudge and let it eat away at my heart and make me vindictive. Or I can try to move on and forgive Gwen.

"Darian told me you aren't sure if your parents are gonna let you go to senior prom," I say.

Gwen sighs. "Yeah. They haven't made a decision yet, but I'm sure it's not gonna happen."

I fall silent when the teacher looks up from her desk.

"I'm gonna return my dress tomorrow," she reveals. "It's just a stupid dance, right?"

It isn't just a stupid dance. It's our last school function before graduation. And maybe I'm putting too much emphasis on it, but if it's important to me, it's important to

Gwen, no matter how much she's trying to hide it.

"Why'd you do it?" I ask. "Why'd you send the picture to Jacki?"

Gwen stops writing and sets her pencil down. She seems to hesitate with thought, but I know she isn't going to lie to me. Is she scared?

"I always thought Jacki liked you," she admits. "I've thought it for a while because, well, why else would she be so jealous of you? You were constantly denying that you were gay to everyone, and Jacki seemed absolutely convinced you were."

I wait for her to explain further before saying anything.

"I sent it to her to kind of rub it in her face," she continues. "To show her that, yeah, she was right, you *were* gay, but you weren't interested in her. It was a petty decision that drunk me made. I realized in the morning that it made absolutely no sense."

I'm dumbfounded, but Gwen's logic might've made *some* sense, in a real twisted way. Jacki had been the first to come out in our class, which then caused a wave of people to do the same. I had wanted to but never found the courage. Was that why Jacki flaunted Jamie in my face? To make me *jealous*? Had the feeling of rejection fueled Jacki's desire to out me?

The thought enrages me.

First hour ends and I go on with my day. I try to think of reasons why Jacki would do such a thing, but nothing adds up in my head. The need to know the truth becomes unbearable. I need answers. I need them because if I *didn't* get them, I would never get over what had happened.

Jamie meets up with me on the way to fourth.

"You look like you're in deep thought," she observes.

"I'm trying to figure out why Jacki outed me," I admit. "Because I don't understand why Jacki, who had the opportunity to come out on her own terms, *outed* me, someone who wasn't ready. Like, she of all people should understand?!"

Jamie falls silent as we grab our supplies and head to our nearly finished mural.

"You know just as much as me," Jamie says. "You've also known her longer."

"Nothing comes to mind."

"Well, maybe you should ask her."

I should. I should confront Jacki because I deserve the truth. I deserve it so I can find closure in all of this. We had fifteen days left of high school, and I want to leave all of this behind me once it was over. I couldn't do that if I never learned Jacki's side of the story.

Then, as soon as we start on finishing up the mural, a voice summons me over the intercom. Again.

"*Peyton Kelly, please report to the principal's office.*"

Thirty-Five

BEING BACK IN THE PRINCIPAL'S OFFICE doesn't feel good, especially after the last time I had been here and what that meeting had consisted of. I sit alone because he had stepped out for a minute. I can hear him talking with someone, but I don't recognize the voice. I have a bad feeling, but I should have nothing to worry about, right?

Then the door opens. The principal, along with a man dressed in a suit paired with a police badge enters as well. The principal closes the door.

"Peyton, this is detective Warren," he introduces the man. "He's the officer that was investigating the vandalism months ago when someone ruined your mural."

Warren holds out his hand for me to shake and I do

hesitantly.

"Detective Warren has identified a main suspect after the blog incident and is wondering if he could ask you a few questions," the principal finishes.

"Uh, sure?" I answer.

My concern must be noticeable because Warren relaxes into the chair next to me.

"Peyton, you're not in trouble," he assures. "We're just trying to find out who did it."

Well, I know who did it.

But instead of saying anything, I just nod and watch him reveal a small notepad from his jacket pocket.

"How long have you known Jaqueline Ross?" he asks.

"Well, pretty much my entire life..." I begin.

And after that, it just pours out. We talk about when her feud with me started, if she ever said anything that indicated she had something to do with the vandalism, and the blog that had inevitably outed me. By the way Warren was talking by the end of the conversation, it sounded as if he knew *exactly* who was behind it. He just needed my side of the story to confirm it.

"Thank you for your time, Peyton." Detective Warren stands. "If I have any further questions, would you be willing to answer them?"

"S-Sure."

Then he nods to me and the principal before leaving. I look at the man sitting behind the big desk and lean forward in my chair.

"Is Jacki in... *legal* trouble?" I ask.

He folds his hands with a sad expression.

"Peyton, vandalism is a crime. Breaking and entering is *illegal...*" he informs. "I'm not saying I believe Jacki's guilty, but after the blog post and student testimonials... it's become clear that she has something against you."

My heart is racing. What is really happening? Is Jacki going to get *arrested?* Is there really a full-on investigation happening right now?

"I'm sorry to pull you away from art for this," he apologizes. "You're free to go."

I stand in a daze. Honestly, I should be happy this is happening to Jacki, but I'm *not.* As much as I hate her for the things she did, I can't imagine Jacki getting charged for this. It would alter her entire life.

"And Peyton," the principal calls. "It's best not to tell anyone about this. Understand?"

I just nod and head out the door. As much as I want to believe not telling anyone is in my best interest, I have to tell Jacki, and I have to tell her soon.

Thirty-Six

IF I'M BEING HONEST, what I'm about to do is stupid. Everyone thought staying *away* from Jacki was what I needed to do. Hell, even a part of *me* thinks I should stay away and just let the investigation pan out on its own. But I couldn't.

"Are you sure this is a good idea?" Jamie asks.

"It's not a *good* idea," I say. "But it's all I could think of." I hand Jamie the keys I had been gifted to work on the mural. "Besides, it's the only way I'll actually get her to talk to me."

Jamie just looks at me with a worried expression. I hadn't told her about the investigation, or that I planned on warning Jacki about what was going on. All I had told her was that I needed to talk to Jacki once and for all.

That's all she needs to know. At least, for now.

"Alright," Jamie agrees. "I guess I'll just wait out here?"

I just nod to her as I wait for Jacki to show up. *If* she shows up.

I rest against the wall and stare up at the mural. It's nearly complete. Jamie and I would finish it tomorrow afternoon since we aren't working on it today because of the whole Jacki thing. Besides, judging isn't going to take place until this weekend anyway.

My heart starts to race at the thought of finally having a conversation with Jacki. If she complies, of course. Jacki will probably try to place the blame for her suspension on me, even when it wasn't even *my* fault any of this happened. All in all, I'm unsure what to expect, because I couldn't remember the last time Jacki and I had, had a civil conversation.

Then, a familiar voice pulls me out of my head.

"Is this a joke?" Jacki says from the door.

I look at her but refuse to say anything.

Luckily, she steps inside the hall with me instead of leaving. I guess she must have some things to say to me too.

"Jamie said..."

"Jamie lied," I interrupt. "For me."

That's when I watch Jamie shut the door behind Jacki and lock it with the key I had given her. Jacki turns around abruptly and tries to leave, but quickly realizes that isn't going to happen. Does she feel threatened? A part of me hopes she does.

"What the hell are you doing?" she asks.

"We need to talk," I start. "It's long overdue, don'tcha think?"

Dark eyes face me. She looks scared but also pissed. I can't blame her. A lot has happened over the past few weeks. None of which was *my* fault, of course, but she still has the right to be upset.

I expect her to say something, *anything* really, but she just looks at the mural. Her expression turns from angry to cynical instantly as she laughs to herself.

"You still finished it," she observes. "And it's good. You're gonna win."

"I guess I have you to thank for that," I say sarcastically. "If you hadn't ruined the first one, Jamie and I wouldn't have come up with this."

She just laughs at me. "You're so convinced it was me."

"It *was* you," I accuse. "I know it was. That's why you're locked in here in the first place."

She shakes her head as she folds her arms in front of her chest. There's still a hard expression on her face, but what I was about to say would ruin all of that.

"There's a detective investigating the vandalism and you're pretty much his prime suspect." I inform. "So, you can stop acting like *fake bitch*, Jacki."

That does it. Her tough demeanor cracks and crumbles like it's made of nothing but plastic.

"*Fuck* you, Peyton." She laughs manically. "You ruined

my life once, and now you're basically *warning* me that it's gonna happen again?" She storms over to the door and bangs on it. "Let me the fuck out, Jamie! Right now!"

I ruined her life? What the hell is she talking about? Has Jacki officially lost her mind?

"What the hell do you mean *I* ruined your life?"

"Don't play stupid. You know exactly what the hell you did." She yanks on the door. "Jamie, open this goddamn door!"

"She's not gonna open it until I tell her to," I say. "Now answer my question."

That's when she stops yanking and rests her head against the door. Her hands tremble against the bar, and then she begins to cry. Is Jaqueline Ross really... *crying*? Has Hell frozen over?

Then she turns around.

"How was it?" she asks through her tears. "When you came out to your parents?"

I'm blindsided by the question. My face must show that because she doesn't give me a chance to answer.

"Did they threaten you with boarding school?" She steps closer to me. "Did they consider *shipping* you off to conversion therapy, where they basically torture and brainwash kids into thinking like them? To think *normal*?"

"Jacki, what the hell are you...?"

"Is your mom gonna pull you out of soccer? Is she gonna choose your clothes and make you learn how to wear makeup and set you up on dates with the neighbor's son? Is she gonna make you go to youth group every Saturday night and church Sunday morning in hopes that *God* will curb your sexuality?"

I can't even get a word in at this point.

"Because that's what *my* mom did to me when *you* fucking outed me!" Jacki sobs. "But apparently you don't remember, because it was just a stupid kiss to you."

That does it. Everything comes rushing back, like that specific moment had been buried in the depths of my brain, in the untouched corners with cobwebs and old, insignificant memories.

"Peyton, can you help me?" Jacki asks as she lugs two bags of soccer balls.

"Sure," I agree.

I take a bag and follow her to the equipment closet and throw my bag on top of hers. Then all the balls spill out. We both groan in annoyance.

Jacki laughs. "Seriously?"

I laugh along with her. "I didn't mean to!"

We enter the room and start picking up the balls together and shove them back into the bag. After the last one, I tug the string tight to where they couldn't come loose again.

"Can I ask you something?" Jacki wonders.

"Of course," I answer.

"Do you ever..." She sighs. "Do you ever think about kissing girls?"

I feel dizzy at the question. I feel dizzy because I had

thought about it and had tried to unthink it ever since. I also feel blindsided because I thought I was the only one.

"N-No," I lie. "Why? Have you?"

She shrugs. "N-No, I just... I saw it on TV, and it looked fun."

Is Jacki lying? It seems weird that she would randomly bring this up if she hadn't thought about it before. And here I am thinking I'm alone in this. Maybe I should just be honest.

"I-I mean," I stutter. "I may have thought about it once..."

Jacki's eyes light up. "Really? With who?"

"Coach Megan." I laugh in embarrassment.

"Oh my God the coach?" Jacki laughs too.

"What about you?" I ask. "Who have you thought about kissing?"

She looks at me but just shrugs. "You don't know her."

"Oh c'mon."

"No," she says with a smile. "But I might get to one day."

"Have you ever kissed a girl before?" I wonder.

She shakes her head. "I haven't kissed anyone before."

I lean against the door and study Jacki. She refuses to look at me for longer than a few seconds. Why doesn't she want to tell me? I thought we were friends. I feel bad. She looks like she really wants to kiss this person she's talking about. She keeps fidgeting with her hands, which means she's nervous. She always does that when she's nervous.

Then suddenly, she takes a deep breath, leans in, and awkwardly presses our lips together.

I'm stunned. I've never kissed anyone before, much less a girl. There's this stirring in my heart and this clenching in my stomach, but maybe that's normal? I don't know.

Then she pulls away.

"Don't tell anyone," she whispers. "Promise?"

I nod in shock.

"Promise."

I was eleven. That was *seven years* ago. But I remember exactly what I did that night now that she had brought it up. I had gone home that night and asked my mother if it was normal for girls to want to kiss other girls. She had asked me why I had asked such a thing, and I had tried to lie about it as best as I could.

Of course, my mom didn't buy the lies, then forced me into telling her that Jacki had kissed me after soccer practice. She had been appalled, explained the Adam and Eve story, and then sent me to my room to do my homework.

"I didn't out you." I shake my head. "I didn't..."

"You did!" she accuses. "You did, because *your* mom called *my* mom, and *that's* why I was pulled off the soccer team. That's why I couldn't be in any after-school clubs until high school. It's why I couldn't go to swim parties and sleepovers..." she fumes. "All because of *you*, Peyton."

I'm shocked. Utterly appalled at the ugly truth that has

been presented. I hadn't meant to do that to Jacki. I didn't know...

"I *told* you not to tell anyone!" she cries. "I trusted you."

All I can do is stare at Jacki in shock.

"And then I had to watch you rise to the top while my own mother held me down!" she continues. "You were so fucking... *privileged*, and yet, here you are, playing the victim. Again."

"Privileged...?"

"Don't *act* like you're not, Peyton Kelly," Jacki orders. "Yes, you're the soccer captain, but is it only because my mom pulled me out of soccer when we were eleven? Maybe! I was just as good as you! And you won student class president because your mom was off to bring you to all the birthday parties and wealthy enough to buy your friends all the best gifts. Everyone liked you because your parents, *both* parents, made sure of it."

It's disgusting how bad I feel right now. The pain laced in the words she says hurts me because it all makes sense.

"And how was someone like me supposed to keep up with someone like you?" she asks. "A mixed, gay teenager with a single black mother?"

"But you came out when we were freshmen," I remind her. "You were senior editor. You became the top theater student! You got to be *yourself* in high school! You were successful too, Jacki!"

Is that what she's wanted all along? Revenge? Because

that's exactly what she got, and now look at where we were. She's currently under investigation and I'm... fine. I'm fine? So why do I feel guilty?

Jacki wipes the tears from her eyes and shakes her head, a broken smile on her lips.

"Yeah, I *was* successful." She picks up her bag. "Until I get charged and get my college admission revoked. You'll win the mural competition, probably get a full ride somewhere far away from this hell hole of a town and take Jamie with you."

She walks back over to the door and I move closer. I can't keep her in here any longer. She doesn't deserve that.

"Unlock the door," I tell Jamie.

So, she does. The look on her face is just as shocked as mine. None of what had just happened had been expected. None of this is fair.

Jacki leaves, but somewhere deep down, I know this isn't over. It isn't over because it still feels wrong. It all feels so *wrong*... and I have no idea how to fix it.

Thirty-Seven

SOMETIMES PEOPLE DO BAD THINGS. People do bad things for many reasons. Pain, fear, anger, sadness, or just plain ignorance can result in people intentionally hurting others. But just because a person does a bad thing, doesn't necessarily make them a bad person.

In a world where we're told to believe things are black and white, we often get lost in the vast gray area of life. We try to box feelings and circumstances into "good" and "evil." We rarely try to understand how they could be both, and how a "bad" decision could be validated based on the perspective and context in which you look at it.

And as much as forgiveness is preached in our places of worship, we rarely find the strength as prideful beings to do so.

As I pace to the principal's office, for hopefully the last time, I no longer feel confused about what I should do.

The door is open as the crowd inside waits for me to arrive. The principal is there, the vice principal, detective Warren, Jacki, and her mom. I can tell Jacki has been crying. The principal looks as if he can't believe this is happening at his school. The detective holds a passive expression, as usual.

"Peyton," the principal greets.

I just nod in response.

He stands from his desk and looks at both Jacki and me with an expression that oozes with disappointment. He rubs the worry lines on his forehead and takes in a deep breath.

"Jacki has confessed to the vandalism," he informs everyone in the room. "And I have instructed her to give you a sincere apology for ruining the mural and outing you to the entire school."

I force myself to look at Jacki who I have never seen look so broken.

"Peyton, I'm sorry that I vandalized your mural and outed you." She sobs. "I'm sorry that I blamed you for my anger over the years, when I should've blamed our ignorant parents for refusing to accept that people are different."

Her mom gasps. "Jaqueline..."

"I have something to say, too," I interrupt.

Silence. Everyone looks at me. I'm not sure how this is

going to turn out, but I know what I have to do to try and make this right.

"Yes, Jacki vandalized the mural," I say. "And yes, Jacki outed me, but she doesn't deserve to be charged, and she certainly doesn't deserve to have her future ruined because she made a few mistakes."

The principal is shocked. The detective shows an emotion that mimics surprise. Jacki and her mother are still. The pressure and weight of what I'm about to say is heavy, but it doesn't feel wrong. I had thought about this all week.

"If Jacki is charged, she'll have her college admission revoked. She might never be able to get into college at all," I state. "She'll be stuck here, in this town where there are too many bad memories."

The silence in the office is deafening.

"Jacki and I both deserve to leave Branton with a clean slate." I try not to let my voice shake. "She deserves to go to senior prom, and I deserve to find closure, because if we *don't*, we'll never be able to move on and find forgiveness from this situation, and it'll define us."

I hadn't realized how intense this situation was until I pause and realize that everyone is hanging on to my every word. The power intimidates me, but I need to use it for good. I need to use my status for *good*, to help someone, regardless of whether she had made mistakes or not.

"People do bad things, but that doesn't mean they're bad people," I finish. "Jacki's not a bad person. She's learned her lesson."

I lock eyes with the principal.

"You have the power to drop the charges and let Jacki move on from this," I say. "You have the power to give her a second chance to get things right."

The principal looks torn. He doesn't want to regret this decision, but I had made valid points.

"I don't wanna leave Branton with this on my shoulders," I reiterate. "And I don't think you wanna send us off like this, either."

He rubs his eyes and folds his hands atop the desk. I can feel my body shaking in anticipation of his verdict. I need him to let Jacki off the hook. I had wronged her years ago, and I feel like this was my chance at finally getting it right.

"Peyton," he starts. "Are you aware of what you're asking me to do?"

"Yes sir."

"Are you sure? Because this is going to tell other kids it's *okay* to vandalize your school without consequences."

"None of the students even know."

The office falls silent again.

I refuse to say anything else. I'm afraid if I do, I'll ruin the only chance I have to get Jacki off the hook. I'm doing everything I can, but I won't argue any further. He's the principal, after all, but he can see that I'm begging him to let this go. I *need* him to let this go.

The principal leans back in his chair, sighs loudly, and shakes his head. I feel like the room is literally standing on the edge of cliff.

"I'll drop the charges," he states.

I feel the weight immediately lift from my chest. Jacki takes in a deep breath of relief and releases a laugh that's paired with happy tears. The guilt and pain and tension seems to dissolve into thin air as a wide smile stretches across my lips.

"Jacki, you're allowed to go to prom and walk across stage for commencement," the principal continues. "You two may leave, and I do not want to see either of you until graduation. Understand?"

"Yes sir," we say in unison.

Jacki stands, along with her mother, and the three of us head for the door. Once we make it outside, Jacki turns to her mom.

"Can Peyton and I have a second?" she asks.

Jacki's mom nods and walks toward the door.

A minute of silence passes as I wait for Jacki to say something. I imagine she has a reason for making her mom give us space, but maybe she's searching for the right words.

"I don't know what to say." Jacki laughs. "Thank you, I guess, but..."

"Don't thank me," I say. "I just want this feud between us to be over. And I'm *so* sorry for what happened... I had no idea."

Jacki just stares at me.

"You're not a bad person, Jacki," I say. "You were

hurting, and pain makes us do stupid things."

She nods as her eyes fall from mine and focus on the floor. She doesn't seem to have any more words, but that's okay. I don't expect anything to come from this. I wanted a clean slate just as much as she did. This was for both of us.

"Guess I'll see you at prom?" I ask.

"Yeah." She laughs in disbelief. "I guess you will."

I give Jacki one last nod and turn to leave.

If there was one thing I had learned, it was that there would be times when people were going to hurt you, and it was up to you to decide how long you would sit in that hurt.

In this instance, I had found the power to forgive Jacki. I had forgiven Gwen as well, because I knew that they were good people, and sometimes good people do bad things and make awful mistakes.

And once I graduate from Branton, I would start over somewhere else and build the life I wanted without the company of my demons that had hurt me in the past.

Thirty-Eight

I WATCH MY OLDER SISTER pin back some of my hair through the mirror, exposing my face, which is now covered in makeup. I have plenty of anticipation for senior prom, and my friends are going to be here any minute now.

"Are you nervous?" Alyssa asks.

"Very," I answer. "But I'm also very excited."

"Good." She pulls back. "Because I *think* we're done."

I turn my head back and forth, studying Alyssa's work that had taken her about two hours. A smile creeps onto my lips.

"I think it looks great," I say.

"*Great?*" Alyssa scoffs. "It's perfect. Jamie's gonna die when she sees you."

I stand from Alyssa's old vanity and study myself in the full-length mirror. She isn't wrong. I did look absolutely stunning. Then the doorbell rings.

"Perfect timing," Alyssa sings.

I grab my heels and head for the front door to greet my friends. When I open it, Gibbs, Jamie, Darian, *and* Gwen are standing there in their formal attire.

"Well, y'all look fantastic," Alyssa admires.

Everyone thanks my sister and heads inside for a moment. I need to put on my shoes and grab my stuff before we head out. My friends meet up with my parents in the kitchen and distract them for the time being.

Gwen steps forward and I smile.

"Your parents let you come," I observe.

"Yeah." She laughs. "I couldn't return the dress, so they felt bad."

I'm glad Gwen can attend senior prom. It wouldn't have been fair had she missed out on this night. She moves past me and joins Darian and Gibbs in the kitchen.

Then Jamie approaches me. "You look..."

"Great? I know," I boast.

She just laughs and shakes her head.

"You look good, too," I compliment.

Jamie's pantsuit holds a nice balance between masculine and feminine. Her blazer is fitted perfectly to her slim figure, and her pants accentuate her legs and make them look amazing. I mean, they always looked amazing, but today they're exceptional. She wore heels, but they were short, which prevented her from towering over me.

"Where are your shoes?" she asks.

"Right here." I flash them. "I just need to put them on, and we can go."

Jamie then kneels to help me put them on. I feel my heart flutter in my chest. Her gentle hands graze my skin while fitting the shoes against my feet before tightening them around my ankles.

When she's done, she stands up. I try to hide how flustered I am.

"I'm ready when you are."

We walk into the kitchen and spot my parents laughing it up with Gibbs and Darian. Gwen stays in the background because I'm sure she still feels a little uncomfortable, but we're working on it.

"We're ready," I announce.

My parents look at Jamie and me, and I can't tell if we should run for the door or not. We hadn't talked much about my sexuality or if I was seeing anyone, but I figured it was because they were still coming to terms with the truth, and I didn't want to bombard them.

"And who is this...?" my dad asks.

"That's Jamie, Peyton's girl..."

I slap my hand on Alyssa's mouth.

"This is Jamie," I introduce.

My mom and dad shake Jamie's hand and attempt to make her feel welcome. They probably think we're dating too, even if that isn't the case.

"Is everyone ready?" I ask.

"Hell yeah!" Gibbs cheers, and then turns red. "I-I mean, heck yeah."

My friends and I just laugh as we leave the house and pile into Darian's Jeep. Jamie's hand rests on my exposed thigh as my dress hikes up from sitting, and I feel my body heat up. Maybe I wouldn't feel so self-conscious if Gibbs wasn't in the backseat with us.

It takes us all but ten minutes to make it to the venue where our prom is being held. People are already making their way in as the lights from the venue escape when the doors open. I take in a deep breath as Darian parks and my friends start exiting the car.

Jamie senses my anxiety and grabs my hand.

"It's gonna be fine, you know," she comforts.

"I know. It's just..." I pause. "I've never done it like this."

"Well, you couldn't have picked a better person to experience this with," Jamie boasts. "I'm a fun date."

I roll my eyes and smile. "You're also *annoyingly* arrogant."

We laugh and make it inside and take in our surroundings. It looks amazing. I grow proud of the junior committee. They've outdone themselves. Then, in the corner of the dance floor stands Jacki with a few of her friends. Her gaze locks with mine. I give her a small smile, and she returns it.

Jamie and I make our way through the crowd, telling

people hey and having small talk. The atmosphere is electric, and I'm happy to be here as myself with all my peers, but I still feel like I'm under a microscope. I pin it on my anxiety and try to ignore it.

"You still seem nervous," Jamie says. "Are you sure you're okay?"

"I'm fine," I answer. "The constant hand holding is just a lot. I'm not used to being like this, much less with a girl in public."

"I don't have to hold your hand all the time." Jamie smiles. "I just want to. But if you're uncomfortable, I'm fine holding back."

"Thank you," I say. "I promise, it's not because I don't want to. I just... I need to do it myself for now."

"That's fine."

Time progresses quickly after that. My friends and I tear it up on the dance floor and we just enjoy our night together at our last dance. It's nice. It's everything I hoped it would be.

No, circumstances weren't how I imagined. Everyone is still recovering from the previous weeks of drama, but we're trying to move on from it. I didn't want the negativity to crumble my high school experience, because my experience was *so much* more than being outed.

Then a slow song comes on, which puts a stop to the dancing. Couples hold on to each other and start to fill the dance floor. My eyes instinctively search for Jamie, but she had told me she wouldn't initiate anything anymore. If I want to dance, it's up to me to do so.

I take a deep breath. Okay. I can slow dance, and everyone here knows the truth now. It won't be a shock if Jamie and I dance together. Hell, there's at least *one* other same-sex couple dancing right now...

C'mon Peyton. This is what you've always wanted, right?

"Will you go and dance with her, already?" I hear behind me.

I turn to see Jacki also looking at Jamie, who's conversing with Gibbs across the room.

"I don't know why I'm so nervous," I confess.

"It's always scary at first," she assures. "But no one here cares. I promise."

I turn to face her. "Not even you?"

She laughs. "Jamie's great but... I think I just convinced myself that I liked her because I could tell she *really* liked you."

I roll my eyes and smile. "You've gotta chill with the competitiveness."

"I will when you do."

We just laugh together.

"Do it, because this song's already halfway over," she orders. "I'll request another one, but no guarantees."

She's right. I need to do this now. I want to. I know that much. That's all the reason I need.

I start toward Jamie and stop when she looks at me.

"I wanna dance," I claim.

"Oh my God, with *me*?" Gibbs teases and giggles like a little girl.

I grab Jamie's hand. "Let's get away from this weirdo."

I pull her onto the dance floor and follow her to the rhythm. She looks happy that I had made the decision to dance. I am too, regardless of the fear I feel from being watched by my peers.

"Relax," Jamie pulls me closer. "It's fine."

I settle into a rhythm and allow Jamie's swaying to comfort me. My head leans on her chest and I feel like a million butterflies are flying around in my stomach.

"I saw you were talking to Jacki," she tells me.

"She was trying to convince me to dance with you."

"I'm still trying to figure out how you got her off the hook." She continues to lead. "And *why*?"

I shrug. "Everyone deserves a second chance. I don't wanna leave Branton with a bad taste in my mouth. I'm sure Jacki didn't either. We all mess up."

"That's really... *bold* of you."

I smile and look up at her. "Thanks."

"So, how does it feel?" Jamie wonders. "Dancing with me, here, in front of everyone?"

"Scary but really good," I admit. "Thank you."

"For?"

"For everything," I say. "For being patient with me, for helping me finish the mural... for everything."

She smiles a toothy grin. I momentarily wonder what would come after this. We only have ten days left of school, and then graduation. I have a speech to prepare. We still have to find out who had won the mural competition... There's still so much to do, but so little time.

But I refuse to worry about that right now.

Right now is for me, and my friends, and Jamie. Now is the time to let loose and just *enjoy* being a teenager. Something I feel like I haven't had the opportunity to do.

The song ends and an up-tempo song starts playing, forcing the couples apart that had previously been dancing close together. Jamie moves to the beat and looks at me playfully. Then my friends join us back on the dance floor.

This is what happiness is supposed to feel like from being able to be yourself. It should always be this easy. If it were, maybe there wouldn't be so many kids like Jacki and me in the world.

Because this is real freedom, and it feels *amazing*.

Thirty-Nine

MY HANDS TREMBLE IN MY LAP as they nervously squeeze the sheet of paper that holds the last speech I will give as a high school student. I try to take in five deep breaths and restrain my legs from bouncing. Everything I had worked for over the past four years has all led up to this.

My valedictorian speech.

The principal and my English teacher had approved my speech earlier this week but the one I was preparing to give is a little... *refurbished*. I pray that this much-needed speech wouldn't result in my diploma getting held.

"And now, I'd like to take the opportunity to introduce our senior class valedictorian, Peyton Anne Kelly," the principal announces. "Peyton is the daughter of Annette and Ken Kelly…"

His voice fades into the distance. My heart is pounding so loudly in my head that I can't help but tune out my introduction. All he's going to do is hype me up to the families of the graduates and make me sound cooler than I actually am. All the accomplishments he rambles on about will mean nothing in the grand scheme of things. Because, he *wouldn't* mention my biggest accomplishment, which is the fact that I had overcome all the adversity surrounding my sexuality and still have the courage to stand up on stage to give a speech.

"… And last but not least, Peyton's most recent accomplishment is winning the Borell Foundation of the Arts' first-place donation for their district-wide mural competition, which will grant Branton High's art department twenty-thousand dollars for the upcoming school year," the principal boasts. "And Peyton's asked me to give credit to Jamie Kendall, who helped her with the mural after transferring here from Chicago at the beginning of the school year."

I take a deep breath and prepare to stand up.

"Peyton will attend the University of Pittsburg in the fall." He takes a breath. "Now please, give a warm welcome to Branton High's senior class valedictorian, Peyton Kelly."

The white noise in my head is loud enough to drown out the applause that follows my introduction. My legs carry me to the podium that overlooks my senior class and everyone's families. It feels as if I float to the front of the stage. When I make it to the podium, I straighten out my revised speech and take one more deep breath.

I allow myself to gaze out and lock eyes with my peers. I frantically search for a friendly face and settle on Gibbs, who gives me a warm smile. He mouths "you got this, Peyt." I release the breath I had been holding.

"Good afternoon, everyone," I start. "You know, I slaved over this speech for close to two weeks, debating on whether I wanted to make today easy or knowledgeable or inspirational or if I just wanted to get downright real with you... I didn't know. So naturally, I chose all of the above." I pause momentarily. "I mean, when all of the answers sound correct, that's the bubble we're told to fill in, right?"

The students sitting in front of me release a wave of laughter. My eyes then find Jamie, sitting there in her cap and gown, smiling up at me. She gives me a wink of encouragement.

"I learned a lot in high school," I continue. "I'm sure we all did, except we've probably forgotten most of it by now, but that's okay. That's what the internet's for." I pause for more laughter. "I learned a lot in high school, but I learned *the most* during my last year, and let me tell you, I'll never forget it."

Silence settles following my reference. I refuse to look back at the principal who is now probably well aware that I'm straying away from my original speech he had reviewed. I force myself to continue.

"I learned about acceptance, about love, about friendship, and forgiveness. I learned about pain, hate, anger, fear, and how these very common emotions rule the world around us." My eyes lock with my parents. "I learned that certain people are put into your life to teach you lessons, to expose your weaknesses–*or* strengths–to test your morale or to simply show you something you've known all along but were too afraid to admit."

The farther I stray from my original speech, the harder I have to work to keep my voice from shaking. I force my eyes to stay locked on the back wall to keep me grounded.

"Often times, life is described as black and white. We think a situation or a person or an idea is either good or bad, but rarely try to see how they, or it, could be both based on the perspective and context we're given." I lock eyes with Jacki this time. "And then we have the gray area. Gray, numb, foggy, and emotionless... But the gray area of life is rarely numb, right? Most times, this 'gray' area is filled with righteous reds and bellowing blues. The 'gray' area is blessed with the presence of passionate pinks and obnoxious oranges..."

"What I'm saying is, most decisions, most *stories*, are better explained in this 'gray' area. They're better understood when you see both sides of the coin. A bad situation can sometimes be justified if you look at it from a different angle. A bad idea can be turned good with just a little modification. And a good person can do a bad thing, because sometimes pain, anger, and fear get the best of us."

C'mon Peyton, you're almost there...

"So, I'll leave my fellow classmates with this..." I continue. "We have our whole lives ahead of us. Some of us will go off and start families. Some of us will travel the world and fall in love, *a lot.* Some will go off and become business owners, musicians, artists, mechanics, dentists, doctors... The possibilities are endless, really."

I read the last paragraph of my speech and sigh.

"I ask you, as someone who had to find forgiveness and acceptance in all areas of my life this year..." I look up. "... To do the same. Refuse to let the opinions of others dictate how your day will go. Refuse to believe winning is everything. Refuse to let hate and anger and fear control you and your decisions. Refuse to let ignorance pass you by without attempting to educate. Refuse to seek meaningless justice and refuse to become complacent..."

The clapping from the crowd begins to silence my monologue. I smile at the response and try to hold back tears.

"And refuse to be anyone but your damn self." I lock eyes with Jamie one last time. "Because you never know who you might save by doing so."

Forty

AFTER COMMENCEMENT, I DECIDE to stay behind and visit the mural one last time. The gym is far enough away for me to escape without anyone noticing, and the key I had been gifted earlier this year had been returned to the principal this week. It's really my last opportunity to see it before the school is locked up for the summer.

Jamie and I had won first place, and from what I *heard*, by a landslide. It's a miracle we had finished, given the circumstances, but it's the legacy we could leave behind when we leave Branton High.

"How did I know I would find you here?" a voice calls from the door.

I smile. "Because you know I'm sentimental."

"You're right about that." Jamie stands next to me and admires the mural. "Your speech was amazing."

"Thank you," I say. "The principal wanted to be mad but, everyone loved it."

We stare at our work in silence. What I feel in this moment is nothing less than amazing. I'm convinced it will become one of my favorite memories.

"It doesn't feel real," Jamie admits.

"I know, it's amazing-"

"No, I mean you leaving for college." Jamie faces me. "It doesn't feel real that you're leaving."

"Not 'til August," I remind. "We still have like, two and a half months."

She nods. "I know."

I feel the need to search for Jamie's hand, so I do. Her grip is soft as I lean into her. I didn't want to think about leaving her right now, not when I still have the entire summer to be *myself*. I didn't want to worry about the future until I absolutely had to.

"You wanna go get burgers?" I ask. "I'm starving."

"Only if you agree to share a milkshake with me."

"But I want my own!" I argue.

We laugh together as we make our way to my car that's sitting in the school parking lot. Jamie's hand never let's go of mine, not even on the car ride to the diner. It feels natural. It feels *right*.

And I fearlessly agree to share a milkshake with her after.

About the Author

Lauryn A. Brooks is an LGBTQ+ fiction writer who has been creating inclusive and diverse stories for over a decade. She grew up in a small, southern Louisiana town and started sharing her stories on the free-reading platform, Wattpad, back in 2012.

She currently resides in Nashville, Tennessee and aspires to be a full-time, self-published author.

Thanks for reading! If you enjoyed my debut novel "The Mural", please let me know with a short review on Amazon!

To keep up with future projects, please follow me on Twitter @laurynabrooks and visit my blog at **www.laurynslgbtbookshelf.com**.

And don't forget:

Be Proud. Stay You.

— Lauryn